A SCRYING SHAME

A Blood Visions Paranormal Mystery

By Donna White Glaser

A SCRYING SHAME

By Donna White Glaser
CreateSpace Edition
Copyright 2015 Donna White Glaser.
This book is a work of fiction. The characters, incidents, and dialogue are drawn from the author's imagination and are not to be construed as real. Any resemblance to actual events of persons, living or dead, is entirely accidental.

Credits:
Cover design by Cormar Covers
Editing by Red Adept Editing and Kindle Press

ALSO BY DONNA WHITE GLASER

THE LETTY WHITTAKER 12 STEP MYSTERIES:

The Enemy We Know
The One We Love
The Secrets We Keep
The Blood We Spill
COMING SOON: *The Lies We Tell*

THE BLOOD VISIONS PARANORMAL MYSTERIES:

A Scrying Shame
COMING SOON: *Scry Me a River*

To my family—

The whole nutty, sprawling bunch of them

CHAPTER ONE

The lights hurt. She blinked until her vision cleared, and the room came into focus.

Hospital. *Damn.*

Her mother stood at the foot of the bed, staring down at her. Arie closed her eyes again.

"Are you awake?" Evelyn's sharp voice sliced into Arie's brain like a scalpel. "Arie?"

No. Arie let herself sink back into the darkness. Maybe, she thought, just maybe she could find her way back to the Light—the real one—the Light that bathed her in warmth and an all-encompassing, no-words-for-it love. It had to let her back in. She didn't think she could stand living if it didn't.

The next time she awoke, her father's gentle smile greeted her. Arie let the warmth of his eyes spill into her own, feeling simultaneously grateful and . . .

disappointed. The love that she had always reveled in felt pale, almost sickly. A wave of guilt flooded into her for making such a comparison, but even her father's love couldn't compare to the Other.

"Hi, Daddy," Arie whispered. Her throat burned.

"Hi, baby." Her dad placed the straw of a plastic mug with the hospital's logo on it to her lips. Water—cool and pure.

Her throat still hurt. Arie reached her hand up to it, grimacing at the pain.

What?

Her fingers ran across the cloth lump of gauze bandages and sticky tape. *Had something happened?* Strange that she could remember being there with such stinging, poignant clarity, but she couldn't remember anything about what had happened to her body right before.

"Was I in an accident?"

Her dad hesitated and looked away. Arie's heart thumped. Although a quiet man, Ed Stiles was a pastor and not one to avoid questions, especially hers.

"Arie." He cleared his throat and took a sip of her water. "It wasn't an accident, hon. Somebody tried to hurt you."

"Hurt me?"

Her dad nodded.

Something felt wrong. Arie struggled to remember but only managed to work up the beginnings of a wicked headache. "Who?"

"We don't know." Her dad's smile faltered and melted away. "We were hoping you did."

The fluid dripping into her arm was clear this time. Probably a good sign. Her mother sat on the bed next to Arie, holding her hand. *Oh, crap, I must be dying. Wait. That's a good thing.*

"Hi, Ma."

"Don't call me Ma. You know I hate that." She sniffed and cleared her throat.

"Are you crying?"

"Don't be silly." She brushed her daughter's hair back from her face, then held a straw to her lips.

Water. Arie swallowed. The cool liquid simultaneously burned and soothed as it went down.

"It was amazing—so beautiful." A wave of frustration made Arie's head pulse, proof her heart was still beating. The puny, everyday, *earthly* words weren't enough to explain what she'd seen and where she'd been.

"I don't see what's so amazing about getting stabbed in a parking lot in the middle of the night." Her mother's face, devoid of makeup for the first time Arie could remember, contorted in pain. She stood and paced at the end of the bed.

"That's not important."

Her mother spun, face twisted with incredulity. "Not important? Honey, you were attacked."

Honey? Another first.

The endearment and the residual effects of the Other Side created a joy bubble that rose and spread into a wide smile. Probably looked goofy as hell. *Well, not hell.* If the Other Side was anything to compare it to, hell probably shouldn't be taken lightly, either. Arie pushed that thought aside. The things she'd seen were all that really mattered.

Arie tried sitting up, but tubes tethered her to the bed. She fell back, weak.

"I saw heaven. It was . . . I can't even begin to—"

"Arie, that's enough. You're getting too excited. You need to rest."

"But—"

Her father walked in, holding two cups of coffee. He was wearing his favorite Christmas sweater—a faded green wool sprinkled with appliqués of tiny reindeer pulling teensy Santas all over it. Arie had given it to him when she was twelve and he'd worn it every December since. His brown eyes sparkled when he saw her. "Well, look who's awake." He handed his wife her coffee, then took her spot on the bed.

More hair brushing. Must be a thing people do in hospitals.

Arie tried again. "Dad, I went to heaven. It was beautiful."

"Oh, for crying out loud," her mother snapped. "Not this again."

"Evelyn, it's okay."

She whipped around. "Did they say her medication would do this? I'll check with the nurse." She strode out of the room.

"It's not my medication. It was so real. More real than this is. And there was a . . . Light. It was love. I knew who It was. It was as if I'd always known."

"Shh." Her father covered her hand. His touch was soothing.

"But why is she mad?"

"She . . . honey, she's not mad. She's just upset."

Not a foreign state for Evelyn Stiles. But how could a pastor's wife be upset about heaven? Arie was so tired she almost couldn't force the question out of her mouth.

"Arie, I know something's happened to you. Something . . . life-changing. And I want to hear all about it when you're able. I do. But you need to understand; something happened to us, too. The doctor . . . honey, the doctor told us you were dead. We thought we'd lost you. We were still sitting with him in that awful little room, trying to comprehend what happened, when a nurse came running down the hall. I think your mother is still trying to process everything. She needs time."

"Daddy, it was so beautiful."

"I know, honey. You're going to tell me. But not now. Close your eyes." He trailed his fingers over her forehead, a magical touch from her childhood. It erased the day, he'd said every night as he tucked her in.

"But—"

"Shhh."

Arie's eyes fluttered. *Maybe just for a minute . . .*

CHAPTER TWO

The small room felt like a coffin, hot and stifling, all the air used up in the swelter. People always talked about Wisconsin as if it only had winters, but summer, though as fleeting as a butterfly kiss, also carried a punch.

If there was any air conditioning in the office, Arie couldn't feel it. The one small window had two file cabinets jammed up against it. Dusty manuals and three-ring binders piled on top killed off any hope of fresh air. Arie angled her arms away from her sides, irrationally hoping for a stray breeze to offset the dark circles forming there. Another trickle of sweat slid down her spine, pooling along the waistband of her skirt.

The man sat silently across the table from Arie. Basil Gallo wore his cropped black hair short, tight to his scalp, broken only by a crescent-shaped scar over his left ear. The scar trailed across the side of his head like a little pink worm.

Arie tugged at the scarf she'd used to hide her own wound curling at the base of her throat. The fabric was itchy and didn't help matters with the heat, but with only a few months having passed since the attack, the gash was still puffy and an ugly dark red. She hated it.

Gallo's leg jiggled manically as though he was trying to siphon off an overflow of energy. Darting black eyes scanned the wad of papers he clasped.

Arie couldn't help staring at his hands. When not scrutinizing papers, he gestured wildly, accenting every statement with emphatic jabs of his stubby fingers. Dark patches of silky hair scattered ever so lightly across his knuckles, adding shadows to the movement. His hands were so clean. Her gaze returned like a cognitive tic to stare at his hands, wondering how he got them so clean. Nobody else would notice or even care, probably, unless they knew what this man did for a living.

She needed this job. And considering the nature of it, she hadn't thought there would be a lot of contenders for the position. But the stack of applications next to the guy's elbow was disconcerting.

Arie cleared her throat nervously. Gallo looked up sharply, but she had already plastered on an appropriately pleasant expression. Her left eye twitched at the effort. She faked a cough into her fist, using the distraction to scoot back in the chair. Her pantyhose were in full mutiny; one side half-twisted clockwise in an attempt to cut off the circulation to her leg, and the other surrendered to a snag that, despite a blob of iridescent Tango Mango nail polish, threatened to uncase her thigh like an over-boiled sausage. She silently cursed her mother's relentless indoctrination in "how to be a lady." What other twenty-five-year-old wore pantyhose these days?

"So, Arie—"

He pronounced it "Airy," an image she would never relate to.

"It's Arie, like the initials R. E. Arie Stiles." They were the initials for her given name, which Arie told only to the IRS and God. She tugged at the scarf again.

"Fine. Arie. What makes you think this is something you can handle? It ain't like TV. I don't care what you see on those stupid crime shows. There's nothing exciting about death."

Arie was tempted to tell him just how familiar with death she really was, but she wasn't sure whether that would make her appear more qualified or just weird. Instead, she merely said, "I know it's not. Blood doesn't bother me—other people's, that is."

She didn't think it did, anyway.

"Blood is the least of it. Wait 'til you go home and find someone's brain stuck on your shoe. Besides, it's the smell that gets to people."

She swallowed hard. "The . . . um?"

"Smell. Death has a smell. It gets in your clothes, your hair, your mouth, everywhere. You're gonna be tasting it days later. I'm tellin' you. It gets *inside* you." Smiling, Gallo tapped the cage of bone that protected his heart, assuming he had one.

"Providing this kind of service"—his eyes held Arie's, as though daring her to challenge the euphemism—"is not for the weak. We take care of the problems no one else can handle." His hand—that clean hand—cut through the air, sweeping the "problems" away. "Don't kid yourself that this is just some small-town outfit. We're right here next to the I-94 corridor. We run jobs from Madison to Milwaukee and wherever else we need to. We go in; we handle the situation. We're what you might call the specialists of death." His fingers twitched quote marks over the last few words.

"It's nice that you take, um, pride in your work." An errant, sweat-dampened tendril of brown hair flopped over one of Arie's eyes.

"What d'you expect? It's a business." Gallo squinted at her. "That's what you gotta keep telling yourself. A business. Keep the emotions out of it. And what you gotta ask yourself is: Can you do it? Can you handle it?"

Arie cleared her throat. *Could she?*

"Don't forget," he added. "If you work up to full time, after a year, you get three sick days and a week's vacation. Also health insurance. It's crappy, and the premiums are killing me, but still."

Thank goodness. Death had benefits.

CHAPTER THREE

"I don't understand. Did you say 'BioClean'?"

Arie could see the war waging beneath the facade of her mother's near-perfect control of her facial expressions. Despite the barest Mona Lisa smile that a lifetime of cloaking her emotions automatically carved out of her mother's lips, disgust showed in the infinitesimal tightening of her eye muscles and in a shadow curling at the corner of Evelyn's mouth.

"What exactly is this BioClean, sweetheart?" Dad asked.

"It's a crime scene cleanup company. I interviewed last week, and the owner called this morning to offer me the job." Arie almost overdosed on the toxic levels of perkiness her own automatic response produced.

"But, why on earth . . . ?" Her mother's voice trailed off. It did that a lot. Her long, pale fingers touched the amber beads around her neck that coordinated perfectly with the rich earth tones she favored. *The perfect pastor's wife.*

Exhausted, Arie dropped into her usual spot at her parents' kitchen table—only four long strides from the back door or seven to get through the door leading to the living room. She'd known the measurements since she was fourteen.

Arie sighed. She'd never acquired the stamina to sustain social falseness the way her mother had. "I need the job. I haven't worked in over six months."

She decided not to bother with the obvious. Her parents were well aware of the circumstances that ended her last job. After all, working late nights at the bar had killed her. It wasn't her fault it didn't take. And her parents didn't know that her rent was already three months past due, and she'd started hiding her car in back alleys to avoid the repo dude—when she could rally herself enough to get off the couch, that is. The eviction notice had finally penetrated the haze of depression she'd been living with since being squashed back into her body shell against her will. Some wills were bigger than others.

At any rate, Arie needed a job. Any job.

Her mother lifted her fingers to her temples, rubbing at the tension that details of her daughter's life inevitably brought her. She threw in a grand display of in-through-the-nose, out-through-the-mouth breaths designed to illustrate her control and dropped her hands to her teensy waist. "What about the job at the bank? I gave you the application, didn't I?"

"Yes, but it's only part time, and it only pays minimum wage. *And* no benefits."

The latter fact scored a direct hit, what with the hospital bills that kept piling up after "the incident," as Evelyn insisted on calling it.

Sitting quietly at the kitchen table, her dad nodded slightly at the point Arie made, but his wife slid a quelling glance in his direction.

"Besides . . . " Arie eyed the back door. *Just four strides.* "It's temporary. Just while I figure things out. You don't understand what it's like to have been—"

"You're right; I don't understand. I've never understood what you're doing with your life." Evelyn reverted to her usual back-up weapons: a main course of disillusionment with a topping of guilt. "Regardless of what you think happened during that incident, you still have to make your way in the real world with *real* people doing real things. You can't keep living in this fantasy world that you've decided . . . " Evelyn pressed her fingers to her temples. When she finally spoke again, her voice was I-am-calm, I-am-peace saintly. "You have such potential. All of your teachers said so. Didn't they, Edward?"

Permission granted, her father nodded.

"Ma—"

"Don't call me Ma. You're not a sheep. And you know I'm right. If you would just apply yourself, you could do anything. What about college? You only have a year left. Don't you want to matriculate? I don't know how you can just leave your education dangling. Of course, you need to rethink that silly degree you insisted on. I mean, really? English Lit? Is that going to help you get ahead in this economy? You should have taken something in computers or business, like your brother. He's doing so well—"

"Mother, stop." Arie's shoulder muscles scrunched so tight they almost twanged. *Not again.* "I'm not Brant."

"And we don't want you to be." Arie's father stepped in on cue. "You just need to buckle down, that's all."

"Edward." Evelyn reclaimed the conversational helm. "You can't tell me that you think this disgusting cleaning job is a good idea?"

He cleared his throat. Loudly. "I can't say I like the idea—"

"There. You see?"

"But if this is what Arie wants—"

"And that's another thing, this ridiculous refusal to answer to her own name."

The screen door banged against the frame on Arie's way out, the same bang as when she was fifteen and forbidden to go to Leanna Schwarz's birthday party because Leanna's mom worked as an "entertainment specialist" at the Boys Only Club. It had happened again at seventeen, when nobody had believed her story about burglars taking the minivan on a joyride up to Madison and, in an amazing coincidence, left it outside Abercrombie & Fitch, Arie's favorite store at West Towne Mall.

After all, criminals had a right to dress well. Besides, there had been a sale on summer dresses.

As usual, after a fight with her mother, Arie ended up at her best friend's place.

"I seriously don't get what the big deal is. You'd think your mom would be all Kübler-Ross about dying, right? I mean, she's a minister's wife. And what's wrong with being dead? It's not like you *stayed* that way." Chandra's voice came out squished as she pretzeled around her knee, daintily polishing her toenails purple-black. Chandra was heavy into body art, although thus far, she had managed to limit piercings to her left eyebrow, her nose, and a tiny angel kiss above her upper lip. The rest of her body was her palate, although she hadn't started on tattoos. Yet.

Arie sat on the faded floor pillows that were her best friend's only furniture. She sighed, pulling her feet out from the cramped, crossed-leg position that had stopped being comfortable when she was twelve. Her right foot tingled one notch below falling asleep. Arie wiggled it.

"You need a couch," she said irritably.

Chandra looked up. "You need a nap."

"Which I could take if you had a couch. And I'm not crabby."

Arie considered snagging the bag of Doritos that she knew Chandra would have stashed in the kitchen. Her mouth salivated. But no. She tamped down the craving. She'd promised herself she'd stop using chips and ice cream as antidepressants.

Chandra snorted, turning back to dabbing the inky liquid onto a stubby pinky toe.

"You smeared," Arie pointed out, earning a glinting, green-eyed glare. Sighing, she thunked her head back against the wall.

Of course Chandra didn't get it. She'd been born and raised in Southern California and had moved to Oconomowoc, Wisconsin, just before middle school. She was used to being thought of as weird—reveled in it, in fact. Arie, on the other hand, came from a long line of proper, beige-y Midwestern ancestors. She had never fit in with them, but they'd never lowered their expectations.

"So let me get this straight," Chandra said. "You don't want to discuss the fact that you were bumped off, died, and had a layover in heaven, but you got a job cleaning up dead people anyway?" She finally untangled her long legs, straightening them across the floor.

Arie knew ignoring her wouldn't work. Chandra would just keep vulture-circling the subject until Arie gave in.

"I don't mind talking about the death part. I just don't want to talk about the attack."

Again.

Dying had been . . . beautiful. But getting mugged—*killed*—for the measly few tips she'd earned bartending was decidedly not. The police had grilled her over and over again about the little she could remember about leaving the bar and walking to her car and for what? They hadn't caught the guy.

Fortunately, Chandra had a fascination with the Other Side—in all things weird and paranormal, actually. From the moment Arie had gotten out of the hospital, the NDE had been all Chandra wanted to talk about. Or maybe she'd simply been more sensitive than Arie gave her credit for.

"Obviously, I'm not afraid of death anymore," Arie finally said. "It doesn't bother me, so why not make money off it? I could sure use it."

Chandra squinted at her best friend. "I think it's an awesome job. The fact that it tweaks your mom's butt is just an added benefit. When do you start?"

"I already did. I went in for training yesterday."

"And you're just now telling me?" Chandra looked stunned.

"I wasn't sure I was going to go through with it. Besides, it's like being on call. I have to wait until someone dies. And I won't be on the first team called out either, unless it's a big job. I had to go in for a bunch of hep-B shots, though, and the training is, like, three days.

I guess I'm still not sure how I feel about the whole thing."

"It's kind of weird hoping that someone dies, huh?"

"I guess." *Not really*. Death was wonderful. But Arie didn't want to start all that up again. "It's not only death scenes, though. It might be a meth lab or something. From what Basil Gallo said, there are a lot of those projects up north."

"Geez, that could be dangerous." Chandra met her gaze. "All those chemicals. What if you blow up or something?"

Then I die, Arie said to herself. *Again.*

CHAPTER FOUR

At least the first job wasn't a murder. Leonard Petranik died all on his own, although nothing about his death could be termed natural.

"Hoarder," Grady said.

Short, squat, and built like a stump, Arie's new partner spoke with the authority of his senior status. He'd been with BioClean for nearly a year and was already their third most experienced employee. This did not generate confidence in BioClean being a long-term employment option.

They stood outside a small ranch-style home in one of those working-class neighborhoods that were deserted during the day. Arie looked at the call sheet and tried to figure out where Grady got the information that their "client" was a hoarder. The only items listed were the homeowner's name—Leonard Petranik—the address, lots of insurance information, and a small box checked Unattended Death. She followed Grady to the back of the van where he pulled out supplies.

"How do you know he's a hoarder?"

Grady pointed at the ranch's windows. A sun-faded Dixie flag and a dingy-looking beach towel hung in place of curtains in the large picture window. In addition to the dubious decorating choice, there was something else off about it. It took a few seconds for Arie to realize that neither flag nor towel hung free. Instead of falling in loose folds, the fabric was mashed against the panes, flattened nearly to the top of the windows where it bunched unevenly. One corner of the flag had slipped off the rod, or whatever it was attached to, exposing a triangle of jumbled colors. Arie's brain told her that something must be holding up the bit of flag, but it looked as though it was levitating. The kaleidoscope of colors added a festive splash to the otherwise dreary exterior.

A second set of windows, smaller and lacking even a towel for privacy, were situated at the far end of the house. A bedroom, maybe? An assorted mix of boxes of varied shapes and sizes blocked the bottom six inches of the windows.

"Maybe he was moving in?"

Grady pointed again, this time to the one-car garage located at the opposite end of the house. The bifurcated door bulged askew, the left side prevented from closing by layers and layers of newspapers wedged underneath.

Grady was already pulling on a yellow Tyvek biohazard suit. He leaned against the back of the van, tugging the fitted "bunny suit" up over his tennis shoes, wiggling his way into the protective gear. Arie had tried one on during training and wasn't looking forward to the stifling heat. She wished she had thought to wear shorts and a tank top like Grady. She was stuck in a short-sleeved T-shirt, jeans, and a pair of ratty tennis shoes that she had already determined could be thrown away if needed.

Her second discovery was that yellow Tyvek did absolutely nothing for her curvy hips. Arie stared down at herself. She looked like a lumpy, ambulatory banana. She copied Grady by wrapping a strip of crime scene tape around her middle to take the suit in. Now she looked like a lumpy banana with criminal tendencies. Sighing, she watched Grady pull on a second pair of disposable booties.

He didn't explain why they needed double wrapping, and Arie didn't ask. She had already figured out there would be things she wouldn't want to dwell on.

The odor assaulted her halfway up the sidewalk. Grady looked over his shoulder, and Arie waited for words of encouragement and inspiration. He was, after all, her supervisor.

"If you have to puke, make sure you get the mask off," Grady said. "It really sucks to hurl in your mask and have it wash back up in your face. And don't puke on the scene. We'll just have to clean that up, too."

Words to live by.

There were tunnels. The garbage had been piled to nearly ceiling height in most of the rooms, but Petranik had constructed a rabbit warren of burrows. The walls of trash were divided into stratified layers, separating into different eras like an archaeological dig. The eighties, which predated Arie's birth by a decade, hit about shoulder high. In one small section, Arie spied the black edges of VHS tapes, a five-inch-thick VCR, a boxy gray dinosaur of an IBM computer, and a squashed-flat box that previously held "The Clapper." A small, multicolored pyramid poked out of the wall. She grasped it, dislodging a small shower of Bubble Yum wrappers and Styrofoam fast-food sandwich boxes. The wall shifted ominously, and Arie held her breath. She had nearly caused a trash avalanche over a rescued Rubik's Cube. Being smothered to death under a pile of trash was not appealing. *Unless . . .*

Unless it meant a chance to return to the Other Side. Arie wondered if Petranik was there now. A wave of jealousy almost doubled her over, making her drop the toy.

She had also lost sight of Grady. Then Arie heard him foraging up ahead. Another sound, a low-pitched humming, filtered through her mask, growing louder and louder the farther down the hall she walked. The sound, an atonal vibration, snuck past her respirator and seeped into her ears. Arie froze, mouth dry. It was almost—not quite but almost—like the sound from the OS, as Arie had taken to calling the Other Side, a pervasive, surround-sound of disparate beings joined in a harmony of noise. A green bottle fly bounced off Arie's face shield.

Oh. This wasn't heaven's harmony she was hearing, but a symphony of flies doing what flies were created to do.

Arie joined Grady at the door to a bathroom. Leonard—under the circumstances, Arie felt they should be on a first-name basis—had killed himself in the bathtub. Considerate of him, really. Maybe he'd expected any spray from his sliced wrists would land on tile, making the clean-up job easier for whoever was faced with the task.

Unfortunately, Leonard must not have factored in what several days of undetected death would leave.

Or maybe he wasn't considerate after all.

A writhing curtain of flies covered the walls and ceiling, coating the now empty tub like a roiling black rug. The bathroom floor was littered with insect husks. An entomologist's dream: the life cycle of the fly from egg to desiccated hull and all the wiggling mass in between.

Arie stepped back into the hall to reassess her newly chosen career path.

Grady stood in the door, watching while she grappled with the horror show in the tub. Arie tried to focus on the scene in the detached way she imagined Grady did. *I'm a professional.*

It might have worked except when she rubbed her forehead, she jostled her face mask, letting the smell squeeze underneath. The breathing space filled with the lingering odor of rotted, decaying meat. Once it was under the rubber seal, there was no escaping it.

Grady said something. The mask muffled his voice.

"What?" Arie pointed to her ear.

He leaned in, speaking loud and slow. "Take your mask off." He gestured at her respirator, miming raising it.

Was he nuts? *"Why?"*

"Come on." He gestured impatiently and began pulling his off, which convinced Arie there must be some reason for this idiocy. Maybe he needed to tell her something.

Arie noticed his puffed cheeks about two seconds too late. The smell knocked her upside the head like a physical blow. Tears flooded her eyes—the reaction either a physical response, an instinctive flushing to protect the orbs, or an emotional one as her brain reeled in horror. If her skin could have curled back, it surely would have. Arie's knees buckled, and she retched.

Bellowing with laughter, Grady resettled his respirator. Stomach still heaving, Arie was afraid to put the mask back on. Grady grabbed her elbow and shoved her back down the hall. Arie stumbled through the house, heading blindly for the door. Her body was in full flight mode, propelling her toward fresh air.

In the yard, she dropped on all fours, simultaneously retching and gulping for air. It was not fresh air—not by a long shot. The odor still lingered. Arie's lungs sucked it in anyway. Her eyes continued to water, and then her nose joined in, snot running freely down the front of her suit. She shook so hard her muscles ached.

She vowed to whip Grady's ass just as soon as she regained a minimal amount of control over her body. The bastard had followed her and was leaning against the van, still hiccupping in the wind-down phase of hysteria.

Pulling herself to her feet, Arie tried to incinerate him with her eyes. It would have been more effective, she knew, if the front of her banana suit wasn't covered with her own snot.

"Welcome to BioClean," Grady said. "Grab the camera."

CHAPTER FIVE

The turnover rate at BioClean suddenly made perfect sense. But Arie had lived—and died—through scarier things than the remnants of a body recycling itself back to nature. She glared at Grady, who still grinned like a buffoon.

Dude doesn't realize he's dealing with the undead, does he?

Saying nothing, Arie snatched up the camera and went back through the house, documenting both the levels of trash in each room and the tiny, cramped bathroom. When she was done, Grady checked the digital display and grudgingly nodded.

"What next?" Arie asked.

They returned to the bathroom. Grady crossed to the fly-curtained window and tried to open it. It had been painted shut, so he ended up going to the van for a crowbar. When Arie had pictured wielding the tools of the trade, she had thought of disinfectant, rubber gloves, and paper towels. Her training taught her to add crowbars, Sawz-Alls, wet-dry vacs, and putty scrapers.

Once Grady got the window open, the flies dispersed. The room looked better already.

"We've only contracted for the blood," Grady said. "I don't know if his kids even know about the hoarding issue, but that's not our job. Not yet, anyway. Since only one of us can fit in here at a time . . . "

He gave Arie an I've-got-seniority look that left no doubt as to just who would be working in the bathroom.

"Right." Arie thought about what she would need and headed back out to the van. Grady followed, and Arie realized this was an on-the-job, pass-fail test. She assembled the supplies and turned to head back into the house.

"Wait."

Arie paused warily.

"Doing the first run-through and for the camera work, we only need the light suit and the latex." He wiggled his gloved fingers at her. "For the real work, you add the heavy ones over the top. Make sure you tape the wrists off."

"Why the change in attitude?"

Grady grinned. "Well, you didn't actually throw up. Guts bet me twenty bucks you would. He always bets the newbie will hurl, and he's always right. 'Cept for today."

"Guts?"

"Gallo. Basil Gallo. Ol' Blood and Guts himself. He's gonna be ticked when he finds out he lost."

Grabbing one of the kits—a plastic milk crate filled with a surprising number of things—Arie made a show of stomping away, but her heart lightened. *Everyone else threw up the first time, huh?* She decided it was a good thing she'd skipped breakfast that morning. Maybe she'd end up a legend in the biohazard-cleaning world.

Arie had only been cleaning for about ten minutes when a sense of profound sadness washed over her body. She'd been scrubbing a particularly recalcitrant streak of blood caught in the tile grout when it happened. Up 'til then, she'd felt pretty spunky, knowing she'd cost her boss twenty bucks in the will-she-puke bet. Knowing she could handle the awful things the job would dish up was a relief, too.

Overwhelming sadness. Tears pooled, and her hand rose of its own accord to clench in a fist over her heart. A thick gray fog materialized before her eyes, filling her nostrils until she thought she would choke. *How was the fog getting past the mask?*

Knowing she shouldn't, Arie sank down to the closed toilet lid and curled over on herself.

What the hell was happening?

A little zing of anger flashed through her body, and that really scared her. The emotions didn't feel like her own.

Shake it off. Arie blinked and rubbed her eyes, then literally gave herself a shake and picked up the wall scraper she'd accidentally dropped. Gripping the bottle of disinfectant as though she was preparing to duel, Arie returned to the section of tiled wall she'd been working on.

Splashes and dots of blood glimmered. The edges of her vision grew blotchy as though she were about to faint. Arie took a deep breath. She sprayed and started scraping, trying to ignore the wash of sadness and . . .

was that loneliness? She focused hard on the thick streak of blood.

An image of a beautiful, dark-haired woman bloomed in her mind. Sunny, a voice inside Arie's head said. She throws her head back in laughter, that endearing gap between her front teeth flashing. My heart feels like it will explode with love.

My heart? A brilliant flash of light burst in Arie's mind's eye. Then . . .

A boy and girl ride bikes in front of the house. The kids . . . my kids . . . so young.

Another flash.

They kneel in their pajamas in front of the Christmas tree. My son unwraps his gift. A Rubik's Cube tumbles in a rainbow of colors from the wrapping paper.

Flash.

A Ford F-250, a blue so dark it almost looks black. Sunny darts around the bed of it, flinging a sodden and soapy sponge at my head. Laughs.

Flash.

The house—empty, except for things. All of their belongings are all around me. Everywhere my hand reaches, I can touch them. I'm surrounded by the pieces of my family. Every bit of it as important as their heartbeats to me. Every bit of—

Arie broke out of the trance, stumbled backward, and tripped over a bucket into the hallway. Eyes wide, Grady came dashing around the corner. The hall had been narrowed by rows of boxes lining both sides. Light backlit Grady's end, and for one brief, hopeful moment, Arie thought she was going back There.

"What the heck happened?" Grady asked.

"Uh . . . I saw a spider." Arie hauled herself to her feet, not an easy feat in a banana suit.

A forty-something man dressed in slacks and short-sleeved button-down shirt followed on Grady's heels.

Grady's head tilted in an are-you-nuts expression. The client, Arie presumed, looked even more concerned. He glanced around in distaste at the piles of trash, and pulled his narrow shoulders in a little tighter. He held the Rubik's Cube in his hand, twisting it nervously.

"I'm afraid of spiders," Arie said. "It's a phobia. I'm okay now."

"Why don't you go take a break?" Grady said.

Arie saw that he had shed his banana suit for a white lab coat. He held a clipboard filled with forms—the contract, maybe. Grady was probably writing up a new estimate to include dealing with Mount Saint Trash Heap all around them.

Memories.

Arie's gut heaved at the reappearance of intrusive thought. She shook her head, trying to rattle the voice out of her skull

"Take it," Grady said in a no-nonsense voice.

She hadn't meant to decline the offer. As Arie shuffled past the client, he shot her another nervous smile. A gap separated his front teeth.

Just like his mama's.

Breaking out in another deluge of sweat, Arie scurried out the door to the van, where she stripped out of her suit and gloves, disinfected, and grabbed a sports drink from the cooler in the front compartment of the cab. She lowered herself to the ground next to the van and sipped her drink. Chills documented the history of her fear in goose-bump Braille all over her body.

What the heck just happened? At least that thought was all her own.

CHAPTER SIX

"I thought I wouldn't mind cleaning up after other dead people, ones who stay dead, I mean. Not like me. I thought the ick factor wouldn't be an issue, you know?"

Arie was avoiding her landlord, so she hid out at Chandra's. After listening to Arie whine about her lack of furniture, Chandra had splurged on a bright yellow beanbag chair from Target. It reminded Arie uncomfortably of the banana suit, but she didn't have the heart to tell her friend that her new furniture triggered thoughts of decomposing bodies. Also, since her body ran to the Dolly-Parton-style of womanhood, her scrunched position forced her knees up to her chest and her chest up to her face, threatening her next death to be attributed to asphyxiation by décolletage.

"You really don't mind cleaning up blood and stuff?" Chandra sounded dubious. In addition to the new "furniture," she'd indulged in a new hairstyle—raven black and very short with bangs. The ends curled around her jaw, and she kept jiggling her head so that they swished around her face.

Cleopatra with a twitch.

"I don't like the smells or the flies," Arie said. "Those really are hard to get used to, but the rest . . . I just remind myself that it's all part of biology. The real person isn't there, anyway. I think dead bodies freak people out because we're still thinking of them as people. They're not. They really are just . . . meat, I guess. What's left of them, anyway."

Chandra gasped. "Are their bodies still there?"

"No, not their whole bodies, but . . . well, there are always pieces, you know? Especially if they've been decomposing."

"If the people aren't still there, then how do you explain what happened with the hoarder dude? I mean, that is some *freaky* shit." Chandra's eyes sparkled.

Arie couldn't answer that.

"Okay!" Chandra said. "So, this vision. You saw stuff and felt it, too?"

Arie nodded. "The Rubik's cube, a pretty woman, and two kids. But I'll be honest. The thing that really freaked me out was the emotions. They took over my body. I can't even explain it. I was feeling this horrible despair, but at the same time, I knew it wasn't mine."

"Kind of like being possessed?"

"I wouldn't go that far." Arie shuddered. "But what I can't figure out is why did that happen to me? I mean, I've had already had a Near Death Experience. Isn't that enough weirdness for one lifetime?"

"Two lifetimes, technically. But maybe," Chandra said, "they *aren't* two separate things."

"Meaning?"

"Maybe the NDE and the psychic stuff are both part of one thing. Maybe you were led to working with these dead people."

Chandra loved woo-woo stuff. Arie never really paid attention to that kind of thing. For starters, her mother would have killed her. Chandra turned to a cheap particleboard bookshelf against the wall. The top two rows sagged with fantasy and mystery books and a whole section of angsty werewolf and vampire young adult novels. The bottom shelf had been set aside for nonfiction: a few leftover college texts, but mainly paranormal and psychic related tomes.

Woo-woo stuff.

Chandra pulled out a volume and paged through it. Shaking her head, she stuck it back and grabbed another. She must have found what she'd been looking for because a beatific smile lit her face.

"Scrying," she said.

"Gesundheit."

Chandra rolled her eyes. "Scrying is the practice of using reflective surfaces to see clairvoyantly. You know? Like seeing images or visions by using crystal balls or bowls of water."

"Are you suggesting I'm psychic or whatever?"

"Tell me exactly what happened," Chandra said. "What were you doing right before the vision hit?"

"Can we order a pizza first?"

"Focus. What were you doing?"

"Cleaning. Wiping blood off the tiled walls. That was it."

Chandra heaved a sigh. "I need more detail. Tell you what. Close your eyes."

"Chandra—"

"Close. Your. Eyes."

Arie complied.

"What does the tile look like?" Chandra softened her voice into a soothing tone. "Like, what color?"

"White," Arie said. "Except for the blood, of course. That's what made the blood stand out so much. It was stark, you know?"

"Good. Keep going."

"I'd already cleaned one of the walls, the one with the lightest spatter. I figured I'd start there and kind of work up to the others. It was on the second wall that it happened. There was more blood, lots more in some places. Streaks of it, instead of just dots or a mist."

"What did the streaks look like?" Chandra's voice grew weaker.

Arie couldn't help smiling. For all her friend's fascination with vampires and paranormal activity, she seemed a little squeamish on the matter of blood. Arie considered giving her a break and keeping it as gore-free as possible.

Still, Chandra *had* asked for details.

"The wall I was working on and the one behind him were the worst," Arie said. "I think he must have hit a vein or an artery or whatever. The streaks were pretty wide, kind of like ribbons, but starting thick and then getting thinner, and all kind of crisscrossing each other."

Arie opened her eyes. Chandra had turned green and seemed to be swallowing a lot more than usual.

"Don't you barf on me." Arie flailed around in her squishy pillow prison, but Chandra waved her back.

"I'm fine," she said, in a definitely not fine voice. "Okay. You're scrubbing away at the . . . uh . . . ribbons, and then what?"

Once again, Arie tried to picture it. "I was getting really hot and sweaty. Obviously, the suits have no airflow. I mean, that's the point. Guts makes us take water breaks every hour if possible, but I hadn't even been working twenty minutes. The first side cleaned up pretty easy. The second wall, though . . . It was a lot harder. I was concentrating. I really wanted to do a good job, especially since I'd passed their barf test."

"Their barf test?"

"Everyone pukes on their first job. Except I hadn't, and Grady was going to win the bet he'd made with Guts. Twenty bucks."

"Your coworkers have some serious issues. You know that, right?"

Arie sighed and felt compelled to point out the obvious. "*They* aren't the ones getting sneak peeks at heaven or having their bodies taken over by dead people."

"Not that you know of, anyway."

That wasn't as reassuring as she might have thought it would be.

"Okay," Chandra continued, "so getting back to this. You were hot and sweaty and concentrating. Then what?"

"Then, what I already told you: this awful rush of sadness. I sat down and . . . and then I started seeing the stuff. That's when I freaked out and made a fool of myself in front of Grady and the client."

Arie flopped out of the beanbag and lay face down on the floor. "Chan, I can't lose this job. I just can't. In fact, I'm probably going to have to take another job, too, because Grady and I only get called out if Rich and Bruno can't make the job. They get first choice. As soon as my landlord catches up with me, I'm going to be evicted. And the hospital bills? I can't even imagine how long it will take me to pay those off."

"I thought your parents were helping with those."

Arie rolled her head to look at her friend. "They are. But Chan, come on. I'm supposed to be a grown up. How many twenty-five-year-olds are still trying to figure out what they want to be when they grow up? I quit college to work in a bar, for crying out loud."

"You loved your job."

"My job killed me. Literally."

"Technically, that was the creep in the parking lot, and he only killed you a little bit." At Arie's glare, she amended her statement. "Well, not permanently, anyway."

"Benefits. Retirement. Investments. Savings. Why didn't I ever think about those?"

"Because, duh. You're in your twenties. Who does that?"

"Brant," Arie said, which wasn't really fair because, for her first child, Evelyn Stiles had apparently given birth to a forty-five-year-old in a baby costume. "You could already see it in his baby pictures. He's sitting there in his diapers, but it's obvious he was already comparing insurance quotes or analyzing stock dividends or something financial and prudent."

"I've seen the pictures. He looks constipated. He always does."

"But he's a grown-up," Arie persisted. "He didn't wipe out my parents' retirement savings in a single blow. I mean, even you! You're more of a grown-up than me."

"Okay, I'm not sure how to take that 'even you' part, but how am I a grown up? I make cakes all day. Believe me, I'm definitely not thinking about pensions or whatever while I'm doing it."

Arie turned to look at her friend. "You should, though. We both should. And you don't just make cakes.

You design amazing, one-of-a-kind pieces of edible art. You're following your dream, but you're still being practical about it."

"I am not. I'm an artist. I'm only doing this stupid cake job until I get enough paintings to do a show. It pays the rent. That's it."

"I'm just pointing out that you can pay your rent. You, um, wisely took a job so that you could still follow your dream. You're making it work. That's awesome."

Chandra's kohl-lined eyes had narrowed at "wisely," but she seemed to accept it. Then she gasped and sat up straight. Her eyes looked like golf balls with little green dots.

"We should experiment," she said.

CHAPTER SEVEN

Arie's mind scrambled to catch up with her friend's grasshopper-flitting ideas. "What are you talking about?"

"Let's see if we can coax a little psychic vision out of you right now." Chandra smiled like a little girl who'd been promised that Christmas would come every day from now on.

"And just how are we going to do that?" Arie could almost hear the clicks and whirs as Chandra's brain buzzed with ideas.

"Let's start out with something simple, like just concentrating."

Chandra plumped the yellow beanbag and waved her friend back into it, claiming a pumpkin-orange floor pillow for herself. Sitting crisscross, she rested her hands softly on her knees, closed her eyes, and breathed deeply. A little Egyptian hippy. She looked so earnest, Arie struggled not to smile. When she tried to copy Chandra's pose, her foot instantly cramped. She settled for sticking her legs out in front of her.

"What am I supposed to do?"

Chandra cracked her eyes open and frowned at Arie's un-Zen posture. Arie obediently crossed her legs again.

"Close your eyes, and take deep, cleansing breaths," Chandra intoned. "Let your aura unfold."

"My aura is folded?" That question earned Arie a dirty look. "All right, all right." Arie relaxed, letting her aura do whatever auras did.

"For now, concentrate on your breathing," Chandra said. "In and out. Nice and slow. Release your negative energy on the exhale. Breath in peace on the inhale."

Wondering when an automatic body function had gotten so complicated, Arie breathed. Her right foot started to tingle. She wiggled it and breathed some more.

Ice clunked down into the refrigerator's icemaker, making Arie jump. Chandra's breathing remained as steady as if she'd fallen asleep sitting up.

Arie made an effort to sync her breathing with the Dalai Chandra. *In and out. Slow and deep.* She wasn't sure whether it was peace she was breathing in or dust. Chandra wasn't big on cleaning. Arie's other foot tingled. She ignored it for as long as she could before wiggling the blood back into it.

The blood . . .

Chandra made a gurgling sound, and Arie peeked at her. She decided it must have been a stifled burp, so she closed her eyes again and went back to breathing, letting her aura unfold. Relaxed but concentrating.

Arie's nose itched.

Outside in the corridor, someone walked past Chandra's apartment, and Arie wondered if they were delivering pizza. Or Chinese. It had been a long time since she'd eaten Chinese.

"This isn't working," Arie said.

Chandra sighed and opened her eyes. "Did you feel *anything*?"

"My nose itched. That's about it."

A bigger, more exasperated sigh. "Were you even trying?"

"Maybe that's what's wrong. I wasn't trying when I was cleaning. It just happened."

A thoughtful look came over Chandra's face. "That's a surprisingly good point. Are you guys done with that job?"

"No, we go back tomorrow and should finish up, at least, unless the client wants us to empty out all the junk."

"Is the blood all cleaned up?"

"Yeah," Arie said. She straightened her legs and tried to wiggle the blood back into them. "We'll disinfect one more time, then do the walk-through with the client. Guts wants me there so I can watch Grady in case I ever have to do it."

"See if you can get some time alone in the bathroom. Then go to that same spot, and see what happens. Try using the tile as a reflective surface. Think you can do that?"

Arie gave Chandra her best "duh" look. "I've been going to the bathroom by myself for over twenty years. I can manage." The doubtful look plastered to Chandra's face was not reassuring.

The next morning, Arie made it to the job site before Grady and found Neal, the hoarder's son, waiting next to his car in the driveway. She knew better than to take him on a tour of the cleanup, but there was no reason she shouldn't make polite conversation while they waited.

Arie introduced herself, something she had skipped during her freak out the day before. When she held her hand out to shake, the man gave a moue of disgust and turned away as if he didn't see the appendage dangling there, all friendly and professional. Arie's first reaction was to be offended, but she remembered in time that the man had seen her scraping fragments of his daddy off a wall with a putty knife just the day before. She decided to cut him some slack.

"This must be so difficult for you, Mr. Petranik," Arie ventured. "Do you have any other family to help with everything?"

Besides the sister I only know about because your father keeps playing "This Is My Life" in my head, I mean?

"Call me Neal, please. Mr. Petranik is my father." Neal blanched. "Was." He cast a despairing look at the house where his father had died.

"It must be pretty overwhelming, Neal. Did you grow up here?"

He nodded, still staring at the house.

He hadn't answered the question about family members, so Arie decided to try again. "Did you have siblings?"

Neal still looked distracted. "My sister is coming in from Detroit, but she had to take care of some things before she could set out. I don't know what we're going to do with all of this. We can't sell it in this condition, can we?"

"Uh, I'm not sure. Grady will be the one to ask. He should be here any minute."

Just then, Grady pulled up in a BioClean truck. When he saw Arie standing next to the client, he frowned. She waved cheerfully, then hurried to get in another question before Grady caught up to them.

"Did your dad give you that Rubik's Cube?" Arie asked. "The one I saw you holding yesterday?"

Now, Neal looked a *lot* confused. "What a strange . . . the Rubik's Cube?"

Grady appeared at their side.

"I saw you with the Cube yesterday. I thought maybe it was a, um, talisman or something. A keepsake."

Grady's eyes widened at the unusual topic. He frowned at Arie, then reached forward and shook Neal's hand. Neal, so distracted he actually consented to the skin contact, continued staring at Arie like the imbecile she already felt like. Clipboard in one hand, Grady put his other on Neal's shoulder, guiding him toward the front door. They'd gone about three feet when Neal stopped and turned back.

"It was a Christmas present."

They stared into each other's eyes for a long moment, then Grady nudged him forward, casting a distinct WTF glare over his shoulder. Arie slunk behind, but Grady stopped her.

"Why don't you wait outside, Arie?" Technically, it was a question, but his tone made it obvious that it wasn't.

"I'm supposed to watch you in case I have to do the walk-through someday."

He gave an "as if" snort.

"I'll be quiet. I promise."

As Grady started shaking his head again, Arie added, "And I have to go to the bathroom. Really bad."

He closed his eyes in exasperation, but the "I have to go to the bathroom" excuse—bane of teachers and parents putting their kids to bed—was impossible to ignore. Arie considered giving a little pee-pee dance hip wiggle just to seal the deal, but didn't want to be disrespectful. The man standing next to them had just lost his father, after all.

Grady stepped back with a sigh, letting her enter.

"We only have the one bathroom," Neal said.

Arie scooted down the hall, leaving Grady and Neal to go over the trash removal estimate. Despite her earlier assertion that she was supposed to listen, Grady wasn't waiting. Arie couldn't blame him. She felt like such a moron.

That feeling didn't change when she finally pushed the thumb lock on the bathroom door. Chandra had made it sound so simple, but now that she was there, staring blankly at the clean tile, she was at a loss. Arie walked over to the bit of wall where she'd had the vision. She remembered to take cleansing breaths and tried to concentrate. Or wait—was she supposed to concentrate or not? She couldn't remember.

Someone knocked on the bathroom door, and Arie almost collapsed into the tub. It didn't matter how well she had cleaned it. That tub was *not* her happy place.

"I'm in here," Arie called.

"No kidding," Grady said. "Are you planning on ever coming out? 'Cause Mr. Petranik needs to sign off on the Completed Work form, and to do that, we need to inspect the work."

Grady's voice left no doubt as to his irritation.

Arie was going to lose her job for sure.

She whipped open the door to find the two men waiting in the cramped, overstuffed hallway.

"I'm so sorry," Arie said. "I just . . . This is my first job and, uh, I just wanted to make sure I hadn't missed a single thing. I wanted it to be perfect."

Grady's face relaxed a bit, and he shot a glance at Neal.

Neal smiled. "That's very nice, Miss . . . uh, Amy. I'm sure you've done a fine job."

Neither Grady nor Arie corrected his error about her name. Instead, Arie slid past the men and headed for the exit. It would probably be best if she stayed out of the way. *Way* out of the way.

CHAPTER EIGHT

BioClean didn't get the trash removal job, but at least Arie didn't get fired. If the Petraniks had gone with a different cleaning company, she probably would have been, but the family took what Guts called the cheap route and decided to take care of the trash themselves. It was a shame because Arie could sure have used the money.

As she had quickly learned, biohazard cleaning paid well but, unfortunately, not often. It also didn't help that Grady and Arie were only called out for every other case, alternating jobs with the other team. Both suspected Guts of funneling extra work to Bruno and Rich. Their team had a new hire, too, so they were able to handle larger jobs. Stan, the other newbie, and Arie had gone through the all-too-brief twelve-hour training together. They hadn't bonded.

Stan closely resembled an ambulatory cadaver, and his sense of humor was about as animated. His former job, carpet installation, had in no way trained him for biohazard cleanup, unless you counted a certain facility with utility knives as a benefit. He'd been laid off at the start of the housing crisis, and with a wife and kids to support, he was apparently willing to do anything.

Bruno and Rich, on the other hand, had both been with Guts since the start of the company. Bruno looked and acted exactly as one would expect a Bruno to act. From the blocky, muscleman body to the thatch of black hair covering his entire body, he looked like Popeye's rival. It took enormous effort for Arie to refrain from calling him Bluto. His partner, Rich, was blond with wavy surfer hair and a runner's physique, and had gone to school with Guts. A distinctly unfair advantage—one of the few things Grady and Arie agreed on.

Worse? Arie's landlord had finally tracked her down and hand-delivered her very own, first ever eviction notice. She'd never been so ashamed. By now, she was nearly four months behind, and even though she could drag the eviction out, she didn't want to accrue that kind of debt. Chandra had offered to let Arie crash at her place, but she lived in a studio apartment. That kind of arrangement would only work temporarily, and Arie wasn't quite that desperate. Yet. She kept telling herself she had options.

Well, one option. And one obstacle.

Arie's mother had perfected the art of saying the proper things while broadcasting her true feelings through weary sighs, a regal uplift of an exasperated eyebrow, or a slight shaking of her perfectly coiffed head. She even had a way of blinking that signaled her despair of ever understanding her daughter.

"Four months?" Evelyn said after Arie finished fessing up.

"Three, actually. Not counting this month's rent."

She got the eyebrow.

"I guess that is four," Arie relented. "There isn't a lot of stuff to move—"

Evelyn gasped. "Edward, you'll never guess what I've just thought of."

Her dad's typically placid features crinkled into slight worry. "What would that be, Ev?"

"It's perfect. Absolutely perfect. You know how we've been fretting over what to do with Grandpa Wilston? Well, here is our answer."

Evelyn beamed and clasped her hands under her chin. She loved it when her plans came together, especially before she'd even made them.

Arie's father shrugged, and he gave her an "I'm sorry" look that terrified her even more than her mother's creamy expression of satisfaction.

"What?" Arie asked. "What's perfect?"

"We can have her set up in no time, Edward. We can probably even borrow Norm Kenwick's pickup truck and save money on a moving van. It's not like she has much, anyway." Turning to her daughter, Evelyn said, "Can you be ready by Saturday? That's if we get the truck, of course. I can't imagine Norm not loaning it to us, but I guess we'd better be sure. Edward, let's give him a jingle right now, and—"

"Mom. Stop. What are you planning? I don't even know what you're talking about."

"Grandpa Wilston, of course."

"Grumpa?"

Evelyn's face emptied as if a plug had been pulled.

I should be so lucky . . .

"Don't call him that. Grandpa Wilston has been a bit of a concern lately." Evelyn closed her eyes as if suddenly weary. Maybe she needed a nap? "Do you know, just the other day, he gave his social security number to a telemarketer? A scam artist, really. And then—"

"But what does this have to do with me?"

"If you'll just be patient, I'll tell you. Your father and I have been worried sick. I went over last week and found four boxes of those Ginseng knives. The ones on the TV? I couldn't believe it! Who needs four boxes of steak knives? We always knew we would have to make this decision one day, but I, for one, thought we were many years away . . . "

Arie let her mother prattle on. It would be a good five minutes before Evelyn stopped circling the conversational airport and landed the plane. Meanwhile, icy foreboding seeped into Arie's heart.

She had always wanted a grandpa to love. Her father's parents had died before Arie was even born, and she'd always been jealous that Brant had known them, even if he'd only been four when first Bapa, then Nana had passed. When Arie had died and gone to the Other Side, she'd looked for them, but she'd been forced back into her body before she'd had a chance.

Grumpa, though. He was a grandparent of another color. Gray, mostly. Maybe a little murky brown thrown in.

It explained a lot about her mother, though at the moment, Arie wasn't able to feel sorry for her. She was too busy resenting the continuous machinations her mother went through to arrange Arie's life. Maybe she just didn't have the energy.

"And so I said to your father, something has to be done. We can't just ignore the problem."

"*I'm* the problem?" Arie said.

"I never said that. We're discussing your grandfather and his living arrangement."

It was no use. Arie could feel herself being sucked in as usual.

"What about his living arrangement?"

Evelyn sighed and rubbed her forehead. "His living arrangement is now your living arrangement. We're going to move you in with Grandpa Wilston and kill two birds with one stone. Perfect. Like I said."

Perfect.

CHAPTER NINE

"Dude, you're creeping me out!"

Grady's voice cut through the home movie version of Agnes Weaver's life that had been playing in Arie's head. It had been so beautiful.

She struggled to erase the silly grin from her face. "Sorry," Arie stuttered. "I was only—"

"I don't wanna know. Get busy. We're only contracted for eight man hours. Guts doesn't pay overtime if we go over the estimate."

Arie struggled to pay attention to the task at hand. They hadn't had a job in over a week, and Arie was desperate not to screw this one up. No matter how she dreaded the situation, she'd about resigned herself to an eighty-three-year-old roommate with telemarketer issues. Not that he had agreed to the arrangement yet; her mother was still working on him. But even that couldn't spoil her current mood.

Death had gotten it right for Agnes—a pleasant surprise for both her and Arie. Even though her left-behind body had remained undiscovered for three long summer days, the actual leaving of it had been welcomed, by Agnes, anyway—or so her visions told Arie. The dead woman's relatives were far less sanguine about the event, and after several days of the body left untended, were understandably squeamish about doing the cleanup themselves.

Grady's phone rang, startling Arie all over again. He went outside to answer it. Despite her good intentions, Arie hurried back to the small spot of blood caught in the grout of the kitchen tile. Agnes must have hit her head when she'd fallen. Arie stared at it.

The mist swirled—green this time, like apples and springtime and a new love. Joy rose in her chest like a bubble, and the most profound sense of peace she'd experienced since her visit to the Other Side settled over her.

Flash.

Pat Boone's on the jukebox singing "Ain't That a Shame," makin' my foot tap. Well, now. Who's that fellow headin' my way? He's a tall one, ain't he? A curl of black hair falls over his face, and I laugh when he brushes it back. He actually blushed! And oh my . . . them eyes. Hazel, maybe. A girl could get lost in them eyes.

Flash.

Smoke is rollin' from the oven. Burns my eyes. Oh, lordy! The roast! Bennie's laughing so hard he can't hardly throw water from the pitcher on it. I guess this means PB and J for supper again. Lordy.

Flash.

Dang this wind. The sheet flaps against my whole body, twisting me up like a mummy. My arms ache from wrestling to get these stupid linens on the line, and the clothespin keeps slipping from my lips. But it's gonna smell so good tonight. Tonight, when Bennie holds me—

Arie pulled out of the vision right before Grady walked back in. She coughed to cover the lingering smile, but he didn't notice this time.

"Almost done?" he asked.

"Yep. How's it look?"

Grady peered at the floor. There was still a dark spot, but the kitchen hadn't been remodeled in twenty years— one dark spot among a multitude of coffee spills and grease stains. Agnes had been a good cook once she'd learned to use the oven timer.

Arie's grandfather had worked most of his adult life as a member of the most hated profession ever created. Being an IRS auditor had suited him. Unlike Agnes Weaver, his personal life hadn't. All her life, an aura of mystery had surrounded any mention of her grandma. From the little bits that Arie had unearthed, she knew Lily Wilston had stayed in the marriage just long enough to produce a daughter for her chronically cranky, perfectionist husband, and then had abruptly vanished.

After living all those years on his own, Grumpa wasn't any more eager for the transition than his granddaughter. In fact, he had refused to discuss the possibility for nearly two weeks. He had even hung tight in the face of his daughter's thinly disguised threat of sending him to a retirement community. When, in seeming retreat, she'd shifted tactics and given her father a choice between his granddaughter moving in or "hiring a nice, respectable lady from Happy Helping Hands," he too had given in to the inevitable.

Moving everything Arie held dear really only took one afternoon. As pastor of the smaller of the town's two Baptist churches, her father had plenty of resources to tap into. For the cost of a half-dozen pizzas, the youth group had shown up en masse to transfer Arie's things from her apartment to Grumpa's house. The adolescents cheerfully hauled boxes, garbage bags, and a couple of suitcases through Grumpa's sunken living room and then down the hall to the former guest room. A few paused to remark favorably on the retro look of the furnishings. The sunken living room with the red brick fireplace received the highest raves.

While Arie didn't mind the decor—in fact, she agreed it was kind of funky—she hated the plastic-covered couch and the plastic runners that had been laid down on the high-traffic areas of the carpet. The couch made the backs of her legs itch, and she knew from childhood that if she tried to lie down, she'd end up with a pool of sweat puddled under her cheek.

Ignoring Evelyn's frantic efforts to keep them organized, the laughing, hyper teens poured around the adults like frothy water in a babbling brook. Grumpa grumbled loudly about the invasion and scolded any who stepped off the plastic runways.

Arie decided staying out of the way was the best choice, and she made for the front door. Sneaking out, she hid around the corner of the garage, where she pretended to supervise the unpacking process.

Instead, she called Chandra. "Where are you?"

"Calm down," Chandra said in a voice dripping with patience. "I told you I wouldn't be there 'til after lunch. Any pizza left?"

"Are you kidding? These kids are like a hoard of locusts. They swarmed the pizza delivery guy while he was still in the driveway. The boxes never even made it to the kitchen table. I didn't even get to *smell* the pizza." Arie's stomach rumbled.

She peeked around the corner of the house. "I can't believe I'm doing this. I forgot all about the pink bathroom. Did I tell you about that? It looks like a flamingo experienced epic amounts of intestinal discomfort in there. The whole room is pink—tub, sink, all the tile. Even the *toilet* is pink. And do you realize I have to share it with Grumpa?"

"Holy crap," Chandra said. "You have to share a bathroom? That seems, like, medieval. Can't you use the guest bathroom?"

"There is only one bathroom in the entire house. One. And Grumpa has his Aqua Velva and his shaving stuff scattered all over the place. And get this, Chan. He leaves his denture goop and the glass he sticks his teeth into at night right there on the counter."

Chandra's groan rattled through the cell phone.

"All night long," Arie continued in a horrified voice. "If I get up to go to the bathroom in the middle of the night, they're going to be there, *smiling* at me."

"I'm on my way, and I'm bringing sustenance."

Arie clicked off and rested her head against the siding. She didn't even care if there was bird poop on it.

"Yoo hoo!" Evelyn called from the side of the truck. "What are you doing over there? We need you. No time for breaks."

Arie sighed and trudged over to her mother.

"You need to make sure those children aren't just tossing your boxes every which way. They're just impossible. I told your father—"

58

She left before her mother could get a full harangue going and headed inside the house, avoiding the kitchen where Grumpa had retreated. She could hear him muttering about the "herd of buffalo" that had been set loose in his house.

Despite the chaos, the teens were doing a decent job. A trio stood in living room under the blue chunky-glass Lucite orb dangling from the ceiling by a large-linked brass chain. One of the girls looked over at Arie and pointed at it. "I love it!" she squeaked. "It's a light, right?"

"Yeah." Arie walked over and felt along the electrical cord that wound around the chain until she found the switch and clicked it on.

"Ooh, it's so pretty," the girl cooed.

"Uh huh. Gorgeous."

A crash at the other end of the house set her heart racing. She hurried down the hall and discovered her father shooing two boys out of her room.

"We're fine," her dad said. "Just a little mishap."

Arie checked to make sure his smile didn't have the little worry lines that bracketed his mouth whenever he had to initiate soothing-pastor mode. They were absent, and she relaxed.

An hour and a half later, the teens piled back into the church van to follow Norm Kenwick's truck over to the Stiles' home in order to stack the odds and ends of furniture that wouldn't fit in the space Grumpa had allotted her. Evelyn scurried to her car, anxious to beat them to the house. She was still calling out directions even as the van backed down the driveway.

Arie sighed and forced herself to return to the house. Quiet had finally descended. She headed to her room and discovered her father placing knickknacks on the shelves of a curio cabinet that had been temporarily relocated from the guest room to the hall. For a moment, Arie was reminded of Leonard Petranik's narrow hallway, and she shivered. As she moved around her dad, she accidentally jostled the cabinet and caused several figurines to fall over with a clatter. Arie picked one up. A ceramic boy with enormous round eyes. *Grumpa collected Precious Moments figurines?*

The noise brought Grumpa stomping down the hall to them. "Here now! You be careful there. Don't you have any respect at all? This isn't going to work out. I can't have all this commotion. And I'm not going to have you crashing around and destroying my things. You never could—"

"Now, Harlan, let's just relax," Ed interposed. "Nothing was broken, and it's just as much my fault as Arie's. Neither one of us meant to disrespect your belongings."

"Oh, really? Well, if we're talking about disrespect, none of this was my idea, was it? If barging into a man's home and forcing him to play nursemaid to a—"

"It wasn't my idea, either," Arie said. "And, for the record, I'm the one supposed to be watching you."

"That's enough, you two," Ed said. "This is going to help both of you. In fact, I'm sorry to have to point this out, but neither of you has a choice. Instead of snapping at each other, you should be grateful."

"Grateful?" Grumpa snorted. "Grateful for—"

"Yes. Grateful. Now, we're going to need to find a new place for this cabinet. It sticks out into the walkway, and it's going to get bumped again. Do you want it in your bedroom instead?"

"I want it back where it belongs." Grumpa pointed through the open door of Arie's new room.

"I understand you don't like change, but Arie has to have a place for her things, too. How about the den?"

"No, it doesn't belong there."

"Harlan—"

"It can stay right here until she gets her own place, and then it can go right back where it belongs. The girl can be careful, can't she?" Grumpa didn't wait for an answer before marching back to the kitchen.

Arie sighed. "Dad, I can't—"

"Honey, this is just temporary. Heaven knows it's not ideal, but really, what can you do? Not that I would mind, but if this doesn't work out, you'll have to move back in with your mother and me. And that means your grandfather would end up in a nursing home. Either that, or he moves in with us, and you find other arrangements. Or, heck! We might all end up living together—one big happy family."

Father and daughter shuddered.

"Okay, but what about when I'm back on my feet?"

"We'll cross that bridge when we come to it. At any rate, with you living here, we'll have a better understanding of Harlan's situation. He seems sharp as a tack to me, but your mother's worried. And he has made some unusual choices lately."

Arie sighed again, then went into her room to unpack. She wanted to make it as comfortable as possible. She had a feeling she'd be spending a lot of time there.

CHAPTER TEN

A few days after she'd settled in with Grumpa, Guts finally called. The job was on the rich side of town. The huge white van with BioClean emblazoned on the side was parked in the lot, letting her know she'd found the right address. As Arie pulled in next to it, she noticed a man walking away from the building. As he crossed in front of her car, their gazes met and held.

Wow.

The blue of his eyes almost stopped her heart, but it restarted with a bang when he tossed her a wink. He was parked two slots down, and Arie got a nice, long bonus view of his butt while he walked to his car. She snatched her gaze away when he glanced back, but not before he caught her.

She waited until he'd driven off before getting out of her car. She noticed a sleek black pickup with the same logo parked next to the van. *Oh, crap.* The boss was here, and she was loitering in the parking lot, ogling strangers.

She thought about the guy's wink and decided it had been worth it.

Guts stood next to Grady in the pristine white living room, issuing instructions. Grady had his clipboard out, and was nodding and taking notes. He wore his suit, too, but Guts was keeping it simple with jeans and a navy blue T-shirt with the BioClean logo. Arie hadn't seen Guts since her interview and wondered if Grady had told him about her weird behavior at the hoarder job.

As she approached the men, Guts was saying, "Took the cops forever to release the scene. I was starting to think we weren't gonna get the job, but the head of the HOA finally called and gave us the go-ahead.

"Bruno and Stan are gonna hate missing this one, but they're on another job. So make sure you don't eff this up. This is the big leagues here. The broad was a famous writer. Made a boatload o' cash with some girly book."

"Cool," Arie said. "What did she write?"

"How should I know? You think I got time to read? I got a business to run here."

Arie decided to fade into the background. She really didn't want to call attention to herself. Given recent events, she had no idea how she would react to a murder, and she certainly didn't want to risk having a vision in front of her boss.

As soon as Guts left, Arie started hauling supplies to the apartment while Grady set up a clean zone—an uncontaminated area they could use as a base for supplies and equipment. In a job this "wet," booties and gloves were changed each time anyone on the crew crossed the barrier. In this case, the wide, square foyer was the obvious choice for the clean zone, and little more needed to be done.

Grady and Guts had done the preliminary inspection. The murder itself had taken place in the victim's bedroom, but according to Grady, other areas were involved, too. Apparently, the victim had tried barricading herself in the bathroom, but then the attack crossed the hall to the bedroom.

Arie listened carefully as Grady outlined the plan.

"Okay, first we grab and bag. Then we do a preliminary wash down of the walls and exposed surfaces. I'm guessing we'll have to dump the mattress. After all that, we'll pull the carpet and see what we got to deal with then."

"What do you mean?"

"If she bled out on a tile floor, there might be a chance that the underlayment wouldn't be too bad. But a carpet? No way the underflooring won't be a mess. This one time? The blood soaked all the way through to the apartment below." Grady grinned. "That was a pretty good job there. It turned into a two-fer. We got called in to deal with the overflow in the downstairs place."

Crime scene cleanup had its own special kind of humor.

Arie decided to do a preliminary look-see, so she'd know what to expect. She started with the bathroom. It wasn't as bad as she'd feared, but nevertheless, it was obvious that an attack had occurred there. Bloody footprints and streaks smeared in long swaths across the tiled floor. Arie could tell the victim had attempted to hold the door shut against the intruder. She avoided looking directly at the blood. For now, anyway. She wasn't sure how she would handle it when she had to, and she didn't want Grady popping in until she did know.

Following the blood trail, she saw that the attack continued across the hall into the victim's bedroom. Once a pristine white oasis, the room now looked like an abattoir. Most of the furniture was covered with a fine layer of fingerprint dust. As nearly as Arie could tell, Grady may have gotten his wish about the mattress. It looked as if it had been spared.

Unfortunately, the carpet did not fare as well. Arie swallowed. Grady had said they might have to remove floorboards. How could that much blood come from just one person? That was when Arie made her mistake. She looked at the blood dead on.

A red haze covered her eyes, and utter panic flooded her body and soul. She grabbed the edge of a nearby dresser to steady herself.

As before, the blood shimmered with an almost painful radiance. Arie tried to take a deep breath, but her lungs would only cooperate with short, raspy pants.

Fear—no, panic—scattered her thoughts. Lossst. The thought intruded like a knife into her skull. So lost. Where am I? Good question. Not hell, Arie decided. But definitely not the place Arie had visited during her own time on the Other Side. Lossst. She sensed the voice coming from a place of confusion and despair. Arie felt it trying to take over her mind. There was an unearthly wailing and an endless stretching of time. A low, moaning chorus filled her ears.

"Holy, holy, holy."

It took a minute for Arie to understand why Grady didn't burst through the door. She wasn't hearing with her ears but with her mind.

She began to hyperventilate. The white flash exploded in her head. Then . . .

Frenzied movement. A knife arcing through the air. Hands—a man's hands—clutching at my throat. They grip like a vise, fingernails digging into the soft flesh of my throat. The pressure . . . closing around my neck. . . the red haze deepens.

Flash.

"Holy, holy, holy."

Flash.

Head bowed, his honey-blond hair hides his face. He slips the ring on my finger. Thank goodness I've just had a manicure. I reach with my other hand to stroke his hair.

The engagement ring—an exquisite solitaire-cut diamond so large it weighs my hand down—sparkles like sunlight reflecting off a crystal-clear lake.

Church bells pealed so loudly that Arie instinctively flinched. She choked on the mingled scents of roses and lily-of-the-valley, so thick she could taste them.

Flash.

Hands clutch my throat. Pressure . . . building. . . the dark is coming.

Flash.

A voice thundered, *"The blood cries to Me."* Arie stumbled to her knees, grabbing at her ears, even though the sound was internal.

Flash.

My old Raggedy Ann doll is in her place on the shelf next to the journal: cracked red leather, a silver lock and clasp. And a key—dull, though, and too large to fit the diary's tiny lock. Rags. Keep it safe.

Flash.

The bathroom is filthy, of course. The tub's loaded with dirty dishes, pots, and pans, just like it always is. They shut the water

66

off ages ago. I'm filthy. I turn to the sink. It's just as dirty. I'm not supposed to use the jug of water for bathing; it's for drinking. But I have no choice. I'll never make it out of this dump if I let myself—my outside self—look as nasty as I really am. I refuse to look in the mirror. There's nothing there I want to see, anyway. I open the medicine cabinet, as much to avoid the mirror as to get the mouthwash I have stashed inside. Cockroaches scatter, as chaotic as my thoughts. I slam the cabinet door shut. And there I am—almost a woman, blond, green-eyed.

Flash.

A wash of bleach filled Arie's nostrils, so real she choked and her eyes watered.

A two-inch stack of typed papers sits on the desk in front of me. The black ink nestles against the white background like a million spiders on a web. My book, and it's finally finished. It's going to be even better than before.

Flash.

The diary again. The smell of bleach lingers.

"What the hell are you doing now?"

Grady's voice pierced through the red haze that enveloped Arie. She gasped, almost as grateful for the fresh air as she had been during Grady's initiation test back at Leonard's house.

Grady stared at her as if she'd lost her mind. Maybe she had. He crossed his arms and waited.

Arie stood and gave herself a mental shake. "I, uh, I was just . . . "

"Listen," Grady said. "It's just another job. You can't let what happened here get to you. Don't start imagining things. That's what's getting Rich into trouble. Imagining things. He's letting it into his head, and that's a bad scene."

"What's going on with Rich?" *Maybe he had some weird psychic power, too?* "I thought he was Guts's go-to guy."

"He is. He's been with Guts since the beginning. But look at his life now. His wife took the kids and left him a year ago. Moved back to Utah with her family, and now he never sees the kids. He used to be on the bowling league, went to church, you know? He had a *life*. Now all he does is wash his hands a hundred times a day and run around disinfecting his house. Cleans all the time. He's got this sweet Corvette he's been working on for years, and now he won't even go near it."

"What happened?" Arie asked the question even though she'd already guessed the answer.

"This job happened," Grady said. "He started seeing things." At the look on Arie's face, Grady shook his head. "Not like imaginary things. He just started seeing how things happened, you know, like, to the victims. You work here long enough, you start to figure things out. Probably every single one of us could be one of those CSI techs. Take this job—it's obvious she tried hiding in the bathroom. If you let your mind go there, you can see it. Her running to the bathroom, some dude chasing her. She gets there, she thinks she's safe, but he gets there, too. And she can't get the door shut. There you go. You can see it, right? The whole thing. And that's just the start. 'Cause then you can see them cross the hall. Maybe he's dragging her. Maybe she took off, trying to find the phone. Whatever. It's all right here, laid out like a story. If you start telling yourself that story, you're going to lose it. You can't let that stuff into your mind. You'll go crazy. And you won't be the first."

If he only knew.

After they had fully suited up, Grady handed Arie a box of red, heavy-duty garbage bags. The bathroom was too small for them to both work inside, so Grady settled in there and sent Arie to the bedroom to start clearing away items contaminated by fingerprint dust.

"But how do we know if the family wants some of this stuff?" Arie asked.

"You got to make a judgment call. The more personal it is, the more you know you gotta keep it. Just make sure you mark the bags and set them aside for the family. And for Pete's sake, don't mix them up."

Arie steeled herself as she went into the bedroom. Like the living room, the decor was white-on-white, except, of course, for the surfaces that had been splashed a gory brownish maroon or coated in black fingerprint dust. A four-by-five puddle of blood pooled at the foot of the bed. There was no way the carpet could absorb the amount of blood that had been shed there. As Arie stared the center of the pool, it began to shimmer and glisten. A tendril of fear twisted through her body.

Arie shut her eyes and took a deep breath. When she was certain she wasn't going to succumb to another vision, she opened her eyes, careful to look away from the puddle.

Her eyes fell on an object on the floor near the walk-in closet. It was easy to understand how she'd missed it. Like everything else in the room, it was white.

And it would certainly qualify as a personal item.

Arie walked closer and picked it up. A wedding dress. An expensive one, by the look of it. A bloody shoe print on the embroidered bodice was its only imperfection. She checked the label. Yup. Vera Wang.

The dress reminded her of the engagement ring from the death vision. That had also been pretty spendy. The embroidery glittered. So pretty. An alien trickle of pride flittered through Arie's chest. Arie shuddered, dropped the dress, and backed away.

Closing her eyes didn't help this time. Someone else's fear swamped Arie, flooding her from the inside out.

Flash.

The hands at my throat . . . squeezing . . .

A crash from the bathroom jolted Arie out of the trance. She leaned against the dresser, trying to catch her breath.

"Sorry about that," Grady called from the other room. "I knocked over the bucket."

"No problem," Arie managed to say.

"You okay in there? You don't sound good."

"I'm okay. I just, uh, it's just hot in this suit."

To Arie's relief, she heard Grady mutter his agreement from the bathroom. With grim determination, she grabbed a fresh garbage bag and approached the Vera Wang as if there could be a cobra hidden in its folds. A thought occurred to her.

"Hey, Grady? This dress has blood on it. It's evidence, isn't it?"

He came and stood in the doorway. "If it was evidence, they would have taken it."

"But look." She spread out the dress. "It's got a bloody footprint. Maybe they missed it."

"I doubt it. Cops don't miss things like that." At her expression, he sighed. "Okay, stick it in a separate bag, and we'll have Guts call 'em. And see if you can hustle a little bit more. You should be done clearing by now."

This was going to be a long day.

CHAPTER ELEVEN

Grady wiped the walls as Arie continued clearing the room of blood-contaminated objects. She started with the Vera Wang. The bloody smear seemed to hum when she picked up the dress, but she took a deep breath and forced herself to stuff it deep into a large red biohazard trash bag. She moved to the dresser, a modernistic black-lacquered monstrosity. Its surface was so shiny, her face loomed out of the black depths when she peered down at it. Suddenly, a red haze misted over her reflection. An atonal chorus sang, "Holy, holy, holy . . . " Arie gasped and pulled back as though from an abyss.

The blood cries to Me . . .

Teeth chattering, she cleared the dresser, tossing a hairbrush and a deodorant stick into the bag as she went. When she came to a jewelry box, she set it aside. There wasn't any blood on it, but it was covered in fingerprint dust and needed to be wiped down.

Arie moved to the nightstand beside the bed. Sprays of blood streaked across the top, and it looked as though it had been shoved to one side. A drawer was open a few inches. Had the victim been trying to reach into it? Some people kept guns in their nightstands for home protection. A can of mace, maybe? Or had the killer rifled through it, looking for something? Arie glanced at Grady. She knew he was right about the dangers of speculation, but she found it nearly impossible to resist.

She glanced at the small pile of books on the stand. Romance novels. Something stirred inside Arie. She bent over and picked one up.

Not a romance this time. This was a hardcover in a paper jacket. The title, *Rich Bitch*, was embossed in a glittery gold font. A wedding ring set with a rock the size of Gibraltar sparkled just below the title. In fact, the set looked a lot like . . . My engagement ring—so large it weighs my hand down. It sparkles like sunlight reflecting off a crystal-clear lake.

Arie dropped the book, and it slid under the bed.

Grady glanced at her. "You all right?"

"I'm fine. I just, uh, dropped a book." Arie picked it back up and waved it at him.

"Dude, you left your gloves on. That's cross-contamination. Now you gotta toss her book."

"Damn. I'm sorry."

"It happens, but you really gotta watch it. And make sure you never, ever forget and touch your face when you're wearing them. So gross." Grady turned back to his task.

Arie grabbed the nearest bio-bag, but the photograph on the back of the book caught her eye. She looked closer. It was a slightly older version of the girl in the mirror. Something about the woman seemed familiar but Arie couldn't chase down the connection, if indeed there was one. She flipped the book back around to verify the author's name. Marissa Mason.

"Didn't Guts say that the victim here had written a book?"

"Yeah," Grady said. "Why?"

Arie waggled the book again. "I think this is her. The victim. This must be the book."

Grady shrugged. "What's the big deal? She wrote a book. Oh, wait. I get it. You want to read that book, huh? Gonna figure out how to catch a rich guy?" He turned back to the wall and resumed scrubbing. "Can't say I blame you. It's not like I want to be doing this job for the rest of my life, either."

Arie mumbled an agreement and, tucking the book under her arm, grabbed the trash bags. "I'm taking these to the van."

As soon as she reached the parking lot, Arie wiped the smear of blood off the book cover and hid it under the front seat of her car. As she bent over, she realized she'd forgotten to take off the outer layer of booties. *Crap.* She hoped Grady hadn't noticed.

She snatched them off and, intending to throw the bloodstained footwear inside, started picking at the ties on one of the trash bags. Then stopped. At some point, she was going to have to figure out what worked and what didn't with this scrying thing. And for that, she would probably need blood.

Grabbing a wadded-up fast-food bag from the back seat, Arie dumped a couple of straggler fries onto the ground and shoved the stained booties inside. The bag got stuffed beside Marissa's book.

After slinging the trash bags into the back of the van, she hurried back to the condo.

Unfortunately, the rest of the day didn't go any better. Death visions popped up everywhere she looked. Anything shiny or reflective, including liquids, served to channel the dead woman's last moments straight into Arie's brain.

After the first hour and a half, Arie had worked up a migraine and was sick to her stomach. She tried to play it off, but when it came time to pull up the blood-soaked carpet, she couldn't handle it anymore and ended up running for the bathroom.

"Hey! Not there. I just sanitized that room," Grady shouted after her.

Too late.

On her way home, Arie called Chandra and begged her friend to let her sleep over. With all that she had to wrestle, she couldn't handle thought of going back to Grumpa's alone.

"Of course you can," Chandra told her. "Do you want to swing by Subway or somewhere and grab something to eat on your way?"

"Don't even talk about food," Arie groaned. Apparently, relentless visions from murder victims worked as an appetite suppressant. Who knew?

She gripped the steering wheel so hard her knuckles blanched, and her eyes throbbed with the effort of concentrating on the road. Every time her gaze landed on something shiny or reflective—not a rare occurrence on a highway—the threat of a death vision vibrated inside her head. She managed to keep them at bay, but fighting them made her stomach roil. She pulled into a gas station so she could call her grandfather and let him know her plans.

As delighted as Grumpa seemed about having the house to himself, it didn't stop him from complaining. "What am I supposed to say if your mother calls? She might want to know what you made me for supper. That's part of the deal, isn't it? Taking care of your poor old grandpa? I suppose that's too much to ask nowadays."

Arie sighed. *Nice try.* "Of course not, Grumpa. I can come home, and we can spend the whole evening together. Just you and me. I'll just swing by the grocery store, so I can pick up some healthy food. You know Mother wants you on a gluten-free, low-carb diet anyway."

"Never mind. I guess one night won't matter. I can make a sandwich."

"Well, if you're sure." Arie smiled for the first time that day. Her migraine slid back a notch. "And maybe we should keep this between us. We don't want Mother worrying over little things."

"That's true. And she probably doesn't need to know about a couple other things, either."

Arie's eyebrows rose. "Oh, really? Like what?"

"Never you mind, little girl. Never you mind."

They hung up, and this time Arie's grin stretched cheek to cheek. *What was that cranky old man up to, anyway?*

"What do you mean, they won't stop?" Chandra looked horrified.

"I mean the visions won't stop."

Arie scrunched up in the yellow beanbag chair with her eyes closed. "I keep seeing them. It's not just happening in the blood this time. They're constant, everywhere I look."

"What about with your eyes closed?"

"It's okay now. But when they're open, I can't keep from seeing them." Arie burst into tears.

Chandra knelt and wrapped her in a hug. "That sounds hideous. I just can't imagine it. But, Arie, listen. We're going to figure this out."

Eyes still closed, Arie smiled and leaned her head on Chandra's shoulder. Her friend smelled like cake.

They sat like that for a few minutes, and then Chandra asked, "What's different, Arie? I mean, about this particular job."

Arie took a deep, shuddering breath. She'd been too upset to share any of the details. Chandra scooted back to her favorite orange pillow and waited.

"I guess the big thing is it's a murder scene."

"Holy crap. I guess you could call that a difference."

Arie nodded at the understatement. "You know, now that I think about it, there has been something different about each of the scenes. At the suicide's, there was a gray fog I was looking through. It felt cold. But at Agnes's—that was the one where the little old lady just died—the fog wasn't gray. It was green. And it exuded a feeling of happiness."

"That is so flippin' awesome." Chandra hugged herself.

Arie smiled at her friend. "I guess it is. That one, anyway."

"So, you're thinking, what? That the color of the fog matches the way they died?"

"Makes sense, doesn't it? Leonard killed himself. The gray fog, the sadness. But with Agnes it was like . . . it was the same peace I felt when I was on the Other Side. I

76

think Agnes was ready to die. She was okay with it. But with Marissa—"

"Marissa?"

"Marissa Mason. She wrote a book called *Rich Bitch*."

Chandra's face scrunched in thought. "Her name sounds familiar. I'll have to check it out."

Arie got up, grabbed the book from under her purse, and handed it to Chandra. Making an "ick" face, her friend held it with the tips of her fingers.

"I wiped it off," Arie assured her.

"Oh, hey. I *do* know her. I read this."

"You read *this*?"

For the first time in the thirteen years Arie had known her, Chandra blushed.

"Well, I'm not saying it's great literature, but everyone was talking about it. I was curious, that's all." As Chandra paged through it, a stiff rectangle of paper slid out from between the pages and fell to the floor. Arie snatched it up. Creamy white paper embossed with a border of flowers. Gold ink. And just the faintest . . . Arie sniffed the card. Yup, it was scented. Roses again.

"What is it?" Chandra asked.

"It looks like one of those wedding programs. You know, the one that tells you when they're lighting the candles or whatever, and who's in the wedding party?"

"Maybe she was using it as a bookmark." Chandra went back to studying the book. After looking at the table of contents, she flipped it over and looked at the back.

"I can't believe she's dead. She looks like one of those golden girls. You know the type. Like Barbie two-point-oh. It's weird to think of her as just . . . gone."

"Well, I'm here to tell you she's not gone. Part of her is alive and well and currently stuck inside my head."

"Maybe that's the difference, then," Chandra said. "She's got unresolved issues. Isn't that the deal with ghosts? She's haunting you."

Arie shook her head. "This isn't a ghost, or at least it's not like any ghost I've ever heard of."

"The important part is that her death is unresolved. What is she showing you?"

"It's all jumbled up. It was a red fog this time. And I had this feeling of being lost or trying to find something. She did, I mean."

"Marissa," Chandra whispered.

"And there were hands at my throat. They were choking me. I can't even . . . I could feel her dying, and it felt like it was me."

Arie could feel her throat close as the memory grew more vivid.

"Who was it?" Chandra whispered.

Tears welled in Arie's eyes. "I don't *know*. I can't see his face. I've tried and tried, but . . . " A deep, shuddering sob twisted through her body.

Chandra reached over and held Arie's hand. "It's okay. You're doing good. How about the hands? What did they look like?"

Arie pressed her fingers to her forehead and forced herself to stay calm. "I don't know. But I don't remember seeing anything distinctive. No scars or tattoos or anything. At the time, I couldn't really think. It was . . . this feeling that I was about to die.

"You have to understand. When it's happening, it's like I'm them. It's not like a movie. I'm not watching. It feels like it's actually happening to me."

Chandra squeezed Arie's hand and took a deep breath. "Let's take a break. I think I should get something to eat."

"I can't eat."

"You have to try," Chandra said. "You need to keep your strength up. And—I don't know—you need to keep doing normal things."

As if to prove Chandra right, the visions receded a bit while they ate their meal. Arie still felt them, though. They lurked at the edge of her awareness as if waiting to pounce the moment she dropped her guard.

After supper, Arie was able to tell Chandra about some of the other elements of Marissa's death vision—the wedding ring, the diary and papers, the trailer.

Chandra was suitably grossed out by the image of the cockroaches scattering from under the medicine cabinet mirror. "That is so creepy."

"The whole thing is creepy. And I know I'm not remembering everything. It's hard. I can't separate myself from her when it's going on. I can't concentrate. I know I'm forgetting things. Did I even tell you about the weird angel chorus?"

"You're kidding, right? *Angels?*"

"Well, *something* keeps chanting the word 'holy' over and over again. And then this other voice, really loud and booming, says something about the blood calling to him. You know . . . like in the Bible?"

"That's your department, preacher kid, not mine."

"Genesis. Cain kills Abel and God finds out when Abel's blood calls to Him from the ground and, like, tattles, I guess. Then God curses Cain and so on. Don't tell me you never heard that one before."

"Well, yeah," Chandra said. "But I didn't know about blood calling or whatever. So does this mean God's talking to you or something?"

"I don't know." Tears welled in Arie's eyes. "I don't want God to talk to me. I'm freaked out enough as it is."

"Okay, I can't help you with the God thing. *Way* above my pay grade, but as far as forgetting things, why don't you try writing it down the next time?"

Chandra jumped up and rummaged through her bookshelf. She came back with a half-used spiral notebook and handed it to Arie.

It was a good idea. Arie set it by her purse, then retreated to the bathroom to wash her face and put on one of Chandra's oversized sleeping T-shirts. Time for bed.

CHAPTER TWELVE

Arie overslept. Worse, the assault of visions continued, and it showed. She didn't even have time to head back to Grumpa's house for a change of clothes. No makeup either, so she ended up using Chandra's. Her friend favored dark and dramatic. Not Arie's best look.

The more she thought about Chandra's theory that Marissa Mason had unresolved issues, the more anxious she grew. It felt right, but she didn't know what that meant for her. Whatever it was, it couldn't be good.

Grady put them right back to work on the carpet. Guts was coming by to check on the job that afternoon, and they would need to evaluate how extensively the flooring had been contaminated. That meant pulling up the plywood underlayment, and that couldn't happen until the carpet was dealt with.

"How are we going to do this?" Arie asked.

The Mason condo was the top floor of a five-story unit. Arie couldn't imagine how they would navigate the flights of stairs with a sodden, blood-soaked roll of carpet without contaminating their path every step of the way. She was exhausted even thinking about it.

Grady's answer didn't sound any better.

"We're going to cut it into strips, roll them up, and bag 'em. It'll be a lot more trips back and forth—"

"You mean up and down, don't you?" Arie was still thinking about those five flights of stairs. Using the unit's only elevator was out of the question. The condo's homeowners association was already upset at sharing the tiny elevator with "janitors of death" in their banana-yellow spacesuits and crates of cleaning supplies. The residents had voiced numerous complaints—and that had been before they'd started hauling out bright red biohazard bags filled with the gory realities of violent death. The HOA president owned several area bars, and Guts wanted to work out a contract for whenever the inevitable bar fights broke out and involved blood. Guts was determined to keep her happy.

"The whole thing?" Arie stared at the thirty-four-by-twenty-foot expanse of lush wool Berber carpet.

"Nah," Grady said. "Just the blood site. We'll have to take an extra five feet or so of what looks uncontaminated to make sure the blood didn't travel. You'd be surprised. But my guess is it didn't flow side to side." He shook his head ominously.

"You think it went . . . "

Grady jabbed his finger at the floor. "Down. My guess is it soaked into the floor trusses. We'll see. If it did, we can only do so much. That's why Guts is coming over. It's his call."

They got to work. Cutting through the backing of the carpet proved incredibly difficult. The razors in their utility knives dulled quickly. Arie was afraid she was going to cut off a finger. She could imagine Grady bitching at her for recontaminating the area. The only good thing was that, although they had to wear their biohazard suits—they did on almost every job—and rubber gloves, they didn't have to wear face masks. Nevertheless, Arie was sweating like a pig within the first twenty minutes.

They heard the condo's front door open.

"Dammit," Grady said. "Guts is early. He said he wouldn't be here 'til this afternoon. Go head him off, and tell him to come back after lunch."

Arie trudged off down the hall, happy to have a break, but wondering how Guts was going to react being told to go away and come back later.

She rounded the corner and almost ran smack into the amazing-blue-eyes-nice-butt, winky guy.

"Holy crap," he said.

Apparently he'd never seen a life-size ambulatory banana before.

Up close, the guy was even more gorgeous than she'd remembered. Coal black hair, those startling—and now startled—delft-blue eyes, and the hint of dark stubble that made a man in a business suit look rugged and sexy as hell.

"Who are you?" Arie managed to ask.

"No, the question is: Who are *you*?"

He sounded pissed, but Arie thought that was probably because she'd scared the hell out of him. Men didn't take well to bananas leaping out of dark hallways.

Recognition crept into his eyes. "That was you in the red Focus the other day, wasn't it?"

"Uh huh. I was late for work. I'm a cleanup tech," Arie said. *Duh. Like he couldn't figure that out.*

She scrambled to regain her composure. "I don't think anybody is supposed to be here. This is a crime scene."

She almost gasped at the brilliance of his smile. Unfortunately, it vanished almost as quickly as it had appeared.

"I'm aware this is a crime scene. In fact, it's *my* crime scene. I'm Detective Connor O'Shea."

"Oh." Arie's mind, not at its best today anyway, went utterly blank.

They stared at each other. O'Shea's eyes dipped, scanning Arie from her scraped-back-from-her-head-into-a-ponytail hair to her blue-booties-over-yellow-suit feet. Her heart skipped around a little until she remembered he was a cop. They had a tendency to look people over.

And she was blocking the hallway leading to his crime scene.

He raised a sooty eyebrow, waiting for her to figure out she needed to move aside.

"Oh," she said again. She stepped back against the wall, rattling the painting next to her head in its frame.

He slid past, but as he did, she could have sworn he stole another quick peek at the "girls," which jutted out like two cantaloupes. Arie's body flooded with heat. *Damn it.* She was blushing. She snatched up two trash bags and fled to the van.

Arie would have stayed away until she was certain that he had left, but she knew Grady would pitch a fit. As she tossed the bags in the back of the van, she remembered the wedding dress. She'd set it aside as Grady had suggested, but she didn't know if he'd told Guts or not.

When she returned to the apartment, Detective O'Shea stood in the living room. He had a small notebook out and was jotting something down.

"Can you tell me your name, please?"

"My name?" Arie squeaked.

O'Shea glanced up from his notes, and his lips tilted up slightly on one side. He closed the notebook and slipped it into his jacket pocket. "Just trying to be friendly."

"Oh," Arie said. *Good lord, couldn't she think of any other word?* Fortunately, she remembered the dress. She was even able to sound reasonably coherent when she described what she'd found and why she'd set it aside.

O'Shea was already nodding by the time she'd finished telling him about the footprint. "Thanks, we know about it. The dress snagged on the coroner's gurney when they were wheeling her out. One of the guys stepped on it. It's not evidence."

Arie resumed feeling stupid. The reprieve had been far too brief.

"And you still haven't told me your name."

"Arie." Since he was a cop, she added, "Like the initials—R.E."

"What do the initials stand for?"

"You'd have to shoot me first."

This time, he let the smile go, and it spread across his face like the sun. "I'd hate for it to come to that."

Grady ruined the moment by walking into the living room.

"Listen, while you guys were cleaning, did you come across anything like a journal or a diary? Appointment book? Anything like that?" O'Shea asked.

Grady shook his head no, but Arie stiffened at the mention of a diary.

Flash.

Red leather. A tiny silver lock. The smell of bleach fills her nostrils.

It was a mere moment, but the detective's eyes locked on hers. They weren't smiling anymore.

"I don't know where it is," Arie said.

"But you've seen something like that? Which was it?" O'Shea's tone was crisp and professional. He pulled the notebook back out.

"No. Of course not. I don't. . . . no."

O'Shea stared at Arie, his pencil still poised on the notepad. She stared back.

Grady laughed. "Dude, you are so weird." Turning to O'Shea, he said, "This is only like her third day. She's still freaked out. You should've seen her yesterday. Barfed all over the bathroom, and I'd just sanitized it."

O'Shea didn't look convinced, but he slowly put his notebook away. His eyes slid back and forth between Grady and Arie.

When the blue orbs landed back on Grady, Arie's coworker shook his head ruefully. "Newbies."

"Yeah," O'Shea said. "Newbies."

CHAPTER THIRTEEN

Guts showed up as expected right after lunch. He and Grady yanked up the bloodstained, four-by-eight sheet of plywood and then sprawled out on their stomachs to peer into the hole. The flashlight beams darted about while they examined the floor trusses. Arie hung back, trying to stay out of the way. The strobe-like effect of the flashing light bothered her. When the doorbell rang, they all jumped.

"Hey, get that," Guts said. "If it's reporters, send them away. In fact, send anybody else away. We can't have people traipsing around in here with a hole in the floor. Some jackass will fall in and sue me."

"It's been three weeks," Grady said. "It's not going to be reporters."

"Oh, yeah? It's not like it's been solved or anything. The cops have had this place completely sealed off, so now's the time for them to sneak in. I've seen it before. Plus, this chick was kinda famous."

The two went back to examining the trusses while Arie went to the front of the apartment. She opened the door to a middle-aged woman almost as height-deprived as herself. To compensate, the woman had piled her hair into a complicated topknot that wobbled whenever she moved her head. Behind her stood a tall, heavily made-up blonde in her late teens. Despite her youth, she'd acquired a pouty look that seemed permanent. Something about the girl made Arie's skin prickle into goose bumps.

A reflection from the woman's glasses caught Arie's eye, and a faint sibilant hiss whispered . . . So lossst.

"Oh, my gosh." The woman gasped. Her eyes rounded in astonishment. At first, Arie thought she'd heard the whisper, too, but she realized the woman was merely reacting to the banana suit.

"The super said I would find someone here, but when no one answered, I thought maybe he was lying. I don't know what I would have done. If I don't get back to these people—"

"Can I help you?" Arie said.

"I hope so, if you'll just let us in. We have permission."

Arie hesitated, looking over her shoulder to the bedroom. She turned back to the woman. "Let you in to do what?"

The blonde broke in. "We need to go through Marissa's desk."

"Uh, I'm sorry, but no one is allowed back there for now. If you come back tomorrow . . . " Arie started to ease the door shut, but the woman shot her hand out to stop it. The force of her action made her topknot bobble wildly. If not for her apologetic expression, the action would have seemed incredibly obnoxious.

"Detective O'Shea already said we could. You can call him if you want. It'll only take a few minutes."

At the mention of O'Shea, Arie flushed for absolutely no reason at all. She tried to cover it by fake coughing into her hand. "I'll have to check with my boss. The desk is in the bedroom, and there might be some liability issues."

"Well, if I need to talk to my lawyer, I can do that." The blonde piped up for the second time.

Arie smiled, though it was as fake as her cough had been. She held the door open and stepped back as the pair swept past her.

At least they were willing to wait in the living room while she talked to Guts. He wasn't happy. "This is going to suck balls."

Although the room had been decontaminated, and there wasn't a speck of blood to be seen, the cloying strawberry smell of the commercial disinfectant only camouflaged an underlying, murky scent of death. "If one of them faints, I ain't responsible. Come on, Grady. Let's go tell the super what we found. Arie, you stay here and watch over the two broads. Make sure they don't fall in the hole."

The woman started chattering the moment she set foot in the bedroom. "You know, I never even introduced myself. I'm June Shaw. And this is Kelli Armundsen, Marissa's baby sister."

Now Arie knew why she'd felt so funny when she first saw her. The murdered woman's sister. . . . She stole a glance at the young woman. Although they had similar coloring, Arie didn't think she would have guessed Kelli Armundsen was related to the murdered woman, much less her sister. Kelli seemed like the rough diamond to Marissa's polished stone.

"We should only be a few moments," June continued breathlessly. She made her way directly over to the desk, which, set off in the windowed alcove, hadn't been contaminated. Kelli stood off to the side, not bothering to join the conversation. Her gaze darted around the room.

Oblivious, June chattered on. "I just need to make some notes on some of the contracts and agreements that poor Marissa made before . . . well, never mind. But the vendors are going crazy. And Chad, poor dear, isn't able to help with this part. He didn't even know which caterer they were using."

"Caterer?" Arie asked. "For the funeral?"

"Oh, goodness, no. For the wedding, dear. They were getting married." She picked up a small, framed photo of a couple from the corner of the desk and handed it to Arie. The light from the window bounced off the glass.

Flash.

My ring . . .

Flash.

Head bowed, his honey-blond hair hides his face. The ring . . . I stroke his hair.

The images kept popping up. *Good lord, how long will this go on?*

And what could she do about it? Apparently, closing her eyes and clicking her heels together three times wasn't going to cut it. She knew. She'd tried. But that meant . . . Arie shuddered. She'd never been a take-action kind of girl, but heaven knew—*literally*—that she was going to have to figure something out. Soon.

June's voice pulled Arie back to the real world. "I was their wedding coordinator. Did I mention that? As you can imagine, everything is crazy." June waved her hands in the air as though churning up chaos.

Sweat tricked down Arie's face. Luckily, June didn't notice, and Kelli was too busy examining her sister's bedroom.

"Detective O'Shea says we're not to take anything, but I can take notes from Marissa's files. I mean, not *take* them. But I can make notes. Chad will have to sort out the money situation later. Or maybe Kelli will."

June glanced at the younger woman, but Kelli had moved to the dresser and was opening the jewelry box. She must have sensed their scrutiny. She stared back, her hand still on the lid.

"I thought you needed to check the papers? I have a hair appointment in less than an hour. I'm not going to be late for that." She turned back to the jewelry.

June blushed and pulled a white binder from under a stack of papers. It had been decorated with lace and ribbons and had a heart-shaped picture of Marissa and a man. *Was that the same guy whose hair she'd been stroking in the vision?*

"Is that Chad?" Arie asked.

"Yes. Don't they make a lovely couple? I wonder where he's staying now." June looked around the room. "I can't imagine being able to sleep in the same room as . . ."

"They were living together?" Arie looked around at the incredibly feminine decor.

June didn't seem to hear her question. She opened the binder and leafed through the paperwork. "She was so organized. She liked everything just so. Most brides do, of course. And it *is* their special day. Of course, having their own way can sometimes cause problems, too. That's why I don't have any of this information. Usually I would, but Marissa liked having it all at her fingertips and everything shipshape."

June absentmindedly handed Arie a stack of papers to hold so she could jot down the information in her notebook.

Arie glanced down. The top page was an invoice from an upscale florist. She gasped at the amount. Then, out of curiosity, she quickly scanned the form.

"She was just using roses and orchids for her bouquet, huh?" Arie's forehead crinkled. Orchids—not lilies-of-the-valley after all. The roses fit with what the visions had shown her, but the orchids didn't.

"Yes, well, not *just* roses and orchids. The roses were a special hybrid called 'Secret.' Isn't that delicious? Rich cream ruffled petals with a delicate blush-pink color on the edges." June sounded as though she quoted from a catalog. "We picked them especially for their fragrance. And the orchids! Oh, my gosh, don't get me started. What a time we had deciding on those. They were chosen for their fragrance, too. They're called . . . oh, let me see." June took the invoice back. "That's right—'Lady of the Night.'"

Interesting choice. 'Secrets' and 'Lady of the Night' for a woman who had just been murdered. Freud would have had a field day.

"I didn't know people chose their flowers for the fragrance. That's kind of neat."

"That was Marissa. She thought of everything down to the last detail. And even though she loved the scent of lily-of-the-valley, she wanted something different than the usual accent flower. Leave it to her to find an orchid that smelled just like them." June laughed and handed a new sheaf of papers to Arie.

Arie took them automatically, fighting off a bout of nausea. *Lily-of-the-valley?* She swallowed hard against a rising tide of bile and, desperate for distraction, turned to see what Kelli was up to. The younger woman was busily separating Marissa's jewelry into various piles. Arie took a deep, shaky breath and felt a little better. Apparently, watching someone's greed was a stabilizer.

"Oh, gosh," June whispered. She shot a glance at Kelli then turned to Arie. "I guess this won't be an issue anymore."

In her hand she held a legal document. A prenup.

"He was sure kicking up a fuss," June said, still in a whisper. "She was getting so angry . . . "

"She wanted him to sign?" Arie asked.

June flicked another look over at Kelli, who, still oblivious, was trying on a pink cameo ring and holding it up to the light. The subtle elegance of it contrasted with the girl's rather harsh makeup.

"Oh, definitely," June whispered. "She had scads of money, all from that book."

"*Rich Bitch*, right?" Arie whispered, too.

June nodded. "I couldn't begin to tell you how many reporters have been after me for a scoop. Not that I would say anything, of course. I'm a professional, you know."

Then in a high-pitched, phony, we-are-so-not-gossiping voice, she said, "Marissa had the most exquisite taste of any bride I've had the pleasure to work with. Everything she chose—"

"Of course she did," Kelli said. "And she had the money to buy it. In fact, where is her dress? I wanted to put that away . . . for, um, sentimental reasons." Kelli picked her way around the hole in the floor, making for the closet. She flung open the door and peered inside. "It's not here." She swung around to stare at the other two women.

"It was damaged," Arie explained. "We had to—"

"*Damaged?* Do you know what that dress was worth? It was a Vera Wang. That dress was probably worth a year's salary at your crappy little cleaning job. How exactly was it damaged?"

Arie bit her tongue. For real. She'd always thought that was a cliché, but it really worked. She struggled to stay professional. She needed this job.

"I'm sorry, but you misunderstood. Nobody at BioClean was responsible for damaging the wedding dress. That happened during the—"

"Oh, bull. You probably recognized it was a Vera Wang and decided nobody would notice if it happened to disappear."

The blonde crossed her arms and rocked back on her heels, glaring at Arie. Then she smirked.

"On the other hand, I don't suppose you could even dream of fitting into it. Your tits alone would bust the seams."

Suddenly, Arie understood, on a purely visceral level, why she saw red during a death vision after somebody was murdered. Red went well with murder. She made a point to stare at the girl's teensy breasts, then gave her a dripping-with-pity smile.

"Kelli!" June gasped. "I'm sure that's not true. You shouldn't—"

"The wedding dress was found lying on the floor, contaminated with blood," Arie said through gritted teeth. "Per procedure, it was placed in a biohazard bag and removed with the rest of the contaminated materials. If you would like, I can check with my boss and see if we can dig it out of the waste and return it to you or to the next-of-kin. Given that it *is* considered biohazardous waste, you'll probably need to sign some kind of document absolving the company of responsibility."

Actually, Arie still had the bag set aside in the living room where she'd brought it to Detective O'Shea. Still, the "digging it out of the waste" line had been a nice shot.

Kelli narrowed her eyes at Arie and seemed ready to snap off another insult. Then a glint of calculation sparked in her bright-green eyes, and she covered her face with her hands as though about to sob.

June rushed over and wrapped her arms around Kelli, although since she was shorter by at least six inches, she had to stand on tiptoe to do it. She patted Kelli's back as though she was trying to burp her and turned to Arie. "I'm sure she didn't mean that. This has all been so horrible, and on top of all that, the funeral is tonight. She's been so upset." June's gaze flicked to the hole and then back to Arie with a help-me-out-here pleading look.

Arie felt a wellspring of guilt rise up in her chest. After all, Kelli's sister had just been murdered. Then she caught the girl's smirk through her fingers.

Still . . .

Arie ungritted her teeth, and even though Kelli had fired the first salvo, forced herself to apologize. "I'm sorry. I know that was probably very hard to hear, but I didn't want you to think that our company or anyone in it would stoop so low as to steal a victim's wedding dress."

"Of course not," June said.

Kelli flung off June's arm and flounced back to the jewelry box, where she picked up several pieces.

"I don't think you're supposed to take anything yet," June said in a small, tentative voice.

Kelli screwed her eyes shut, and her hands clenched into fists. She seemed about to explode into a Veruca Salt-style meltdown. Then, just as suddenly, she slid a plastic smile on her face and strode from the room. Over her shoulder, she said, "Hurry up, June. I'm not going to miss my hair appointment for this."

"Boy, she's all kinds of scary, isn't she?" Arie said quietly.

"You have no idea."

CHAPTER FOURTEEN

"I can't believe we're about to crash a funeral." Arie rubbed her forehead, behind which an ominous throbbing had started. "And I can't believe you're so excited about it."

"This was your idea, not mine," Chandra said. "But you have to admit, this detective stuff is cool. I mean, we're probably going to be in the same room as Marissa's killer. We might talk to him, and we wouldn't even know."

"That's not exciting. It's . . . stupid."

Chandra took a hand from the steering wheel and patted Arie's knee. "Look, you're going through a lot. I can't even imagine. But you're the one who wanted to do this."

Arie leaned her head against the cool glass of the passenger-side window. "I don't feel like I have a choice. Besides, this feels personal to me. I'm connected to these people, Chandra. Their memories are inside me. When Marissa was being murdered, it felt as though *I* was being murdered. It's not like a movie. It's like I'm really her. And now I'm going to my funeral. I mean, her funeral."

Chandra was silent. She reached over and rubbed her friend's back. "I'm sorry."

The funeral home was packed. A line of mourners ran along the side of the room and then curved around the back row of folding chairs. The cloying smell of funerary flowers clashed with the aftershave and cologne scents emanating from the crowd.

"Dammit," Arie whispered to Chandra. "It's closed casket."

"Now who's being morbid?" Chandra whispered back.

"I wanted to see if I would have a vision if I got right next to her. I'm still trying to figure out what works and what doesn't."

"Are you still having those? I mean, all the time, not only when you try?"

"It's a risk every time I look into any kind of liquid or reflective surface. I couldn't even use the mirror for my makeup."

"I guess that explains it."

Arie ignored her friend's attempt at humor. At least she hoped Chandra was kidding.

"That's why I had you drive." Arie rubbed her head again. "I've been getting migraines."

"Well, you could always use the casket. It's the shiniest black lacquer I've ever seen."

Arie stared at it. Marissa had finally gotten her flowers. Roses and orchids lined both sides of the wall behind the casket. *So wrong.*

The line moved forward about six inches. Arie sighed. At this rate, they'd still be in this line at breakfast time.

"By the way," Chandra said. "Do you smell chili? It's making me hungry."

Arie groaned. "I made Grumpa a pot while I was getting ready. I don't seriously smell like chili, do I?"

Chandra's only answer was a pitying look.

Arie sniffed, but couldn't smell anything. Maybe Chandra was kidding? But then how did she know...? To distract herself, Arie scanned the crowd. She thought she caught sight of June's coiffed 'do, but the woman was so short Arie couldn't be sure.

Kelli stood near the casket, receiving condolences. A stylish woman in her late twenties stood next to her, her hand on the sleeve of a tall blond man. The fiancé, perhaps? What was his name? People ebbed and flowed around the trio in a mournful social dance.

Chandra poked Arie. "I know her."

"Kelli? She's Marissa's younger sister."

"No," Chandra said. "The other one. I went to school with her. We had a couple of classes together. Her name is . . . shoot, I can't remember. It's one of those unusual frou-frou names that nobody knows how to spell."

"Like Chandra? Or Arie?"

"Fair enough. Do you see anyone else you know? It looks like half of Oconomowoc showed up for this. The rich half, anyway."

Chandra was right, a fact that did nothing to settle Arie's nerves. It was the type of crowd that, money or no money, her mother would have blended in with. For one thing, Evelyn would have pulled the perfect saddened-but-not-a-member-of-the-immediate-family dress from her closet with matching I'm-so-sorry shoes and an I-feel-your-pain scarf that she would tie in one of those fancy, complicated knots.

Following step-by-step instructions off of YouTube, Arie had practiced for forty-five minutes with the one scarf she owned. The same one she'd worn to her job interview, in fact. The process had been made more difficult by not being able to use a mirror. She'd ended up tangling her hair into the knot so tightly she'd needed to cut it out. As for her dress . . .

The navy blue was subdued enough, but during the months following her trip to the Other Side, Arie had struggled with depression. Like many, she ate her emotions. Actually, emotions were probably calorie free; it was the cookies and potato chips that had bolstered her curves. Her dress squeezed her midsection like a python. Worse, the plunging neckline let the "girls" come out to play like a couple of wiggling puppies trying to escape a sack. Even the scarf didn't help. She gave the neckline a tug, but it only turned the wiggle into a decided jiggle. Giving up, Arie straightened and came eye to eye with a pair of sapphire-blue orbs that bored into her skull like a drill.

"Detective O'Shea." Arie gasped. The gasp did nothing to help the jiggle issue.

If the twinkle in his eyes was any indication, O'Shea didn't seem to mind. "Arie? I didn't expect to see you here."

"I . . . uh . . . I thought I should pay my respects."

O'Shea turned serious. He glanced at the casket then back at Arie, a question dimming the twinkle. "Did you know Marissa Mason?"

Arie swallowed. "No. Of course not. I . . . "

O'Shea waited.

"I guess I've never known anyone who was murdered before." A situation made especially weird, since Arie hadn't been "introduced" to the victim until after her murder.

Best not to mention that.

A darker shadow crossed O'Shea's face. "So you're here out of curiosity? That's funny. I didn't have you pegged for that kind of thing."

"What kind of thing?"

"A death groupie. But I guess that explains your job." He started to turn away, but Arie grabbed his arm. His eyebrows shot up, and he looked pointedly at the hand gripping his wrist. Arie didn't think it was possible to blush any harder than she already was, but she managed.

"That's *not* why I do my job."

O'Shea's eyebrows stayed raised, but his eyes lifted to hers.

"I . . . I do what I do because somebody needs to take care of them." She let go of his wrist.

He continued staring into her eyes, but a warmth crept back into his. "So do I," O'Shea said. "Maybe we could talk about that some time? Over coffee, maybe. Or, I don't know, chili?"

He turned and walked back into the crowd, leaving Arie shaken and confused and more than a little as if she'd just read the sexy bits in a romance novel. Also humiliated. *Chili?* Arie sniffed her arm. She still couldn't smell anything.

"Holy cats," Chandra said. "Who was that?"

"That's the detective on Marissa's case. I met him this morning."

"And you didn't think to mention that? He's got to be the most gorgeous man I've ever seen. Those eyes . . . "

"I didn't mention him because he probably thinks I'm an idiot."

"That didn't stop his eyes from drinking you in like you were a strawberry smoothie. And I don't think he was thinking 'idiot' when he was staring down your cleavage and asking you out." Chandra glanced down at herself and sighed. "You really have the advantage there."

"Oh, no," Arie said. Shock drove any leftover tingly feelings away.

"No, really. I could probably get by with a couple of Band-Aids—"

"What's Brant doing here?"

"Brant?" Chandra stopped her self-evaluation and followed Arie's gaze. "Your brother?"

Both girls stared across the large room at a man in a gray suit standing against the wall by himself. Objectively speaking, it should have been possible to call him handsome. Blond, tousled hair, light blue eyes, broad shoulders, and a strong jaw line: he had all the individual parts of a Nordic god. Except he wasn't. Despite the genetic favors bestowed upon him, Brant Stiles lacked an indefinable quality that would have made him stand out in any crowd. Arie, with her unremarkable—to her—dark brown hair and eyes, had always resented Brant's inability to work the advantages he'd been given. But then, he'd been given so many.

When he caught Arie staring, he grimaced. She left her place in line and, with Chandra trailing behind, crossed the room to her sibling.

"Brant, what are you doing here? Did you know—"

The realization hit her. She slapped a hand over her mouth.

"Arie—"

102

"Was this *your* Marissa?"

"What do you mean, 'his Marissa'?" Chandra's eyes darted between brother and sister.

Brant clenched his jaw and looked away. "Go home, Arie. I don't need you here."

"I'm not here because of—"

"Dammit," Brant said. "Now he's looking right at us."

"Who is?"

Arie grabbed Brant's jacket sleeve, but he pulled out of her grasp and walked away, leaving his sister to stare at his back.

"Well, that's rude," Chandra said.

"You don't understand."

"Maybe not. How did your brother know Marissa?"

"I'll explain later," Arie said.

"You might have to do some explaining to Detective Gorgeous while you're at it. He's been watching us the whole time you and Brant were talking. Think he's jealous?"

"He's trying to find a murderer, Chandra. Is that who Brant thought was looking at us?"

"I think so. He's headed this way."

"Oh, hell." Arie grabbed her friend's hand and pulled her to the door. "Time to go."

Arie wanted to go to Whelan's, their favorite coffeehouse. Ice cream topped with caramel, pecans, and hot fudge would go a long way toward settling her nerves, but Chandra insisted they go back to Grumpa's house.

"You have to quit avoiding things," Chandra said. "It's your home now."

"I know, but—"

"You have to let your grandfather know this is your home, too. You have to go in there and claim it."

"I don't have to pee on the carpet, do I?"

Chandra ignored her. "After all, if you weren't there, he might have to go in a home or something. He could be at least a little bit grateful."

"Grumpa doesn't do grateful."

This was apparent as soon as they walked into the kitchen. Grumpa stood near the sink, scrubbing at a spot on the countertop. He hadn't bothered brushing his hair, and wisps stood like patches of dandelion fluff around the dome of his head.

"You're trying to poison me, aren't you?"

Arie tempered her reply. "Hi. Nice to see you, too."

"Hello, Mr. Wilston," Chandra chimed in.

"Who's that?" Grumpa glared at Chandra.

"You know her name," Arie said patiently. "You've known her since she was twelve."

"Whatever." He turned and wrung out the dishrag in the sink.

Arie stifled a sigh. "Did you eat some of the chili I made?"

"I'm surprised I didn't have to call in the paramedics. It's obvious you're trying to kill me. In fact, I probably should've saved some for evidence."

"Saved some? You mean you ate the whole pot? Grumpa, that was supposed to be for both of us, and there should've been enough left over for lunch tomorrow."

"Well, there wasn't. And I had to make the cornbread by myself. You can't eat chili without cornbread."

Arie opened the refrigerator. "Did you at least leave me some cornbread?"

"Of course not. What good is cornbread without chili?" Grumpa stomped off into the living room.

Arie leaned her head against the refrigerator door. The cool surface felt good on her forehead. She heard rustling behind her and turned.

Chandra had pulled a loaf of bread from the breadbox and was digging through a cupboard. She pulled out a nearly empty jar of peanut butter.

"I don't suppose Ol' What's-His-Name has any grape jelly in there?"

Although Chandra had decided that peeing on the carpet was the way to go, Arie led the way to her bedroom. She plopped on her bed while Chandra perched on the dresser.

"This feels like high school," Chandra said.

"Tell me about it."

Arie reached into her purse and pulled out Marissa's wedding program. She passed it to Chandra. "Is the woman from the funeral in Marissa's wedding party? She seemed pretty in with the immediate family."

Chandra squealed. "She sure is. Riann Foster. In fact, she owes me for her B-plus in Eastern Religions."

Arie quirked an eyebrow at her friend.

"She flunked the midterm and barely passed the final. Her only hope was the final essay, and believe me, this girl couldn't pull together a ten-page paper on her own. She was one of those perpetual students, always changing her major. And she was a major party girl if the rumors were true. I gave her a little help."

"You mean you cheated."

Chandra shrugged. "Yeah, but let's face it, it was Eastern Religions. I also had her in Astrology, but she managed to get by in that class." Chandra frowned. "Or else she found someone else to help her."

"How about any of the other names? The fiancé, Chad Atwater?"

Chandra studied the names but shook her head. "Looks like one of the groomsmen might be a brother or cousin. Same last name as the groom. But I don't know any of these others. Just Riann, and really, I barely knew her."

"I'll try to Google them later."

A long pause ensued. Chandra finally broke it. "All right, maybe you'd better tell me about Brant now."

"I can't even imagine where to start." Arie scrabbled through her purse to find her bottle of ibuprofen. She would need that plus caffeine to take the edge off the pounding headache that had finally erupted. She simply had to figure out a way to stop the visions.

"I take it Brant knew Marissa," Chandra prompted.

Arie nodded wearily. "They were engaged."

"Engaged? Are you kidding me? How come I never heard about this?"

"It was the only secret we ever really shared. And it was a while ago. Two years, maybe. I ran into them at the movies and made Brant introduce us. If he could've gotten away with just ignoring me, he would have. She seemed really sweet, though."

"I still can't believe you never told me."

"Anyway, they broke up about three months later."

"How come he wanted to keep her a secret?"

Arie shook her head, which only made her headache worse. "I don't know. He acted . . . embarrassed, which was crazy. I mean, like you said, she was one of those golden girls. You know, one of those Barbie dolls with a sparkly smile and perfect skin. I can't believe I didn't recognize her from the book photo. Back then, though, the only thing that surprised me was how Brant ever got her to go out with him in the first place."

"I don't suppose you know why they broke up."

"Nope. I didn't see him for a couple months, not 'til Thanksgiving. He covered it up, but I could tell he was really sad. When I asked him if he was going to tell Mom and Dad about his engagement, he said there wasn't anything to tell them. He wouldn't talk to me about it."

"Okay, well, here's the big question: If it was so over, why was he at her funeral?"

"Maybe it was over for her," Arie said. "But not for him. Besides, that's *not* the big question."

Chandra quirked her eyebrows in a question.

"The two really big questions are why was Brant so upset about O'Shea watching him, and why is O'Shea watching him in the first place?"

After Chandra left, Arie pulled out Marissa's book and studied the author photo on the back. After a few minutes, the page's edges shimmered, and Arie felt another wave of nausea roll over her. She tore her eyes from the photo and dropped the book. It fell open to the dedication page. Arie leaned over and picked it up.

To B—

Whose love and encouragement brought a sweet light into my darkest days.

All my love,

M—

CHAPTER FIFTEEN

Arie skittered around the corner of the van and almost careened into Grady.

"Whoa, dude. You're late," he said. "Not going to be a habit, is it?"

"No, definitely not. I—"

"Save it." Grady pulled their supplies out of the van. "Long as we get this done today, I don't care. Unless it happens again." Grady gave her the evil eye, but the banana suit took some of the punch out of it.

Arie stuffed herself into her suit as fast as she could and followed Grady up the stairs to Marissa's apartment. She wished she'd been able to stop for coffee, but had overslept and nearly been late to work. Lack of sleep and no caffeine made her stumble on the steps. After seeing Marissa's dedication, she'd kept reading through the night. *Rich Bitch* could have been used as a training manual for the International Coalition of Gold Diggers, if such a thing existed. Considering how many women bought the book, there seemed to be a need.

Thing was, it didn't read as though the Marissa Brant had been dating could have written it. The one time Arie had met her, she'd seemed . . . sweet.

At any rate, it looked as if she and Grady would be finishing the job that day. Maybe she'd get a little relief from the visions if she wasn't in direct contact with Marissa's things.

But, Arie feared, maybe she wouldn't.

They had to disinfect the hole in the floor one more time, but then it was mostly just hauling bags and crates down to the van.

When Arie walked into Marissa's bedroom, she saw it in a new light. *Had Brant ever been here?*

Yesterday, the furniture had been pushed to the other side of the bedroom to give them space to work on the gaping hole. The bloody section of the carpet had been removed. The whole thing would have to be taken out, of course, but that wasn't BioClean's problem.

Arie grabbed a crate and started picking up tools and cleaning supplies. A utility knife slipped from her fingers and fell behind the dresser.

"Great," Arie mumbled. She lay on her stomach and stretched her arm as far as she could under the dresser. Her boobs got in the way. She twisted onto her side, and her eye caught a glint of metal. She strained to reach it, and the metal object tickled her fingertip and then squirted out of reach.

Arie heard the front door open and then male voices conferring in the living room. She hated the idea of Guts finding her like this. She could leave the knife. Nobody would know.

But retrieving it had become a *thing* now.

As footsteps started down the hall, Arie's fingers closed over the object.

She pulled it out and jumped to her feet. Even before looking, she knew it wasn't the knife. A key.

And not just any key. Arie recognized it as the key from Marissa's death vision. She tucked it into the palm of her hand.

Detective O'Shea walked into the bedroom. Arie jumped in surprise and squeaked something that came out sounding like "eep." A hank of sweaty hair fell into her face, and she suddenly remembered that, in her haste to get to work that morning, she'd forgotten her deodorant.

O'Shea pulled out his notebook.

Oh, crap.

It wasn't wariness Arie saw in Connor O'Shea's eyes. Or was it? No, it was an absence of emotion, a neutral professional blankness that had encapsulated the detective like a thin layer of galvanized steel. That someone could have such complete control over his emotions made Arie shiver with superstitious awe.

"Last night," O'Shea began, "when you attended Marissa Mason's funeral, you were seen talking to a gentleman. His name is Brant Stiles. Blond, blue eyes, about six feet. What do you know about him?"

Arie felt her mouth fall open, an inherently unattractive look, she knew. "Brant? Is he a suspect?"

"You know him?"

Oh, more crap. He was serious.

"I do."

An image of O'Shea taking his wedding vows inserted itself into Arie's mind, and she almost giggled. She started to put her hand over her face and then remembered she was holding the key. For some reason—

and it might not have been her own—she didn't want O'Shea to see the key.

"He's my brother."

"Your brother," O'Shea said. It wasn't a question. Now his face did register something. His lips thinned briefly, and he looked off into some middle distance. "I thought you said you didn't know Marissa Mason."

"I didn't. I mean, I didn't know I did. I only met her once, and it was two years ago. I didn't recognize her from the little picture on her book, and the funeral was closed casket."

He finally showed an emotion. Unfortunately, it was incredulity.

"They were engaged. Do you really expect me to believe you didn't know her?"

"I really didn't."

Arie clung to the truth, even though she knew how ridiculous it sounded. But it *was* the truth. Besides, her mind was racing so fast she couldn't have come up with a decent lie if her life depended on it.

There was a long pause while they both assessed the new situation and took measure of the other. After a few moments, O'Shea nodded slightly to himself.

"So you didn't know Marissa Mason, even though you had met her at least once, and even though you say she was engaged to your brother for a period of time. You showed up at her funeral, even though you didn't know her, out of some altruistic desire to care for the dead."

The words hung between them, adhering themselves to the bitter chemical smells and the underlying coppery odor of blood that still lingered in the room where Marissa Mason had died.

Arie swallowed. Her mouth had grown so dry her lips were gummy. "I didn't know her well enough to recognize her. I met her once, as you said, and it was over two years ago. Yes, she was engaged to my brother, but it was a secret engagement. Why do you think Brant has anything to do with this?"

Without answering, O'Shea nodded again. He opened his notebook and said, "I'll need your full name."

Arie was already shaking so hard she thought she might rattle the remaining floorboards loose. She took a deep breath and reminded herself that, whatever he had done to make O'Shea think he was guilty of murder, her boring, staid, predictable brother was not a killer.

O'Shea was waiting. Reluctantly, she told him her full name—no initials this time—and endured the blank stare he gave her.

"It's a family name," she whispered. "That's why I just use the initials."

"I don't blame you," O'Shea said.

It could have been a bonding moment. It wasn't.

"Address?"

After Arie had answered all of the detective's questions, the two stood in indecision. Arie's heart knocked against her chest as if it were trying to escape her body. *Was she going to get hauled in for questioning or something?* A bigger, deeper fear lay curled in the bottom of her stomach. *Brant, what have you done?*

And how was she going to find out?

Just as the tension became almost unbearable, Grady walked in. Apparently sensing the crackling energy, he swung his gaze back and forth between the two. As soon as O'Shea turned to look over his shoulder at Grady, Arie slid the key into her glove. The metal felt cold against her sweaty palm. Strangely, a feeling of peace—the kind she hadn't felt since she'd gone to the OS—settled over her.

"Uh," Grady said. "You about done in here, Arie?"

O'Shea turned back, his eyes assessing her.

"I'm not sure." Staring at O'Shea, Arie asked, "Am I?"

Another long pause. Then O'Shea said, "For now."

Didn't look like they'd be getting that cup of coffee anytime soon.

CHAPTER SIXTEEN

As soon as Grady cleared Arie from her duties, she jumped in her car and sped to her parents' house. She was in no shape to deal with her mother, but this couldn't wait. How well did she know Brant after all? They traveled in different circles; they had different lifestyles; they had different lives. Brant was always . . . Brant. He got good grades, followed the rules, and met or exceeded expectations of anyone in range to set them.

And he was as boring as hell.

Arie couldn't believe that Brant would ever be swept away by any emotion long enough to kill another human being.

But did she really know him?

Doubts and worries bounced around in her head like the Fisher-Price vacuum popper she'd pushed from room to room as a toddler—until her mother had donated it to their church's rummage sale, that was.

When Arie pulled in the driveway, the garage door was open, and so was the trunk of her dad's Buick

LeSabre. Bags of groceries were loaded in the trunk, awaiting the last leg of their journey. Arie sighed and grabbed two of them, the brown paper crinkling in her arms.

Ed opened the door as she neared it.

"Well, look who showed up in the nick of time."

Her father's smile was like a soothing balm. He held the door for her, and Arie pecked his cheek as she went by. Her mother, she knew, would be moving back and forth between the kitchen table and the cabinets, stowing the food in its proper place. Her parents had long ago fallen into a pattern of sharing household duties. Her father probably didn't even know where the tomato soup was stored. His job was to show up for the expedition to the grocery store, tag along behind his wife so he could reach the items that were shelved too high for her, and finally, to haul the bags to the kitchen table. Evelyn was in charge of everything else.

"What are you doing here?" Her mother softened the question with a bright smile.

Sometimes, Arie had to remind herself that her mother really did love her, despite her bustling, energetic, controlling nature. An almost overwhelming urge to lay her problems on her mother's table, the place where so many other problems had been dumped then solved over the years, rose in Arie's chest.

But this problem? This wasn't like failing algebra (Arie) or who dented the side panel on the station wagon (Arie) or which of the four colleges offering scholarships should be chosen (Brant, of course.) This was a frantic woman chased from room to room, her blood sprayed across walls. This was death. And it had no place at her parents' kitchen table.

But if her mother ever found out that Arie knew Brant was in this kind of trouble, and hadn't told her? Arie shuddered at the prospect. She had to find another way of digging into Brant's past without asking her parents. Not yet, anyway. And she wanted to talk to her brother first.

Thinking about Brant's college decision had given her an idea.

Belatedly answering her mother's greeting, Arie said, "I thought I'd stop in for a few minutes. I have some things I thought would be nice to have at Grumpa's."

Her mother frowned. "What things? And don't call him that. You know he hates it."

"Well, let's not tell him. I made him chili the other night for supper, if that helps. Homemade, even, not from a can."

Ed walked in, carrying the last of the groceries.

"Goodness," Evelyn said. "Chili? Isn't that too spicy? You have to remember, Arie, you're supposed to taking care of your poor grandfather."

Ed snorted at the description of his father-in-law.

"I think you should be more careful about his meals," Evelyn said. "But I'm sure you two will overrule me the way you always do."

Arie's eyebrows rose nearly to her hairline. Had anybody ever overruled Evelyn Stiles? But there had been a plaintive tone in her mother's voice that Arie had never heard before. In fact, Evelyn looked almost teary-eyed. It scared Arie a little.

"Now, Evelyn," Ed said. "I'm sure Arie is taking good care of Dad."

"He actually liked it," Arie said. "In fact, he ate the whole pot and all the cornbread."

Evelyn rubbed her temples. "Well, that's good anyway. I just think—"

"I'll be careful about spicy foods, Mom."

Evelyn folded the last paper grocery bag and stored it under the sink. "I know you will. I'm just a little tired today. I'm going to go lie down for a bit."

As Evelyn walked away, Arie turned to her father, a question in her eyes.

He reached over and patted her hand. "She's fine. I think she's fighting off a cold."

"Oh, okay. Listen, I just need to grab a few things from the basement. I'll be quiet."

"Don't worry about that. She likes to read for a bit, anyway. I'll be in my chair if you need anything."

Although the incident with Evelyn, slight though it was, left Arie a bit uneasy, the thought of Ed resuming his usual place in his easy chair, surrounded by his military adventure novels and crossword puzzles, reassured her.

The basement had been finished long ago. Fake wood paneling covered the walls, and the cement floor had been covered with kid-friendly, durable carpet. The air felt damp. Arie would have to remind her father to get the dehumidifier going.

She went into the storage room, with its jerry-rigged plywood shelving that sagged with boxes of Christmas decorations, gardening tools, and miscellaneous boxes filled with knickknacks that had survived the move from the old house eighteen years ago, but had never been deemed worthy of a spot in the new. Arie pushed boxes around until she found the one she wanted.

She knew it was the right one because it said BRANT—STAY OUT in black magic marker with three exclamation marks. It reminded her of the Keep Out signs they used to tape to their bedroom doors, whose only purpose had been to fan the flames of each sibling's desire to breach the barrier and see what was on the other side.

It was the box Brant had lugged home after graduating from Marquette University in Milwaukee. Just one box. Brant wasn't the sentimental type, but Arie hoped it would give her some clues about what her brother was like back then. It embarrassed her how little she knew of him—the real Brant—but she set the thought aside for now.

Opening the box, she found a tattered, well-read copy of Stephen King's *The Stand* as well as a white mug decorated with the entwined navy-blue-and-yellow *M* and *U* college logo. A coffee stain decorated the inside like a lacy brown spiderweb. She pulled out several textbooks and set them in a pile beside her.

The next layer was paperwork: old essays, a class schedule, and a dusty old day planner. Arie wiped off the planner, then realized she was staring down at her own reflection on the glossy black cover. She braced herself for the vision she knew would be triggered. Nothing happened. Puzzled but relieved, she set the book aside and hurried over to the downstairs bathroom.

Despite its no-nonsense functionality, hardly anybody liked to use it. Evelyn kept the white porcelain clean, of course, but since the room was barely used, it gathered a slight layer of dust. It didn't appear to have spiders, but with the chill, dank basement air, it *felt* spidery. Potential spiders were almost worse than ones you could see and therefore avoid. Still, it came in handy at the family Christmas parties or when some—always unidentified—person stunk up the upstairs one.

Arie approached the mirror with care. She'd had trouble looking into any mirror since the death vision at Marissa's. She stood in front of the sink with her eyes squinched shut, quickly opened them, peeked into the mirror, and immediately squeezed them shut.

Nothing.

She opened them again and risked a longer look. Still nothing. She breathed a sigh of relief. *Were the visions over?*

Backtracking, she realized the pressure had lightened the moment she'd pocketed the key in Marissa's bedroom. The moment, in fact, when she'd unconsciously committed herself to uncovering Marissa's murderer.

Arie leaned on the counter and considered this new idea. What did it mean? Did she have to choose between being haunted by a murder victim's memories or putting herself at risk by trying to track down a killer? *That was a choice?*

And what would happen if she couldn't figure it out?

Arie straightened up and decided to pull a Scarlett O'Hara. She'd "think about it tomorrow." Maybe.

Still shaken, she went back to the box of Brant's stuff and picked up the day planner. As she did, a thick white square slid out from between the pages.

A Polaroid picture. Only Brant would still be using a Polaroid.

Arie flipped it over and realized she'd found what she'd been looking for. A much younger version of her brother—although he couldn't have been, really; it had only been two years ago—sat on a blanket with a beautiful blonde curled in his lap. Marissa Mason, of course. A bottle of wine, glasses, and a Tupperware container filled with red strawberries completed the picnic. Arie couldn't tell for sure, but she guessed they were at an outdoor concert. She thought she could see a stage in the background.

She could hardly take her eyes off Brant. She'd never seen him so relaxed. Or happy. No wonder she barely recognized him. Suddenly, Arie felt herself grieving for the brother she never knew.

And it was certainly Marissa sprawled across her brother's legs. She seemed happy, too. They matched. They belonged.

Arie wondered what had happened to take the smiles off those two young, joyous faces.

CHAPTER SEVENTEEN

Arie waited until after she'd gotten home, fed Grumpa a healthy meal of lean pork chops, brown rice, and broccoli—whereupon he accused her of trying to kill him—and took a long hot shower before she tried calling Brant. She'd had to look up his number in her mother's address book. That said something about their relationship.

When Brant's phone clicked directly to voice mail, Arie hung up. There was no way she could leave any sort of message that would make sense.

Instead, Arie called Chandra to fill her in on Detective O'Shea's visit.

"Holy cats," Chandra said. "Is he going to arrest both of you?"

"I think if he was going to bring me in, he would have. Besides, he can't arrest me. I didn't do anything."

A dubious silence hung on the line. Chandra said, "It sure looks bad, though."

"You don't have to tell me."

"What are you going to do now? I mean, you don't really believe Brant would . . . "

"No. Of course not." Another long pause. "Do you?"

"Not really," Chandra said. "He's so blah. It's . . . "

"What? Just say it."

"Well, it's always the quiet, boring guy who turns out to be the serial killer. I mean, I really don't think Brant's a killer, but . . . I mean, if he did do it, it's probably because he, you know, snapped."

"Brant doesn't snap," Arie said. "That's exactly what Brant doesn't do. He's the most un-snappy person on earth."

"Then why does O'Shea think he's involved?"

"I don't know. He wouldn't say. That's what I need to figure out."

"Can't you just ask Brant?"

"I tried calling him, but it's not that easy." Arie sighed. "He'd never trust me with this kind of thing. The only reason he told me about his engagement in the first place was because I accidentally ran into them. From the look on Marissa's face, she didn't know he had a sister. And you saw how he acted at the funeral. Besides, he's going to want to know why I'm involved. What am I going to tell him? I stared into a pool of his ex-fiancée's blood and had a vision of her murder? How is that going to go over? He doesn't even believe I had a near-death experience. In fact, he told Dad I was making it up to get attention."

"Does he think you mugged yourself, too?"

"No, but he probably thinks I was irresponsible and placed myself in harm's way."

Chandra laughed.

"But you were just walking to your car after work. How is that irresponsible?"

"Because it was a stupid job in a risky part of town."

"You know, about that. I wanted to ask you something."

"About . . . that night?" Arie's stomach muscles cramped. "What about it?"

"Well, I was just wondering, if you've tried this vision stuff on yourself. I mean, that's only natural, right? Maybe you could—"

"I can't."

"Can't? Or won't?"

"I tried, okay." Arie sighed and confessed to having pricked her own finger with a needle to get a sample of blood.

"Holy buckets! What did you see?"

"Blood. That's it. And listen, Chan, I know you're trying to help but I don't want to—"

"You can't avoid it forever."

"I can for now. So forget that. Didn't you say you knew that friend of hers—Diane?"

Chandra sighed, but capitulated. "Riann. From college. But it's not like we—"

"Can you figure out some way to introduce me to her?"

"Oh, boy. What are you—"

"Can you?"

Chandra didn't answer right away. Arie waited. If there was anything she had faith in, it was her friend's complete inability to resist poking her nose into other people's business.

"I'm not promising anything," Chandra finally said. "I have an idea. What are you doing tomorrow night?"

"Why does that question scare me?"

"I'll pick you up at six. This is gonna be great."

Arie shivered. She and Chandra had vastly different definitions of the word "great."

Chandra's eyes were bright with excitement as she gripped the steering wheel. "I've been going to her for months now. She's a remarkable woman. I've been wanting you to come see her for ages. Remember, I told you about her?"

Arie groaned. "Please tell me you aren't taking me to your psychic lady. You know I don't—"

"For someone who died and visited heaven and then came back with her very own psychic gift, you sure are close-minded."

Okay, she had a point. So many weird things had happened to Arie recently, and aside from Chandra, she really didn't have anyone to talk to.

Her mother cringed at any discussion of "the incident." In fact, Evelyn still seemed unconvinced that her daughter had actually been dead for four minutes, despite the doctor's affirmation and the medical records. Evelyn didn't even like talking about the events leading up to Arie's death, as if her daughter having been mugged in a parking lot was unseemly.

Arie gently rubbed the puckered, starfish-shaped scar just over her collarbone. The doctors had stated that blood loss was the primary cause of death. Maybe, Arie mused, the blood they'd used to refill her had come from someone with a gift, as Chandra called it.

It didn't feel like a gift. It might be too soon to call whatever she had a curse, but it was certainly a burden and scary as hell. And because of it, Arie didn't feel comfortable opening up to her usual confidants.

Her father had always been there for her. Although she might have kept some of her boneheaded decisions from him initially, she almost always fessed up eventually. And although there might have been times Edward Stiles was disappointed in his daughter, he always forgave her, and he always helped her see the best in herself.

They had been able to talk about her visit to the OS. As a pastor, Ed had no trouble believing in heaven or even rejoicing in it.

But talking about it set him at odds with his wife, and Arie didn't like being the cause of conflict between them. Besides, death visions were a whole 'nother level of freaky.

Chandra pulled the car to the curb in front of a well-kept trailer home, interrupting Arie's train of thought.

The bathroom is filthy, of course. The tub loaded with dirty . . .

Arie felt dizzy and braced herself against the dash of Chandra's car.

"Are you okay?" Chandra's eyebrows furrowed, and she patted her friend on her back. "Maybe you're right. Maybe this is too soon. I thought it might be good for you to talk to somebody who's comfortable with this stuff. I already told Walynda about your NDE."

"I'm okay. I just needed a minute. I think it was seeing the trailer . . . "

"What's the big deal about a trailer?"

"I'm not sure. Marissa grew up in a trailer. Maybe she . . . I dunno . . . got upset?"

Another wave of dizziness flowed through Arie. She'd never really thought of it that way. A dead person was sending her thoughts, her memories, her *life* straight into Arie's head.

Arie sucked in a deep breath.

Wait . . . Walynda? Who named their kid Walynda?

CHAPTER EIGHTEEN

A gypsy caravan had vomited across the whole of the interior. Yards and yards of royal-blue fabric decorated with tiny silver stars, ivory crescent moons, and golden suns draped the windows and the back wall. A round table dominated the middle of the room, and candles, crystals, and incense holders lay scattered across every available flat surface. A maroon wingback chair had been pulled up to the table. Walynda's chair, Arie assumed. The other three chairs ringing the table looked like ordinary dining room chairs with scarves thrown over them.

Walynda arrived.

The decor immediately ceased to be the main attraction because a six-foot-two woman with brilliant purple hair and long burgundy fingernails had her own attention-gaining abilities. The long, flowing white satin choir robe helped.

A pastor's kid, Arie knew her choir robes.

"Welcome. I'm so glad to finally meet you."

Walynda's voice had a soft, otherworldly lilt. She floated to Arie's side and held her by the shoulders. Peering into her eyes, the psychic smiled widely. "Welcome, indeed."

"Thank you," Arie mumbled.

Walynda released Arie and turned to Chandra, adding a cheek kiss to the shoulder-grabbing thing.

Chandra's eyes sparkled. "You did your hair."

Walynda patted her purple tresses self-consciously. "Oh. Yes. I like to go to Becky's Institution of Beauty Art to get my hair done. It's very economical, and it's nice to see all the young girls as they're starting out on their life's journeys." She blushed and patted her hair again. "There are drawbacks, of course."

Leading the way to the table, the psychic offered Arie a seat. Chandra perched on the edge of another chair and pulled a pen and notebook out of her purse. Instead of joining them, Walynda circled the interior of the room, lighting candles. Then she picked up one of the incense holders, a thin stream of fragrant, sandalwood-scented smoke already wafting from the opening, and circled again. This time, she fluttered her hand through the smoke, dispersing it throughout the room.

Arie coughed.

"Oh, dear, are you allergic?"

Without waiting for Arie's answer, Walynda set the incense aside, gathered her skirts, and folded herself into the burgundy chair. She reached across the table and grabbed Arie's hands in her own. Walynda's fingers had so many rings on them they clicked and clattered whenever she used them, which was a lot. Walynda was a hand-talker.

They were still clicking as Walynda opened an intricately carved wooden box and pulled out a deck of tarot cards. Walynda held them lovingly to her chest, closed her eyes, and took a deep breath. After a few moments, she began shuffling them.

"Think of a question while I shuffle, and keep thinking of it as I lay out the spread."

A question? How about ten? Arie tried to narrow it down, but she was nervous, and it was hard to prioritize from the multitude of questions swirling in her mind .

Walynda set out five cards: three side by side in a line, then one above and one below the middle card. The images were brightly colored, a jumbled mix of yellows and blues and reds. She placed a sixth card crosswise over the center card.

"Don't stop thinking of your question," she trilled. To the left of the arrangement, she added another row—vertical this time—of four.

"All right now. Here we go."

Walynda took a moment to study the cards, then suddenly stiffened and swept them up. With a phony laugh, she said, "Whoops. You're supposed to shuffle, not me." As she handed the deck across the table to Arie, her hands shook so hard her rings sounded like castanets.

Arie accepted them warily and shuffled them a few times. They were bigger than usual playing cards and kept slipping through her fingers. The pictures were both interesting and a little frightening, so she turned them face down.

"Do you want me to lay them out?"

"Yes, dear. Just the way I showed you."

Arie laid them out exactly as Walynda had. Not only was the layout the same, as far as Arie could tell, so were the cards. Exactly the same.

"Holy crap," Walynda said in a very nonlilty voice. Out of the corner of her eye, Arie saw Chandra taking frantic notes.

"Is that supposed to happen?" Arie asked. The other two exchanged glances that fully answered Arie's question.

Swallowing hard, she gathered the cards again, carefully shuffled for several minutes, spread them out.

Exact. Same. Cards.

The same reaction, too, as all three women gasped and pulled back from the table. Walynda swept her hand across the cards, blurring their order, then picked them up and stuffed them back in the wooden box. She stood so abruptly her chair rocked back and almost fell over.

"I'm sorry," she said breathlessly. "I have a headache."

She shooed the girls over to the door.

"Walynda?" Chandra spoke for the first time in twenty minutes. "What just happ–"

"Nothing to worry about, nothing to worry about," Walynda sang. "I'm just not feeling very well tonight. I've had a lot of readings this week, and my energy has been drained dry."

As the girls cleared the threshold, Walynda called to Chandra. "Call me for an appointment, dear!"

In the next instant, the door swung shut, and they heard the click of a lock. And then another.

Chandra and Arie stood on the sidewalk and stared at each other.

"Well, that went well," Arie said.

While Chandra ordered their coffees at the counter, Arie made her way to their favorite spot in Whelan's: a small, round table near the white fireplace. She briefly considered ordering a Turtle Sundae. After the unsettling episode with Walynda, she deserved something sweet and gooey.

She sighed. Eighteen pounds since her visit to the Other Side. No ice cream.

When Chandra joined her with a couple of steaming mugs, Arie asked to see the notes.

Chandra scrunched her face. "I'm not sure we should do that. I mean, I know some things about reading tarot, but only enough to know that I don't know enough. We should really—"

Arie waggled her fingers. "Gimme."

With a theatrical sigh, Chandra pulled the notebook from her tote-size purse. Arie spread the notes on the table between them so Chandra could see.

"Okay," Arie said. "There's ten cards, right?"

"In this layout, yeah. She used the Celtic Cross spread. I think it's the most common one. What question were you thinking of while she shuffled?"

"At first, I couldn't think of just one. But then I figured out what to ask: Should I use my gift? Maybe I should've been more specific."

"I don't think the question was the problem. The whole thing is so weird. I can't believe with a layout of ten cards, you picked the same ones over and over again."

"Apparently, Walynda's never seen that, either," Arie said. "She looked at me like she'd seen a toad jump out of my mouth."

"I don't think freaking out your psychic is a good sign."

"D'ya think?"

Arie leaned over Chandra's notes, trying to decipher her friend's scrawl. "So which one of these cards triggered the freaking?"

"You mean, as if pulling the same cards three times in a row wasn't enough?"

"Yeah."

Chandra sipped her chai tea and studied the page. Her finger trailed down the list. "Honestly, there's enough here to freak me out, and I don't even know exactly what I'm looking at. I can tell you what I know about a couple of them, but that's not the point. It's not just what cards are; it's where they're placed. Each spot tells you about a different time or circumstance in your life, so each card's meaning can vary depending on your circumstances and where it was placed in the spread."

"Look, I don't know anything about this stuff, but even I saw the Death card. It was written right on there: Death. Some black knight dude riding on a white horse. Is that the one that freaked her out?"

"See, that's what I mean," Chandra said. "It's not that easy. The Death card is really powerful, but it's not about, you know, *death*. It's about transformation. And, um, in your reading, it was placed in your distant past, not your recent. So it was talking about progressing from your old life to a new one. It means you had an attitude that was holding you back or a challenge that you faced in your past, and you grew from it. It's probably not even about your NDE."

"My mom would agree with the attitude-needing-changing part. So, which one would be about my recent past?"

Chandra tapped the number four card located at the bottom of the cross. She smiled.

Arie leaned over and looked. "Well, of course. I'm a Fool."

Chandra giggled. "Nobody is going to argue with that. But when it's placed here"—she tapped the notebook—"it's a pretty cool thing. The Fool is the first step in a journey. He's like, I don't know, *possibilities*."

"Possibilities?"

"You really need to talk to a medium about this. Pulling the same cards three times in a row—that's majorly significant. But there are aspects of this layout that I couldn't even begin to explain."

The tightness forming behind Arie's eyes told her another headache was brewing. She worked at massaging it away with her fingers.

"Look," Chandra said, "do you want me to find another medium? I've heard about this one lady—"

Arie flung her hands up like a traffic cop. "No. Let's just put it away for now."

Chandra reached for the notebook, but Arie stopped her.

"I'll keep it."

CHAPTER NINETEEN

Several days went by without another BioClean job. One top of everything else, Arie's financial troubles were crushing. At the rate she was going, she wouldn't be able to keep herself in coffee money, much less groceries or rent, if she ever wanted to live on her own again. She needed another job.

Even though she knew it would irritate him, she started scanning Grumpa's newspapers as soon as he set them down. He accused her of putting the sections back in the wrong order on purpose to aggravate him.

There weren't that many jobs she was qualified for. And the ones she was, like waitressing or second-shift factory work, would have meant coming home after dark, which after being knifed in a parking lot and left to die, she wasn't ready for. And maybe never would be.

And that wasn't the only thing preying on Arie's mind.

Finally, one night, after tossing and turning for three hours, she gave in. Flicking on the lamp, she sat up in bed and grabbed her laptop from the nightstand. While she waited for it to boot up, she padded over to her dresser and retrieved Chandra's notebook from her sock drawer, where she'd felt compelled to hide it. It wasn't that she thought Grumpa would prowl through her room; she just hadn't wanted to be reminded of it.

But ignoring it wasn't working either.

Arie entered "tarot" into the search engine and got approximately thirty bazillion hits. She clicked the top one.

Ten cards in the Celtic Cross. Chandra had been right. This particular spread seemed pretty common, and interpreting it depended on a lot of variables, including the question Arie'd chosen. She should probably have been more specific than "Should I use my gift?" but it was what it was. Also, according to the website, there were no bad cards. Just misunderstood ones, Arie supposed.

She took a deep breath and read on.

The first card Walynda, and then Arie, had placed stood for the present. The High Priestess. *Cool.* But what did it mean?

A Major Arcana card, whatever that was. Arie read the description and realized it wasn't going to be as easy as plugging in the card and getting a readout of its meaning. According to the website, this card was "veiled in mystery."

No shit.

The High Priestess seemed to be about the unconscious, the "Inner Voice"—which, for Arie, usually sounded like her mother nagging. Somehow, Arie couldn't picture her mother as "a gateway to realms beyond human comprehension."

One thing did ring true, however. The High Priestess was supposedly a sign that a decision had to be made, that Arie's intuition was sending her a message.

Well, yeah.

She sighed and moved on to the second card: the Tower. It was in the spot indicating an "immediate challenge." As far as symbolism went, this card looked scary as hell. Lightning smashing into a phallic tower, and people jumping headfirst to the cliff below.

No bad cards? Right. Arie's immediate challenge looked like Armageddon.

It was supposed to signify a dramatic change. Okay. That made sense. Being attacked, dying, taking a spin around heaven, and then returning with the ability to read memories in blood would seem to qualify for that. But was that the immediate challenge the cards meant? Because that had already happened.

Uh, boy. Arie read on.

Third card: Death. Distant past. Why would death be in the distant past? Arie would have thought it would be more recent or, given the nature of her job, future circumstances.

Fourth card: the Fool. And *that* was the card representing the recent past. Reading about the Fool made her feel a smidge better. The card didn't mean she was as dumb as a box of hammers. It meant innocence or untapped potential. Arie could picture herself as untapped potential. Her teachers had always talked about her potential. Of course, that was because they were trying to find the silver lining in her failing grades, but still.

Fifth: the Four of Swords indicated the best outcome. Of the reading? Of her life?

Arie's stomach rumbled. Prophesy made her hungry.

The Sword card meant something about rest and recovery. Okay, that could be good. So far, Arie liked this card best.

Sixth. *More than halfway done.* Page of Sword—lots of swords. Arie didn't know what that meant. It had been laid in the immediate future slot. It stood for confusion, learning about her powers, and battling evil.

Shitshitshitshitshit.

Arie forced herself to finish up the last three by promising her Inner Voice and whoever else dwelled inside that she would find something good to eat as soon as she was done.

Seven, eight, and nine were the Seven of Swords, Two of Cups, and Ten of Wands, respectively. The dude on the Seven of Swords was stealing a bunch of swords and running away. Running away . . . Arie's usual approach to problems. It was supposed to stand for factors affecting the situation, but Arie couldn't figure out how stealing swords would be helpful.

Two of Cups: a relationship. That could be cool. The memory of a certain pair of delft-blue eyes made her shiver. But she soon discovered it might not mean a new love. It might mean learning to love herself.

She gritted her teeth and turned to the Ten of Wands. Hopes and fears. The card had some guy in a skirt gathering up a bunch of staves and was supposed to show the weight of burdens. Something about character building and responsibility and blah blah blah . . .

And finally, the last card. Arie stared at the image—a woman in a flowing red robe and crown on a throne. In her right hand, she held up a sword; in her left, a balanced scale. Justice.

Well, goody.

And speaking of goodies . . .

Arie tiptoed past Grumpa's bedroom. The last thing she wanted was to have to deal with him. Keeping the kitchen light off for the same reason, Arie dug busily in the pantry cupboard, searching for a package of chocolate chip cookies she'd hidden there. The side door creaked open. Before she could reach the light switch, a dark shadowy figure slipped into the house.

Death, maybe?

Arie screamed and threw the cookie package at the intruder's head. The intruder bellowed and flung himself sideways, tripping over the garbage can and landing with a thump. Still screaming, Arie lunged for the light switch, then grabbed a meat tenderizer from the drainer and prepared to defend herself.

"I knew it! You're trying to kill me."

Grumpa lay sprawled in the middle of a bilious pile of smelly food wrappers, discarded coffee grounds, egg shells, and a half a head of lettuce that had lain forgotten in the vegetable bin of the refrigerator until it reached a state of near-liquefaction.

"Grumpa?" Arie gasped. She lowered the meat tenderizer. "Why aren't you in bed?"

"What? Are you my mother?" Grumpa struggled to his feet. When Arie rushed to help him, he shook her off.

"I thought you were in bed. Where on earth have you been?"

"None of your business, missy. You're not the boss of me. This is still my house. I can do what I want, when I want."

Grumpa stomped away. Bits of eggshell and slimy wilted lettuce clung to his bottom. They plopped on the kitchen floor in his wake. Staring at his scrawny butt made Arie realize he was wearing stiff new jeans and a red-checked Western shirt. *What the . . . ?*

Before he made it through the door, Arie said, "What on earth are you wearing? And what do you think Mother is going to say when she finds out you've been running around town in the middle of the night?"

Grumpa stiffened and slid to a halt. He turned slowly. His eyes narrowed, and he eyed Arie speculatively.

"Now, why would you want to go and worry your mother like that?"

Arie folded her arms across her chest. As always, her boobs kept her crossed arms floating aloft like a Russian Cossack dancer and drained the gesture of impact. She slitted her eyes to make up for it. "Oh, I don't think she'll be worried. She'll be *frantic*. Of course, she'll want to know why her eighty-three-year-old father is out roaming the streets instead of asleep in his bed, like everyone thought he was."

"Then don't tell her. It's none of her business, either."

"Are you going to tell her that?" Arie chuckled at the thought.

Grumpa glared at his granddaughter for several moments, then nodded thoughtfully. "No. I'm not. Of course, if *you* do, she might have a few questions for you. In fact, I guarantee she'll want to know how you let your poor old grandpa wander outside all alone in the cold, dark night."

Arie scowled. He was good. Better than Brant, even, who had been known to tattle on himself as long as there was any hope of getting Arie in trouble, too.

"It's July. It's not like you're going to freeze to death."

Grumpa wrapped his arms around himself and shivered. "Old people get cold really easy. Thin skin, you know? I could probably even work up some goose bumps if I wanted to. Wanna see?"

Laughing merrily, Grumpa turned and left the room. Arie was pleased to see that he still had an eggshell dangling from his butt.

But what had that old coot been up to?

CHAPTER TWENTY

"Got you a present!" Chandra practically vibrated with excitement. Arie stood aside to let her in, and she danced through the front door.

"Who's making that racket?" Grumpa yelled from the kitchen.

"It's just Chandra," Arie yelled back. She grabbed her friend's hand and pulled her to the bedroom, the one oasis of privacy she had left.

Chandra carried a shopping bag, which she handed to Arie as soon as she shut the door. Arie opened it and extracted a square white box. Something heavy shifted inside with a rustling sound.

Arie looked up warily.

"Go on." Chandra squeezed her hands under her chin and wiggled like a puppy. "You're going to love it."

Uh huh.

Arie opened the box and pushed tissue paper aside. A ruby eye in the middle of the white paper stared up at her.

"Eeaaaghhh!" Arie closed her eyes and thrust the box away.

"Oh, for cryin' out loud. It's a crystal ball."

Chandra pulled it out of its wrappings and shoved it into Arie's hands.

Arie peeked at it. When it didn't blink, she examined it more closely. "Why is it red?"

"Isn't that cool? I could have gotten a regular old clear one, but I knew you would like this better."

"Oh."

"Well, you said you were going to experiment and stuff, right? This makes sense."

It was beautiful; that much was true. But if she had to use a crystal ball at all, Arie wished Chandra had gotten one of a different color, any other color. The deep, translucent red of the ball looked exactly like a perfectly formed drop of blood.

Her stomach rolled. She put the ball back in the box.

Chandra frowned, and a hurt look crept into her kohl-edged eyes. "Aren't you going to take it for a spin?"

"I love it," Arie lied. "I do. Really. I'm getting a headache, though, and I think I'll try it out later."

Chandra sighed and shook her head. The hurt had morphed into exasperation, but she seemed ready to let it slide. This time.

"Oh, guess what?"

Arie was afraid to guess, but Chandra didn't wait for that anyway.

"I figured out how to set up a meeting with Riann. It's going to be great."

"Great?"

"Uh huh. I've got a plan."

"You had a plan last time," Arie said, thinking of Walynda. "I don't think I like your plans."

"Look, you said you wanted to meet Riann. Now, do you want to or not?"

Arie sighed. "What exactly am I letting myself in for?"

"It's perfect. You're going to love it."

The last time Arie had heard those words, she'd ended up with a red eyeball.

"What *exactly* am I going to love?"

"Let's just say your newfound gift is going to come in handy. Leave everything to me."

After Chandra left, Arie pulled the crystal ball back out. If she was going to make sense of this gift—and for a moment, Arie wasn't sure whether she meant the ball or her ability—she was going to have to test things out. She sat cross-legged on her bed, holding the crystal ball in front of her.

She bent over and stared into it. Blinding white light flashed like a disco ball on speed, so fast and so sharp it felt as if it were cutting slices from her brain. Images exploded in between the streaks of light, too chaotic for Arie to make sense of them.

It was so disorienting, in fact, that she ended up vomiting after each attempt. Finally, after the fourth purge, Arie decided to get rid of the thing. There had to be some other, more dependable way of calling up visions.

She remembered the stained bootie she'd confiscated from Marissa's condo.

After retrieving the garment from her car, Arie spread the paper bag out on the bed in front of her and set the bootie on it. She took a minute to gather herself, then stared at the blood smear on the green material. It shimmered and—

Flash.

Losssst . . .

Arie pulled herself out of it. Okay, that worked, but toting around samples of a murder victim's blood might be problematic. She couldn't imagine what a friend of Marissa's would do if Arie pulled out a bootie smeared with the victim's blood to do a little psychic reading.

Definitely not cool.

Arie's foot had fallen asleep, so she stretched and wiggled it. The movement set the crystal ball rolling. It landed next to the bootie.

Hmm.

Arie retrieved the stand and, after sliding the bootie between the stand and the crystal ball, took a deep breath and looked.

Flash.

So lossst . . .

Arie watched the houses grow in size and grandeur as Chandra's little Ford Fiesta rolled along the winding curves of Lac La Belle Road toward Riann's lake house. The synthetic fabrics and department store fit of her never-were-in-season clothes started to itch. A hunk of probably-should-add-fancy-highlights brown hair flopped accusingly in her eye, as if scolding Arie for settling for a "cut" instead of forking over the money for a "style."

As if fate hadn't arranged circumstances for maximum discomfort level, Arie thought she saw O'Shea's sedan pulling out of the driveway as they drew up. She ducked down, clunking her head on the dash. That was gonna hurt.

"What the hell are you doing?"

"Did he see me?" Arie asked.

"Who?"

"O'Shea. Wasn't that him?"

"Oh, fabulous. Now you're hallucinating on top of seeing things."

"Chandra—"

"Get up. We're here." She hauled Arie up from the floor.

The woman Arie had seen at Marissa's funeral waited in the doorway of the spectacular waterfront home. She jumped at Arie's sudden appearance, but she'd recovered her poise by the time they scrambled from the car.

"Channie," Riann greeted her old classmate. "How wonderful."

Despite having agreed to the appointment, Riann acted as though seeing Chandra was a delightful result of serendipity rather than a previously arranged meeting.

The home opened into a tiled foyer with a ceiling so high, Arie knew if she even cleared her throat it would echo. Suddenly, she had a nearly irresistible urge to clear her throat.

It was official. She had no class.

Riann peeled herself off Chandra and, hands clasped under her chin, turned to Arie.

"And you must be Amy! I'm so excited."

"It's Arie, actually."

Despite only being six or seven years older than Arie and Chandra, Riann radiated a sleek sophistication that went well with the surroundings. Reddened, overly puffy lips were the only contradiction to her perfectly groomed appearance.

Collagen injections?

"Channie told me about your abilities, and how you'd been given a message for me. Richard, my fiancé, says I should be more careful of who I trust, but of course, that goes without saying. It's not like I'm stupid or anything, right? Besides, if you're trying to pull a fast one, I'll know soon enough."

A steely glint suddenly knifed its way past the woman's social smile. It made Arie shiver.

This was such a stupid idea.

Arie almost decided to call the whole thing off, but Riann was already leading the way across the foyer and into a white-on-white living room. Arie wondered if Riann had taken decorating tips from Marissa or vice versa. Somehow, she guessed the latter.

Entering the room felt like floating in a cloud. A small, round wooden table had been set up in front of a white couch. The room would have had a magnificent view of Lac La Belle, except half the room in front of the floor-to-ceiling sliding doors had been blocked off by an elaborate model train display. Multiple lines of train tracks ran between several towns, a mountain range, and wide swathes of farm and forestlands. All these were elevated to waist high on plywood platforms of varying widths and heights. The aisles were big enough to allow someone to walk between.

"Oh, wow," Chandra said.

Riann glanced over. Her swollen lips gave a moue of disdain. "That's Richard's."

Without further explanation, she slinked her way over to the white couch. She had a way of walking with her hips thrust forward and her body at a slight angle, a runway walk, Arie guessed. Riann had the body for it, too—long and slender—with a mane of rich auburn hair that looked so natural Arie knew it had to be fake.

Riann sat—no, *reclined*—on the couch. She patted the space next to her.

"I hope this is okay. I thought we would be more comfortable here, although the table is a little high. Richard tried to find us a more suitable one but . . . " Her brows furrowed as though the inconvenience of a two-inches-too-high table was deeply troubling.

Chandra reached into her tote and pulled out the ruby-red sphere and set it up in the middle of the round table. Arie noticed her friend was careful not to dislodge the tiny snippet of bootie they'd placed between the crystal ball and its stand.

Riann gasped. "How beautiful. What a stunning crystal ball. Where did you get it?"

CHAPTER TWENTY-ONE

Arie felt her stomach lurch the same way it had when Chandra had first showed her the crystal ball. After working with it for most of the night, Arie had finally reached a tenuous control of her own mind, but it felt fragile.

Riann squealed with pleasure. "I can't wait. Let's get started. What do you need me to do?"

Arie's heart thumped hard enough to make her boobs quiver. Her mind went blank. "Uh . . . "

Riann's smile slid off her face, and she frowned. Apparently, incoherency was not reassuring.

Chandra created a diversion by dragging over a footstool—white, of course—to the table and plopping herself down. Her chin barely cleared the tabletop, but what could be seen of her face was smiling.

"Arie needs a few minutes to get centered," Chandra explained. "It's always a little difficult for her to transition from the earthly plane to the other realm. In the meantime, you should prepare yourself as well. Take a couple of deep breaths, and clear your mind. In fact, close your eyes. It's better that way."

Reassured, Riann squeezed her eyes shut. Chandra hitched her eyebrows up and shot Arie a get-your-shit-together glare.

"Right," Arie said. "Yes."

Chandra rolled her eyes so hard Arie was surprised they didn't cause a brain hemorrhage.

Arie cleared her throat and scooted closer to the crystal ball. She took a deep breath and peered into it. For the briefest of moments, nothing happened. Then the color shifted, turning more opaque, and began to slowly writhe and swirl. Arie felt herself being sucked in.

She mentally wrenched herself away, refusing to fall into the abyss. Clearing her throat again, she said, "I see a woman."

"A woman?" Riann's eyes flew open. "Is it Marissa?"

"It's an older woman. She's not very tall, and she wears her hair . . . uh . . . " Arie waggled her hands above her head to indicate a fancy hairstyle.

Chandra rolled her eyes again.

When they'd rehearsed, she and Arie had agreed that mentioning June might establish Arie's credibility—as long as Kelli wasn't around, that is. It had seemed like a good idea, but right now, Arie couldn't remember why. She forged on.

"She's talking about flowers," Arie said. "Roses. Roses and orchids."

Riann gasped. "Those were Marissa's signature flowers. So you *are* in contact with her."

No lie there.

"That woman," Riann continued, "must be June. She was Marissa's wedding coordinator. But why would Marissa be communicating about her? Oh, wait! It's probably her way of letting me know she's still with me. I've recently started planning my own wedding, not that I would ever use June. I know Marissa was happy with her, but I always thought she was too ridiculous for words. June, that is, not Marissa, of course. She's so gushy and nicely nice, I could vomit. And let's face it. If she had an ounce of self-discipline, she wouldn't be so fat. After all, if a woman can't even discipline herself, how on earth is she going to be able to organize a wedding like mine will be?"

Every plump cell of Arie's body burned with rage. Under the table, Chandra reached over and squeezed Arie's knee. Her *plump* knee.

"You're getting married?" Chandra asked. "Would that be this Richard you've mentioned?"

Riann tried to blush, but it emerged as a self-satisfied smirk. "Richard Boyette. You've heard of him, right? The financier? *Business Daily* called him 'the most ruthless man of the decade.' He's absolutely amazing, and he's such a dear. I hate to say it, but he spoils me terribly." Her smile turned creamy.

"That's wonderful," Chandra said. "I'm so happy for you. When's the big day?"

Riann flashed a glance at the door leading to the hallway. She covered her conspicuously ringless left hand with her right and shrugged.

"Well, there's a lot to be decided. I don't want to rush into anything, and with all that's happened. . . . What else do you see?"

Arie reluctantly turned back to the crystal ball. A swirling, like reddened smoke against the sky, rose from the depths. At first, tendrils twisted, but they quickly shifted into a dense, roiling fog. A red fog. And then the fog was inside Arie, inside her mind.

Flash.

Lossst. Marissa's despair flooded Arie's soul. Or was it Marissa's soul and Arie's despair? A ring sparkled. My ring. The solitaire was just as stunning as when Arie— Marissa—had first seen it.

Flash.

Back in the bathroom. My skin crawls. Water drips from the faucet, an irritating plink-plink-plink that makes my teeth grind. Cockroaches skitter in the dirty crevices.

Flash.

The key. I reach for it. I have to . . .

Flash.

Outside now, looking at the old trailer. Time to leave this dump. I have to. Rags hates it as badly as I do. Worse, maybe.

A new image: a young girl with short-cropped brown hair and piercings in her nose, upper lip, and in an arcing line of her left ear.

Annie. Her Mudd jeans have holes in the knees that go all the way to her thighs. Rags . . .

Flash.

Church bells clamor, wildly ringing. Arie slaps her hands over her ears, but the violent cacophony peels on.

Someone wants to hurt me. Arie's throat closes. Hand . . . the hand grips my throat.

Someone grabbed her shoulder, and Arie yelped as if . . . well . . . as if she'd seen a ghost. She found herself staring into Chandra's frightened face.

"You're okay, Arie. It's all right."

"Well, what did you see?" Riann asked with all the sensitivity of a rhino in heat.

Arie shuddered again. It had been far worse this time, and she didn't know why. Maybe the proximity to somebody who had known Marissa so well made it more intense. Arie didn't know, but she tried to shake it off. She couldn't afford to be distracted. She studied Riann. Was that tiny dot on her lip from a decades-old piercing? Her ear hadn't healed nearly as well.

"You changed your name." Arie's throat was dry, and it made her voice raspy.

Riann blanched. "How did . . . I did not."

"You did, too. It used to be Annie. And you used to live in a trailer park, didn't you? So did Marissa. You two grew up together."

"Yes, we did," Riann said.

A closed expression had slipped over her face during Arie's revelation, and her green eyes glittered like a cat's. "I was her best friend, the only one she ever trusted."

"What about her fiancé?" Chandra said. "Or her sister. Kelli, wasn't it?"

Riann faked a laugh. "Kelli? Not a chance. For one thing, they were only half-sisters. Kelli was always going back and forth between her dad and her bio-mom's house. She was there every other weekend and maybe a week in the summer. Besides, Marissa left home as soon as she could. They barely knew each other."

"As for Chad," Riann continued, "they were in love, but of course that's not the same thing as a girlfriend. We told each other everything. I can't believe she's really gone. Even at the funeral . . . "

The sadness that had flickered in Riann's eyes slipped away, replaced by a gleam of suspicion as she stared at Arie.

"Hey, didn't I see you at the funeral? How did you know Marissa?"

Arie felt her stomach lurch. "I, uh . . . I felt I needed to be there."

"You mean, like, Marissa's spirit called you to her?"

"Kind of, I guess." Arie had to think fast. She hovered over the crystal ball and slowly moved her hand just above the surface. "I see a man from the past."

"From my past?" Instantly diverted, Riann leaned in, too, staring into the red orb as if hoping to catch sight of the guy.

"Marissa's past. He's blond. About five-ten."

Riann shook her head doubtfully. "She dated a lot."

"I think she was in college. He's handsome, but kind of . . . boring, maybe?"

"Oh! You mean Brant?"

Out of the corner of her eye, Arie saw Chandra squelching a laugh.

"That's him. Marissa is showing him to me. Why would she do that?"

Riann's eyes narrowed into slits. "Because he's the asshole who—"

A slight, elderly man in soft gray pants and a white button-down shirt ambled in. He held a blue-and-white conductor's cap in his hand.

"Oh, I'm sorry, dear. I didn't mean to intrude on your visit."

"Don't be silly. Of course you can join us." Riann's voice reanimated with apparent pleasure, although an ever-so-slight falseness tinged the edges. She'd taken care to raise her voice to a level suitable for someone who might be hard of hearing. She waited until the man had settled in next to her before turning to Arie and Chandra.

"Girls, I want you to meet my darling—"

"Dick." He stuck his hand out to shake.

"Richard." Riann's smile stayed plastered on her face as she pretended he hadn't spoken. "Richard Boyette,

I'm sure you've heard of him. The financier?" Without waiting for their response, she turned back to Dick/Richard. "I've told them all about you. They've been just dying to meet you. Haven't you, girls?"

Arie and Chandra both smiled and verbally stumbled over themselves agreeing.

"Guess what, darling?" Riann spoke over them both. "Arie is a medium. She's talking to Marissa for me."

"A what?" Dick looked puzzled.

"A medium." Riann laughed. When he still looked confused, she said in a louder voice, "A fortune-teller. Like a gypsy. She even has a crystal ball." She pointed to it on the table.

Arie did a mini-Vanna White move over the crystal and immediately felt stupid. Chandra's snort didn't help.

"Oh." Dick's gentle smile showed slightly crooked, never-been-whitened teeth. He twisted the conductor's cap in his hands. "Like Jeane Dixon."

"Who?" It was Riann's turn to look confused.

"Never mind, dear. I can't say I've ever put a lot of stock in such things, but if you're enjoying yourself, I guess it's okay. Just be careful. I don't want you getting yourself all worked up." Dick patted Riann's arm with a frail, liver-spotted hand.

Arie couldn't help noticing that his nails, though clean, were twice as long as many women's. She would've thought Riann would have insisted on his having a manicure, but perhaps her influence—fiancée or not—was limited.

"I told you, Richard spoils me," Riann said.

"It's not spoiling to be concerned, dear. You've been doing far too much lately, and I know you're still upset about your friend's death. You should rest this afternoon. Maybe take a nap."

Riann either had a twitch, or she was struggling against the urge to roll her eyes.

"You're right," she managed. "I do have far too much going on, but a nap would only put me further behind. I have so many things to get ready and set up. Maybe you could help me this afternoon, darling?"

"Not today, dear. I'm meeting Clark about an American Flyer engine he's thinking about selling."

Riann's face transitioned from pouty to sullen to verging on tears in a matter of seconds.

"You could hire a personal assistant," Arie said brightly. "I've heard they even have virtual ones."

"You don't need a crystal ball to see that," Dick said.

Riann brightened. "You know, I've been thinking about doing just that. Honestly. I bet that came to you from Marissa. That's exactly the sort of thing she would've suggested."

"That's probably why I thought of it," Arie said.

Dick harrumphed and shot a warning look to his girlfriend.

A slight glint crept into Riann's eyes. "Oh. I get it. You're looking for a job. That's why you—"

"Me? No, I've got a job."

Arie might have been considering looking for a part-time job, but she certainly hadn't been angling for the position of Riann's personal assistant. Slave, more like it.

"I'm not sure that would work. My hours at my job are a little unpredictable. You'd probably want someone more flexible."

The suspicious look in Riann's eyes had turned to an appraising one that made Arie nervous. It seemed the more she protested, the more determined Riann was to offer her the position.

"Of course, you'll want to interview people, punkin. You need to be careful about—"

"But, Richard! I don't want to bother with all that. Arie would be perfect."

Uh boy. "I really don't think—"

"After all," Riann gushed, "I don't want to spend my time interviewing people. That's, like, exactly the opposite of taking it easy. And think! You would be right here if Marissa needed to talk to me. It would be like texting, but with, you know, a human." She giggled.

"I'm sorry." Arie used a firm voice, the one she practiced in case she ever decided to have kids. "But—"

"Only part-time, of course," Riann said. "Maybe ten hours a week? I don't know . . . Does three hundred sound all right? In cash, of course."

"A week?" Arie gasped.

"Okay, three-fifty. But all of my readings are free."

"When do I start?"

CHAPTER TWENTY-TWO

Arie presented herself at the front door of the lake house two days later. She had the usual first-day-on-the-job butterflies, especially since she was there under false pretenses. After all, her cover would be blown if Kelli showed up. Riann was over a decade older than Marissa's younger half-sister, so they might not be close, but still . . . it was a risk.

Riann seemed as uncertain about her new employee's duties as Arie was. She greeted Arie at the door wearing a silky, pale yellow blouse and gray slacks, an outfit Arie could tell cost more than she'd earned all of last year. Since she'd only been working part-time at the bar that probably wasn't saying a lot.

"Want some water?" Riann handed Arie a blue-tinted bottle and watched her closely. Arie could tell her new boss was waiting for some kind of response.

She uncapped the water and took a little sip. "Mmm. Thank you."

"It's good, right? Richard has it shipped in. You simply can't get it around here."

Arie studied the bottle. *Volvic?* It sounded like something gynecological. She took another sip. Water.

As Riann turned to lead Arie inside, she fake-whispered, "Fifty dollars a pack."

"Fifty dollars for twenty-four bottles?" Arie squeaked.

"No, silly. Fifty for a pack of twelve. Not counting shipping, of course. But it's so worth it, isn't it?"

Arie took another drink. Still only water. She sighed and followed Riann down the hall.

They started in Riann's office—a guest room just off the kitchen that had been repurposed for Riann's use. Although the bed had been removed, there were still divots in the carpet where it had been. Riann sat at her desk, which looked more like a table than any desk Arie had seen. There weren't even any drawers. She guessed Riann didn't do a lot of work there. It held a MacBook, a pencil holder with two pens, and a vase filled with what Arie thought at first were fresh flowers. A closer inspection showed a thin layer of dust on the expensive silk blossoms.

Dick poked his head in. When he saw Arie, he scowled, but merely asked Riann where she'd put his glue gun.

"Oh, Richard, I don't know. It's in there somewhere. But listen. As long as you're here, maybe we should talk about the wedding venue. I know you're a member at the Lake Club here, but I was thinking the Van Dusen Mansion in Minneapolis. It's historic and elegant and—"

"Well, let's talk about this later, punkin. I'm trying to set up a new area for a logging camp." Dick smiled vaguely, then beat a hasty retreat to the living room to fiddle with his train.

Riann frowned.

"Uh, maybe we should talk about my job duties?" Arie asked.

"I guess so." Riann opened the Mac and started it up. "I can't imagine how I've gone so long without the appropriate help. You're going to have to really hustle to keep up with me."

"Sounds good," Arie said nervously. "Where do you want me to start?"

"That's a good question."

Arie thought so, too. That was why she'd asked it. After a long pause, Arie said, "How about your calendar? Maybe we could start there."

Riann perked up at the suggestion and clicked a button on the laptop. A Google calendar appeared on the screen. An *empty* Google calendar.

Riann faked a chuckle and waved an elegant hand at the computer screen. "See why I need an assistant? I don't even have time to write my schedule down."

"I see that." Arie pretended to believe Riann's line of crap. "Maybe you could start by telling me about any appointments you have this week."

"Well, for one thing, Chad is stopping by with a friend later this morning so you can do a reading with him. It's a surprise. The police have practically glued themselves to his back, which is ridiculous. Not only was he out of town, but what reason would he have? They weren't even married yet. Anyway, he's been so down since Marissa died. I thought this might give him some closure. You don't mind, do you?"

"Oh! Well—"

"That's not 'til later, though. After we're done here."

"But Chad doesn't know—"

"I'm not sure exactly when he'll get here, so I'll put him down for an hour somewhere today. That's good enough."

Riann carefully typed "Chad" into an hour slot after lunch, leaving around a hundred or so empty hours to fill in.

"I guess that's a start to getting organized, isn't it?" Arie used a chipper voice.

"I don't need any help with organizing." A peevish tone crept into Riann's voice.

Sensitive much?

"Right. I misspoke. But if we enter things into the calendar, it will help you decide what duties you want me to do."

"I guess that'll work." Still frowning, Riann studied her perfect manicure.

"Maybe I should do the typing."

"Of course. After all, you're the assistant." She rose and did her slow runway walk to a cream-colored armchair near the window. After arranging herself as though for a magazine spread, she looked expectantly at her latest acquisition.

Arie took her place and, with fingers poised over the keyboard, said, "Let's get started now, shall we?"

Apparently, at some point in the exchange, she had transformed into a British nanny.

"How about . . . uh . . . " *What* did *rich women do all day?* "How about exercise? Do you have a regular—"

"Yoga! I do yoga three times a week."

"Great," Arie said. "Which days?"

Riann frowned again. "Which days?"

"Do you go on regular days? Like Monday, Wednesday, Friday?"

"No, I go when I feel like it. Do you do yoga? It's just fabulous, isn't it? So meditative. I can feel peace flooding my soul every time I go. And believe me, with my hectic lifestyle, I need peace."

Arie could relate.

"Okay, but for the calendar—"

Riann airily waved her hand. "Never mind that. I'll just tell you when I'm going to go. Richard calls me his free spirit because I don't like to be pinned down." She giggled. "Except maybe in bed. Sometimes Richard gets a little kinky."

Arie closed her eyes, her mind, and her very soul to the image of Riann and Dick getting freaky in bed.

"I suppose one of the things I'll have you do is research honeymoon spots. It has to be romantic, but I don't want it to be all touristy, either. So somewhere remote. But not too remote. I need to be able to get to the shops, and Dick needs to be by a really great golf course.

"Oh, and definitely a beach resort. Somewhere tropical, but make sure it's not too humid because my hair gets all frizzy. And also, I don't like when the sand gets in my suit. I hate that, don't you?"

Arie let Riann chatter on and on. She had a feeling that was going to be her primary duty, and as such, Riann was paying for someone to listen to her blather on about her wedding plans. Though, as nearly as Arie could tell, Dick hadn't actually proposed. Riann seemed to be operating under the belief that if she acted as if he had, he would start to believe it, too.

Arie didn't think it was working.

She tuned back in when Riann brought up June Shaw, Marissa's wedding coordinator.

"I know Marissa thought she was wonderful," Riann said. "But she always had an attraction to maternal figures. She wanted one, I mean. A mother. Hers was . . . " Riann stopped picking at her cuticles long enough to waggle her finger in circles by her temple—the universal she-was-nuts sign.

"Is that the only reason Marissa liked June?"

"Well, June seemed to know what she was doing, but there's no way I could stand all her fluttering around. And she's always smiling. She gets on my nerves. Nobody can be that happy. And then there was that thing with the cake decorator . . . "

"What happened?" Arie didn't really care, but she was running a Google search for a remote, nonhumid, sandless tropical beach resort with lots of shops and a "really great" golf course.

"It was ridiculous," Riann blathered on. "I don't really know the details, but the cake decorator totally flaked out. There was this whole scene. Like I said, I don't really know, but of course *I'll* never use her. Anyway, June recommended the decorator in the first place, so what does that tell you?"

Since the story was completely devoid of details, it hadn't really told Arie anything. But it did give her an idea. Unfortunately, Riann seemed intent on getting her money's worth out of Arie, and she didn't have time to pursue it.

More to the point, Arie still wasn't clear about what her actual duties entailed. She would have to pin Riann down—and immediately regretted that particular thought as a very unwelcome image of "Master" Dick wearing assless black chaps and holding a leather whip arose in her mind.

"Okay, then," Arie said quickly. "What other appointments do you have? Lunch dates? A standing salon appointment, maybe? Do you have, like, a personal trainer or something?"

"Yes, yes, and yes. We're finally on the same page. I see Evan, he's my trainer, at the gym four times a week."

"Four times a week?" Arie's voice had squeaked with incredulity.

Riann laughed. "If I don't take care of my body, nobody else will. After all, I'm . . . twenty-nine, if you can believe that."

Arie didn't.

"My body isn't merely my temple," Riann continued. "It's my savings account and retirement plan. Have you read Marissa's book? We called it *Rich Bitch* for a reason. It was my idea, you know. All of it. In fact, I practically wrote the whole thing. But anyway, you should really get it."

Riann's eyes narrowed to green slits, and one of her feet jiggled back and forth, churning the air in tight little arcs.

Mood swing.

The nanny responded. "It sounds really awesome. I bet the retirement thing was from you, right? You came up with that?"

"I sure did. Not that she gave me any credit for it. She didn't even dedicate the damn book to me, and she should have. *Everybody* said so."

Placating didn't seem to be working too well, so Arie got back to business. "So, this Evan. You said four times a week. Is that right? Should I put him in the calendar for you?"

"Of course. That would be perfect. Put him down for, like, four days. But not before eleven. I don't like waking up early. Oh, and I have a nutritionist, too. I don't remember when I'm supposed to see her, but she always calls the night before. Oh! And date night. We can't forget that. Di—" She cleared her throat. "I mean, Richard takes me out every Friday night. He makes the reservations, so you don't need to worry about that. But we'll need to put together an outfit in the afternoon so that I look absolutely flawless."

"Retirement plan," Arie said.

"You're damn straight."

CHAPTER TWENTY-THREE

Chad didn't show up until right before Arie was ready to leave, and he brought a friend. He was a bit younger than Chad and Riann, around Arie's age.

Riann seemed surprised and a little put out at the addition.

"Mitch, what a surprise. It's good to see you." The words were right, but the delivery flat. "I thought you were bringing Wyatt?"

With a start, Arie remembered his name from the wedding program that had slipped from Marissa's book. Mitch and Chad shared the same last name—Atwater. Brothers, maybe? Or cousins?

At Riann's unwelcoming welcome, Mitch blushed and dropped his eyes to his feet. Chad put his hand on Mitch's shoulder. "Wyatt couldn't make it, so Mitch agreed. Otherwise, I probably wouldn't have come at all. I'm not really socializing these days."

Arie could believe it. Chad's eyes were red-rimmed, and he walked as though carrying his body was a burden.

Riann took him by the hand and led him into the living room where she'd had her first reading.

At their entrance, Dick left his trains to say hello but excused himself immediately and fled to his own office. Arie envied his escape. In the face of Chad's sadness, she felt awkward and like a complete jerk for deceiving her way into his acquaintance. She'd wanted admission into Marissa's inner circle, but she hadn't prepared herself for how she'd feel when she got there.

On the other hand, this was murder.

Riann arranged it so that Arie sat next to Chad on the couch. She herself sat in the armchair next to it, her face alight with excitement. Mitch hovered by the train display, seemingly entranced, until Riann caught his eye and pointed at a decorative chair against the wall. He showed a little spirit by dragging it across the rug until he was technically part of the group, but he avoided his hostess's eyes. She scowled for a moment at the drag marks in the carpet, then turned her attention back to Chad.

"I'm so glad you came," Riann said again. Although she had folded her face into the appropriate consoling expression, her eyes glittered with excitement or some other emotion. "Kelli told me that you're isolating yourself again. I know it's hard, but you have to get out more. Marissa wouldn't want you shutting yourself off from your friends."

It occurred to Arie how often people seemed to know what the dead person's wishes might be. And how often those wishes seemed to match the speaker's.

Riann finally introduced Arie to Chad and then told him about her new personal assistant's special gift. At the look on his face, she hastened to reassure him.

"No, really," Riann said. "This is on the level. Arie knows things about Marissa that she wouldn't have any other way of knowing. Listen to her."

They all turned to look at Arie. Chad didn't bother hiding his skepticism. Mitch, ignored, continued sitting in silence.

Arie's mind went blank.

"Uh, I wasn't really expecting . . . I mean, I'm not prepared. I didn't even bring in my crystal ball."

Chad snorted and started to rise. Riann waved him back down, but his readiness to leave was all too apparent.

"What about tarot cards?" Riann asked. "Could you use those?"

Arie thought about her last experience with the tarot and shuddered. "I don't think so. I don't really—"

"Listen," Chad said. "I appreciate what you're trying to do, Riann. But this is—"

"Wait. It's out in my car. I'll go get it."

Chad had difficulty stifling his impatience.

"I'll make you a drink while Arie gets set up," Riann said. "She'll be ready in a jiffy."

"It's a little early for drinks, isn't it?" Mitch spoke up.

Nobody answered.

As Riann hurried into the kitchen, Arie turned to Chad. "I know this probably seems really weird, but it's not a scam. I promise."

"Not to be rude, but that's exactly what a scammer would say. But anyway, I'd make a lousy target. Marissa didn't leave me her money. And I didn't expect her to, either. So if it's a payday you're looking for, you're wasting your time with me."

Arie hurried to her car and made it back precisely as Riann returned to the living room carrying two cocktail glasses filled with amber liquid. She set one on the table before her and handed one to Chad.

Mitch and Arie got nothing.

She'd apparently spilled, leaving a wet spot on her left boob, turning the pale yellow blouse as transparent as Saran Wrap. Of course, Riann had chosen that day to go braless.

Flustered, Arie quickly looked away and discovered that Chad had also tuned into Riann's inadvertent peep show. *It was inadvertent, wasn't it?*

Arie wasn't so sure, especially when Riann bent over as she set the glass on the table in front of Chad.

Returning to her armchair, Riann sat with perfect posture, her nipple swinging like a pointer between her guests.

Arie tried hard to avoid looking directly at it—her—but she did notice neither Chad nor Mitch put up a huge struggle to do the same. In fact, Mitch had perked up in direct proportion to Riann's . . . perkiness. But after all, they were men, and presumably, they liked nipples.

How am I going to concentrate with Riann waving her nipple all over the place?

Arie took a deep breath, then another as she stared into the depths of the red orb. For several long moments, nothing happened. As Arie was starting to fear that nothing ever would, the ball began to glow.

The white light flashed.

Chad's face, mottled red with anger, is mere inches from my own. He's screaming so loud my ears ache, and spit lands on my cheek. How can he do this to me? Can't he understand why I need him to sign the prenup for me?

Flash.

The knife slices through the air toward my face, cutting. I duck. I feel a blow on my upper shoulder like a fist hammered into me. Get away! If I can . . . get to the . . . get to the bathroom. Lock the door. Another blow, this time on my lower back. I stumble into the wall, bounce off, and make it to the bathroom. I slide on the tiles. My hands slip on the doorknob. That's my blood. There's so much. How can there be so much?

Flash.

"Holy, holy, holy. The blood cries to Me."

We're fighting. I push him off, and he stumbles against the tub. I can get away. I know I can. I run for the bedroom. My phone. Where's my phone? Oh God—he's right there! He grabs my hair. We fall. He's on top of me, and I can't get up, and he grabs my throat. I can't . . . it . . . he . . . hurts.

Arie tried to force her mind—or whatever it was that had joined with Marissa's memories—to pull back, to look at Marissa's attacker. To *see* him. But as soon as she regained control of the experience, she lost the vision.

When Arie came back to herself, she was on her knees in front of the table, slick with sweat. She gripped the crystal ball with both hands and shook so hard, the stand chattered on the glass tabletop.

Mitch had dropped to her side and had his arm around her shoulders. He tugged her back up to the couch where Arie promptly burst into tears.

CHAPTER TWENTY-FOUR

"I don't know why you won't tell me where we're going," Chandra said. She hadn't eaten yet, and she tended toward irritability when her blood sugar fell.

"Like you told me where we were going when you dragged me to Walynda's? Relax. We're not even going to have to lie this time. You're going to thank me."

An idea had come to Arie when Riann had been talking about June, but after the episode with Chad and the vision, she hadn't been sure she would feel up to going through with it. After thinking about it, she realized it would be a good distraction. It would also be an opportunity to put Chandra in the hot seat for once. Too tempting.

"Can we at least stop for something to eat?" Chandra whined. "I'm starving."

"You're not starving. You had three cookies before we left."

"Why are you talking like a nanny?"

Arie pulled into the next Subway they came to. The nanny-thing was starting to worry her.

Twenty minutes later, they reached the outskirts of the city. Arie used her phone's GPS and made a series of turns that deposited them in front of a tan split-level home. Unfortunately, it appeared to be suffering a garden gnome infestation of Biblical proportions.

Across the yard, gnomes had gathered together in conversational groups of two or three. At least a half dozen peered out like ceramic stalkers from under bushes or behind trees. One adventurous risk-taker even balanced on the edge of the brick chimney chase. The majority, however, seemed to be attending the wedding of a handsome gnome-groom and his rosy-cheeked gnome-bride. A white veil had somehow been affixed to her head, and a faded bouquet of daisies was tied with a ribbon to her wrist.

Arie and Chandra stood for a while on the sidewalk, taking it all in.

The side door of the house opened, and June leaned out, waving delightedly. "Yoo-hoo! Over here. We use this door."

Neither girl was able to tear her gaze away from the gnome-a-palooza.

"That nice lady is yoo-hooing at us," Chandra said in a distracted tone.

"That's June," Arie said. "She's a wedding planner."

"Of course she is. Anybody can see that. Does she work with elves and trolls, too?"

Arie shook herself free of a gnome-induced stupor and led Chandra over to June and introduced them.

"Chandra is the head designer for Cake Connection," Arie said. "Riann told me that there had been some difficulties with Marissa's cake. I thought if you were looking for a new decorator, it might be beneficial for you two to meet."

"Oh," June said with a slight frown. "I thought you said on the phone you had some questions about planning your own wedding."

"Not my wedding, no. But I'm working part-time as a personal assistant for Riann Foster, and she's planning hers. I'm helping with that."

"Ohhh," June replied. The mention of Riann's name seemed to bring about conflicting emotions.

Arie understood.

On the one hand, being hired to plan Riann and Dick's wedding would be a huge opportunity. Dick apparently had boatloads of money and didn't seem to mind spending it on his little darling. On the other, knowing Riann as well as June must have from working on Marissa's wedding probably decreased the attractiveness of the opportunity considerably.

Nevertheless, June led the girls into a small dining room repurposed as Wedding Central. On a nearby sideboard, a Pisa Tower of glossy wedding magazines leaned unsteadily, while open boxes filled with netting, crêpe paper rolls, ribbons, and other decorating supplies lined the walls. Two chairs had been pulled out from the table, and each had a stack of purple and pink three-ring binders labeled with clients' names. A gnome with a maroon preacher's surplice dangling over his neck lay on his side in the center of the table. A miniature Bible, a strip of black ribbon, and a hot glue gun sat nearby, waiting for their mistress to complete his ensemble.

June gestured for them to have a seat and settled herself at the head of the table. She began quizzing Chandra on her cake decorating experience. They talked for a while about basket-weave piping and almond paste and fondant and such. Chandra promised to e-mail June her portfolio the next day. They both seemed pleased with the results of the meeting.

When they'd finished, June folded her hands and turned to Arie. "Well, then. Now that that's taken care of . . . are you telling me Riann is interested in my services as a wedding coordinator?"

Arie didn't want to add yet another lie—especially one that could be checked so easily—to the slew that she already had going, but she didn't want June to stop talking, either.

"I don't think she's made that decision yet. She's really in the planning stages."

"Considering Dick is too smart to get caught by that little gold digger, I'm not surprised. I bet he hasn't even given her a ring yet, has he?"

Arie's eyes almost popped out of her head and rolled across the table.

"Oh, don't look at me like that," June said. "You know as well as I do the old coot has no intentions of proposing. And it's not like I'm talking bad about a client. Marissa was my client, and she was an angel."

"She was?" Arie asked.

"Well, I'm not saying she was my easiest client, but she certainly wasn't the worst. At least she was capable of making a decision when she needed to. She knew what she wanted, and she made sure she got it. But she wasn't completely unreasonable, either. Did you know she grew up poor? People like that either hate where they came from, or they hate who they were. Marissa hated where she came from, so she concentrated on enjoying where she'd gotten. She had fun with her money. She didn't need to treat people like dirt to make herself feel better."

"She and Riann grew up together, didn't they?" Arie already knew the answer, but she wondered how much June did.

"They sure did, but you'd never get Riann to admit that. Or that snotty little Kelli, either. They're the second kind of rags-to-riches. They hate who they were, so they treat everyone like doody to forget how they feel about themselves. They need to prove they're better than anyone else. To themselves, anyway. Nobody else cares. I try to stay away from that kind as much as possible, but in my line of work, you can't always tell. Not at first, anyway."

"But eventually . . . " Chandra said.

"Oh, eventually, they all show their true colors. And funny enough, it's usually when they have to deal with subordinates. Service workers, I guess you'd call them. You know who I mean—waitresses, beauticians, any kind of clerk. The ones who are grateful to have gotten out of wherever they came from treat service workers like regular people. Good work gets tipped, bad work doesn't; no fuss, no muss. Marissa was like that. And she wasn't stingy with saying 'thank you,' either. But those nasty ones . . . give them a little power, and oh, boy. Get out of their way. If you're lucky, that is."

"Riann's been nice so far," Arie said. "But I know what you mean."

"How long of you been working for her?"

"Um . . . about two and a half hours."

June snorted. "Well, good luck with that. You couldn't pay me enough. But then again, maybe she didn't like me. I know she didn't like Marissa listening to me. Every suggestion I made, Riann stuck her nose in with twelve reasons why it wasn't good enough or wouldn't work. Marissa didn't pay her any mind, though.

If she liked the suggestion I made, she approved it. If she didn't, well, never mind. We went on to the next thing."

June sighed. "I wish she could've had her wedding. Such a shame . . . "

"Who do you think killed her?" Arie asked.

June shook her head knowingly. "You know what they say. Look to the loved ones first."

"You think it was Chad?" Arie said. "You said they were fighting about the prenup."

"They were. But I think he really loved her. I'm sure her being rich didn't hurt any, and maybe that's why he went after her in the first place. But I've worked with couples for over twenty years now. I can tell when someone's in love and when they're not. I really do think they loved each other."

"Then who?"

June tilted her head, making her hairdo bobble precariously. "Are you a private eye or something?"

Chandra laughed.

Arie gave her the evil eye. *What was so funny about that?* To June, however, she said, "No, of course not. I'm just interested."

June squinted at her speculatively for a few moments. "I guess I can understand that, especially if you're working for that woman."

"What do you mean?"

"Well, you know they had a fight that afternoon, right? A vicious one. I'd taken some estimates for the reception venue over to Marissa's apartment for her to go over and could hear them plain as day through the front door. Not that I was trying to listen, of course, but—"

"Riann and Marissa?" Arie's heart thudded against her chest. "Do the police know that?"

"I doubt it. They didn't ask me anything about Riann, and I didn't volunteer. But it was a doozy, let me tell you."

"What was it about?" Chandra asked.

Despite the fact that they seemed to have the house to themselves, the three women had lowered their voices and drawn close together in the age-old gossip huddle.

"A man, of course," June said. "Isn't it always? Riann accused Marissa of going home with some guy the night before. I guess the girls were having a night out, but apparently some old boyfriend of Marissa's showed up unannounced. Riann called Marissa a hypocrite—talk about the pot and the kettle. Then Marissa told Riann she was a jealous bitch and always had been. That was probably true. And then Riann called Marissa a whore and a sellout and a thief. And then, let me tell you, it got *really* ugly."

"Okay, if Marissa went home with some guy," Arie said, "I get why Riann might call her a whore, but why sellout?"

"Or thief?" Chandra added.

June shrugged. "You got me."

"And you never told the police? Not even after Marissa's murder?" Arie said.

June sighed again. "I know, I know. It's . . . look, this is all I have." She spread out her arms. "This house. This business. That's it."

"Plus a bazillion garden gnomes," Chandra muttered.

"Brides are always acting up," June went on as though she hadn't heard. "Getting married is the most stressful thing a woman ever has to deal with. They fall apart, and I'm supposed to be there to pick up the pieces. If word gets out that I'm blabbing about their silly tantrums, I might as well close up shop and apply at Walmart."

"But it wasn't only a silly tantrum, was it?" Arie pushed.

"How do I know? Riann was mad, sure, but if she was going to try to kill Marissa, she would've done it right then. I may not like her, but I can't imagine her sneaking back to Marissa's apartment hours later and chasing her from room to room with a butcher knife. Besides, Kelli told me that Riann already told the police about the ex-boyfriend, so they would have known how she felt about Marissa's . . . indiscretion, shall we say."

Arie and Chandra exchanged glances. *Marissa's indiscretion? Brant?*

CHAPTER TWENTY-FIVE

Arie lay twisted in a tangle of sweaty sheets. Flinging them off, she padded out to the kitchen.

Was Brant Marissa's "little indiscretion"?

She rummaged in the fridge for something good to eat. Her mother had stocked the crisper with apples and oranges, but they weren't quite what Arie had in mind. Brant, of course, had always loved fruits and vegetables.

She'd called him earlier, but he hadn't answered. Hadn't—or wouldn't. When she tried leaving a message, she discovered his voice mailbox was full—another very un-Brantlike behavior. Arie's brother didn't let things pile up. He'd been born making lists, preferably alphabetized and in order of priority. Nothing satisfied his neat little soul like crossing off items, one by one.

The uncertainty of not being able to contact him made Arie feel even more estranged from her brother, from her whole family, really. She'd never been close to her mother, of course. But lately, she'd even felt disconnected from her father. It made her feel sad, but also guilty.

Arie hadn't wanted to come back from the Other Side. It had been too beautiful. There really weren't any words capable of describing the place she'd been allowed to visit briefly and then been sent away from.

She sprawled across the table and buried her head in her arms. Crying over her ejection from heaven wasn't a new thing. Arie had been depressed for months afterward, but she'd thought she'd gotten past the raw, aching emptiness.

Guess not.

The kitchen lights flicked on. Grumpa, in a short, ratty green robe, blinked at her blearily from the doorway.

"What the heck is wrong with you?"

Arie wiped her face on her sleeve. "Nothing. Don't worry about it."

"Did you have a bad day at work or something?" He remained in the doorway, his pale, spindly legs sticking out of the bottom of his robe like stalks.

"I'm sorry if I woke you up."

"You still upset over that parking lot thing?"

Arie stiffened.

"'That parking lot thing'? I *died* in that parking lot, Grumpa. I was murdered."

"Look. I'm eighty-three years old. You think I haven't thought about dying? But I realized I've got two choices. So do you, and so does every other breathing animal on this earth. You can focus on death, or you can focus on life. I'm not going to waste the time I have left."

"Oh, right. You're telling me you focus on life? Because it sure doesn't seem to make you very happy. In fact, I can honestly say you suck at it."

"That's because I'm still getting used to it. Happiness is a habit, and I ain't used to it yet. And don't say suck. It's not ladylike."

Arie thunked her head down on the table. Her mother had shape-shifted into a crabby old man in a puke-green bathrobe.

"It's all your fault, anyway," Grumpa said.

Arie picked her head up and glared at him. "Your century-old bad attitude is my fault now?"

"See, that's rude. Who's the one with the bad attitude now?"

Grumpa shuffled over to the refrigerator and pulled the door of the bottom freezer open. His robe was so short that for a brief, paralyzing moment, Arie thought she was going to be treated to the sight of her grandfather's bare butt. She experienced a whole-body shudder that almost tipped her chair over.

"Maybe you should explain that." Arie was getting another headache.

"Well, that parking lot thing. I'd never thought about you dying before me." He was still rummaging around in the freezer. "And then afterward, you got all sad and weepy."

He stood, a couple of frozen Snickers bars clutched in his scrawny hand. Arie's heart lifted, and the possibility of forgiving his chronic insensitivity and general crabbiness loomed. He tossed one over to her and then peeled the wrapper halfway down his own.

Lucky for him. She was not above candy snatching from the elderly, or anyone else, for that matter.

"I figured, if you got that down in the dumps about not staying dead, it must've been pretty nice. So I decided not to worry about it anymore. Death, I mean.

And I decided there were still some things I wanted to do before my time did come, just in case."

"In case what?"

"Well . . . just in case I didn't qualify for that nice place. Sometimes, I'm a little hard to get along with."

"I've noticed."

Grumpa ignored her. "And in case I didn't get a second chance the way you did."

A second chance . . . there was something in that.

"What things do you want to do before your time comes?"

Grumpa looked startled, then his expression folded back into its usual sour lines. "None of your beeswax, little girl. You mind your business; I'll mind mine."

So much for bonding.

Arie had to talk to Brant, but he wasn't exactly cooperating. She'd left several messages, including one at work. When he continued to avoid her calls, she pulled out the big guns. She threatened to—what else?—tell their mother that he wouldn't talk to her.

He called fourteen minutes later, but he was not pleased.

It took a while, but Arie finally got him to agree to a meeting—his place in Madison, where he'd lived since graduating college. Neither of them wanted to chance a run-in with their mother. Arie had to use her GPS to find his house, a small Craftsman-style starter home in a decent neighborhood.

If she'd expected a heartwarming welcome, she didn't get it. Brant answered the door in jeans and an old gray UWM sweatshirt with coffee stains on the front. It was an outfit most people would look relaxed in. On

Brant, however, it only served to illustrate the distress he must have felt.

It occurred to Arie that her brother had suffered a significant loss. She felt a wave of guilt at her insensitivity.

They settled in the living room. Brant seemed distracted and apprehensive. He cleared his throat. "So, what do you want?"

"I want to know what's going on." Arie flung up a hand. "And don't say 'nothing'. We both know you're in trouble."

Brant didn't speak right away. When he did, it was only to ask if Arie had told their parents.

"Not yet," she answered. "But if this gets any worse, they are going to have to know."

He frowned. "What do you mean, worse?"

"Oh, come on, Brant. I know the cops are questioning you about Marissa. And Riann said you showed up one night when she and Marissa went out, and Marissa went home with you."

Brant scrubbed his face with his hands and groaned. "That bitch. Look, you need to stay out of this. I didn't kill Marissa. I loved her"—Brant's eyes met his sister's—"and she loved me."

"She was engaged to—"

"She was going to break it off. It wasn't working out. The asshole was starting to show his true colors, and they were fighting all the time."

"Over the prenup?"

Brant looked surprised. "How do you—"

"Never mind how I know. I just do. Marissa was going through with the marriage. I met her wedding planner, Brant. Nobody has said anything about the wedding being called off."

"Well, she was going to. She was waiting for the right time. It wasn't an easy thing for her to do. She was afraid of him, Arie."

Arie thought about the look on Chad's face when he screamed at Marissa in the vision. She shivered.

"He killed her," Brant said. "I know he did."

"He wasn't even in town."

"So what? Maybe he came home, and they had it out or something. All he had to do is turn around and drive back to Chicago."

"How do you know he was in Chicago?"

Brant blushed.

"She told you, didn't she?" Arie was horrified. "Were you there that night?"

"No." Tears pooled in Brant's eyes. "But I wish I had been. She wasn't feeling well, and besides . . . "

"Besides, what?"

"We never met at her place. She was always afraid the asshole would walk in."

Arie looked around the nondescript room. "She came here?"

Brant shook his head. "It was too far for her to drive. The asshole was keeping close track of everywhere she went and how long she was gone. She'd never be able to explain away a three- or four-hour chunk of time."

"Then where did you meet?"

"Her sister's. Marissa was paying the rent anyway, so it's not like she didn't have some rights."

"Oh, crap." Arie gasped. "No wonder the police think you're involved. Kelli must have told them what you two were doing."

"I don't think so," Brant said. "She seemed cool with it."

"Don't be stupid. Kelli is a spoiled brat. She's not going to cover for anybody, much less her sister's lover."

This time, Brant's voice was laced with anger. "I disagree. She knows how much we loved each other. She's already proved it."

"By letting you two fool around in her apartment? What choice did she have?"

"It's not only that. She's proved it since then, too. She even sent me—"

Brant's cell phone buzzed like an angry bee, vibrating across the coffee table in front of them. He reached for it, but Arie grabbed his arm.

"Brant, Marissa was paying Kelli's way. Of course she's going to keep her secrets and kiss her a—"

Brant yanked his arm away. "Look, never mind. I know you mean well, but it's time to go."

"Brant—"

"It's going to be okay. Leave it alone."

CHAPTER TWENTY-SIX

Arie had arranged her second day with Riann for later that week. Riann, having had more time to think about possible uses for her minion, had a full to-do list all ready. In addition to the guest list for the still nonexistent wedding and updating her calendar, Riann had decided that she needed to start her own blog. She also decided that Arie, despite having no experience as a web designer, should get it all set up so that all Riann needed to do was dictate her posts. Typing was out of the question because it would surely damage her manicure.

After reiterating her almost total ignorance of all things blog-related, Arie asked Riann what theme she would use.

"Theme?" Riann asked. "What do you mean?"

"Well, what will you be talking about?"

"I haven't decided yet. I'll probably talk about whatever comes to mind at the time."

"But is there going to be a consistent topic?" Arie asked. "Like, some blogs are on scrapbooking or working moms. Stuff like that. They usually have some kind of common denominator."

"What's a denominator?"

"Okay, skip that. What sorts of things do you like to talk about? Do you have a hobby?"

Riann shrugged. "I talk about whatever."

This was a fast train going nowhere. Maybe the concept of a theme was too ambitious.

"How about a color scheme? Do you have a favorite color or style?" Arie worked hard to keep the tone of desperation out of her voice.

Riann shrugged again. "I don't know. Something pretty. Maybe diamonds. I like diamonds." She giggled.

"Diamonds," Arie said. She was supposed to design a website based on . . . diamonds.

Before Arie could figure out how to explain to Riann that diamonds weren't a color, the intercom near the front door chimed. While Riann answered it, Arie started Googling DIY blog sites. She reminded herself she only needed the job long enough to find Marissa's killer. Keeping Brant out of jail would be a nice bonus.

Arie's mother-inside-her-head voice was not amused at her priorities. The real one wouldn't be either.

Riann called to Arie from the living room.

"Coming, master," Arie grunted.

As soon as Arie entered the living room, she stumbled to a halt. Kelli sat on the couch with Riann, the two of them chatting in a high-pitched, bubbly tone that dripped with insincerity. Unaware that Arie and Kelli had already met, Riann gestured her over to the couch.

Arie's stomach started a languorous slow roll as fear flooded it with acid.

At first, Kelli didn't recognize her, but as Riann began describing the talents of her newly acquired pet psychic, Kelli's head tilted, and a puzzled look seeped into her eyes.

"Don't I know you?"

"Uh . . . I don't think so."

"I'm telling you," Riann said, "the things she told me about Marissa are simply amazing. I've never—"

"Are you sure? Because you look really familiar."

Riann, miffed at being interrupted, scowled. "Do you want to hear about this or not? Chad met her the other day, and even he was freaked out."

Kelli stiffened, and her attention immediately swung back to her hostess. "Chad was here? What did he want?"

Riann smirked. "He came to see me. You know that he and I have been keeping in touch. It's the least I could do for Marissa."

At that, Kelli suffered a complete fail as she tried pushing a smile through gritted teeth, allowing Riann to score a point in the mean-girls battle they seemed to be waging. Arie kept very still, hoping to avoid notice. She'd never been any good at making hurtful remarks sound as though they were intended as a compliment—a basic skill for any mean girl.

Unfortunately, she was still standing in the middle of the room. And, of course, when Kelli cast about for a distraction, her eyes fell directly on Arie. It was the boobs that did it.

"I *do* remember you. You're the janitor." Kelli glanced around the room as though trying to reconcile the idea of Arie's presence with Riann's pristine palace. "No wonder you know all this stuff."

"What?" Riann looked at Kelli as though the younger woman had lost her mind. "She's not a janitor. She's my personal assistant."

"Actually, I'm both," Arie said.

"What?" Riann's face scrunched up in confusion.

"I'm a hazardous waste technician for BioClean. We do biohazard cleanups, like crime scenes or unattended deaths. That's how—"

"I don't understand," Riann said. Her face had still not unscrunched.

"I work—"

"She's a *janitor*," Kelli said. "She wears a hideously ugly yellow sweat suit, and she cleans up dead people. She must have been pawing through Marissa's things. That's how she—"

"I'm a technician," Arie said.

"You mean, like, for computers?" Riann asked.

Arie closed her eyes. She really hoped Riann was successful at keeping her body a temple because her brain was never going to be a viable fallback position.

"Who the hell said anything about computers?" Kelli asked.

Time to get control of this situation.

"I work for a company that cleans up blood and other dangerous things at crime scenes," Arie told Riann in her nanny voice. "That's how I . . . uh . . . met Marissa."

"Ohhh." Riann smiled in relief. "I get it. Yeah, that makes sense."

"How does that make sense?" Kelli said.

"Because how else are dead people going to find Arie? Do you think they're going to chase her around town? I mean, duh. If she's a psychic—and she is—then that's a perfect job for her to get clients. It's kind of gross, though, huh?" Riann turned to Arie with her nose wrinkled like a little bunny.

"It can be," Arie said. "That's why I have to wear the ugly suit."

"Oh, my gosh, yeah. I don't blame you. Except I wouldn't want to wear it."

Kelli rolled her eyes. Riann, for the most part clueless, caught that.

"Well, Miss I-Don't-Believe-In-Ghosts, I guess you won't want to come to the little gathering I'm throwing together for Marissa's grieving loved ones."

"A party?" Kelli said.

"Well, not really a party," Riann said. "That would be tacky. More like a séance. I'm going to have Arie read for us. I mean, for Chad and Mitch and Wyatt. And, of course, me." To Arie, she said, "This way, you can make up for whatever happened the other day with Chad. That was so freaky." Turning back to Kelli, she continued. "It's too bad you can't make it. In fact, I guess I'll be the only girl there."

Arie looked down to see if her breasts had evaporated. Nope—still there.

"Oh, Riann," Kelli said sweetly. "You know I wouldn't miss that for anything. After all, I'm Marissa's little sister. You know she would want me there."

Now that Riann had regained her ascendancy, she smiled. "I suppose one more won't hurt."

Wonderful.

CHAPTER TWENTY-SEVEN

The gathering at the lake house was everything Arie imagined a socialite cocktail party would be. Soft jazz drifted down from surround-sound speakers, lights had been dimmed, and a bar had been set up in a corner.

The train display had been roped off with theater-style braided gold rope. A trio of guests stood at the barrier, marveling at the miniature world.

Everything looked perfect, except, that is, for their host.

Under an unfortunately form-fitting gray vest, Dick Boyette wore a button-down shirt that seemed an uneasy compromise between teal and mint-green. His tie was . . . plaid. It picked up on the gray and teal, but tossed in stripes of melon and baby blue as well.

Riann probably dressed him. Dick had to be around the same age as Grumpa, but the resemblance ended there. His clothes were certainly more expensive than anything Grumpa could ever afford. Unfortunately, the style was generations too young for the octogenarian to pull off with any dignity. Even Grumpa in his ratty green bath robe and his blue-veined legs sticking out from the bottom would have been more appropriate than the club scene costume poor Dick was decked out in. And judging from his expression, he knew it.

The rest of the small assembly looked like a photo shoot for one of those glossy-paged fashion magazines. Arie started sweating just looking at them. She had mistakenly assumed Riann was only inviting the wedding party, but there were twenty or so guests. For most of her life, Arie had been too short and her boobs too big to have ever been considered one of the pretty people. In addition to physical beauty—both genetic and engineered—the crowd seemed to have a secret way of looking at the world that she'd never been privy to; they spoke a language she didn't understand. Fortunately, she wasn't alone.

Right after Riann had foisted the idea for the gathering on her, Arie had insisted that Chandra accompany her. Riann had balked, but Arie had stayed firm, insisting she needed Chandra's help running the séance. Eventually, Riann realized that Chandra's attendance would make it look as though Riann was so affluent that even her assistant needed an assistant. The idea tickled the hell out of her, and permission was granted.

Her mood carried over to the evening, and she waved gaily at the girls when they walked in. However, Riann seemed the only one in good spirits. There was a strange undercurrent of tension that Arie noticed as soon as she and Chandra arrived.

The fact that she was again woefully underdressed didn't help.

In an attempt to establish credibility as a medium, Arie had chosen to wear a long, black swirly skirt combined with a psychedelic, off-the-shoulder peasant blouse. Unfortunately, that meant either going braless— something Arie hadn't been able to do since she was eleven—or wearing a strapless bra, which, if there was any hope of such a contraption holding up her boobs, meant wearing a bra so tight it came close to cracking her rib cage. It also severely restricted her breathing. Bending over was not an option. She hoped the clanking and jingling of the many bracelets she'd also donned would cover the sound of her shallow panting.

Chandra had dressed with her usual angsty artiste style, which stood out among the chic fashionista tribe like a flamingo at a peacock parade. Chandra laughed it off and, after stopping to fortify herself with a drink, pushed forward to explore the artwork lining the walls of the apartment.

Normally, in these situations, Arie would have headed for the nearest wall and made like a flower, but she'd backed herself into a corner earlier by telling Riann she would need at least an hour to mingle and "absorb the energies" of the guests before she could attempt a reading. In reality, she knew she likely wouldn't have another chance to see the whole wedding party in one place again. She'd met everyone except Chad's best man, but she wanted to get a sense of how they interacted with each other.

Kelli stood at the bar, deep in conversation with Chad. She appeared to be doing all the talking while he did all the pouring. Marissa's younger sister wore a shimmery white cocktail dress that, even dismissing the short time since the funeral, seemed strangely inappropriate.

Actually, it looked ridiculous. Unlike her petite sister, Kelli was tall and wide at the hips. In a room full of pretty people, she looked almost as out of place as Arie felt.

As Arie drew close, she heard Chad mumble something but couldn't catch the words. Kelli's laugh trilled falsely in response, and she reached up to adjust Chad's already perfect tie. He downed half his drink in one gulp, then slid past the girl and made his way over to a man Arie didn't recognize. She wondered if it was Wyatt, Chad's best man.

Kelli scowled as Chad left. Arie didn't feel like dealing with Her Poutiness anyway, so she pretended she'd been heading somewhere else and angled away. She kept her eyes on Chad and his friend.

Whoever the other guy was, the two made a striking contrast. Chad was an obvious product of wealth. He wore his tailored clothes with ease. His blond hair looked as if it had been genetically bred to flop casually over one eye. His teeth were the result of careful attention by a team of hygienists, dentists, and orthodontists. All in all, he was handsome but in a blurry, generations-of-soft-life kind of way.

His buddy? Also blond and handsome, but that was where the resemblance ended. As Arie examined him, the word that came to mind most often was *sharp*. His face, all angles and planes, looked as if it had been carved from marble. His eyes constantly scanned the crowd in watchful, hypervigilant darts. His clothes . . . his clothes *seemed* right, but he held his shoulders too stiffly, and he fingered the collar of his buttoned-down shirt too often for him to pull off the casualness of the "haves." When he smiled, Arie spied a tiny chip in one of his front teeth. And underneath it all, he exuded an energy of raw ambition that rivaled even their hostess's.

Watching Riann approach the two men, Arie remembered her pseudo-boss's disappointment when Chad's brother Mitch had shown up with him that afternoon. Although Riann slipped her arm through Chad's, her smile seemed solely for his friend's benefit. He smiled back.

Unfortunately, as Arie moved to join the trio, so did Kelli from one direction and Dick from the other. Dick slid his arm around Riann's waist and tried to deliver a testosterone-laden glare to Chad's friend.

Kelli handed Chad a drink, which he reluctantly accepted. From the way he chugged it, Arie didn't think his hesitation had been about the drink itself, but rather the provider of it. He excused himself and made his way to the door, presumably heading to the bathroom. He had acquired that too-careful walk that signified his level of intoxication had breached the dam of good sense.

Kelli watched his retreating back with narrowed eyes.

Riann, perhaps as much to distract from the various tensions as for good manners, introduced Arie to the stranger.

"Arie, I'd like you to meet Wyatt. He was going to be Chad's best man, and he knew Marissa almost as long as Chad did, didn't you, darling?"

Not noticing Dick stiffen—or perhaps not caring—Riann reached up and stroked Wyatt's cheek with her thumb. "Sorry, darling. I left a little lipstick when we said hello." She smiled impishly at Wyatt, who chuckled and casually sipped his drink.

Riann preened, but then Wyatt leaned down and whispered something in Kelli's ear. The younger woman giggled but stopped as soon as she spied Chad returning from the bathroom. She abruptly pulled away from the group and crossed back to the bar where Chad had stopped to pour another drink.

Wyatt frowned. "Why can't she leave him alone? She's practically stalking him."

"My goodness," Riann said. "If I didn't know better, I'd say you were jealous." A sly smile bloomed on her pretty face. "Oh, I get it."

"Shut up, Riann. He's got enough problems. If the cops think he's interested in another woman—even if it *is* Kelli—he's going to be in even deeper trouble than he already is. Of course, you'd like that, wouldn't you?"

Riann's lips thinned as much as her collagen injections would allow. "Oh, right. Like Chad has anything to worry about. He's got an alibi, remember? But I wonder . . . do the cops know about your history with Marissa? I know Chad doesn't. That really would be awkward, wouldn't it?"

Although Wyatt tried to seem unaffected, Arie saw his mouth tighten behind the raised glass. His eyes flicked over to Kelli and Chad. Just as quickly, he turned the charm back on and met Riann's challenging eyes. His lips twisted into a conspiratorial smile.

"Marissa and I never dated, and you know it," Wyatt said. "You love to stir up trouble, don't you?"

Riann's giggle cascaded lightly. "You know me so well."

Dick cleared his throat. "My dear, you aren't still planning on holding this séance thing, are you? I don't think it's appropriate to—"

"Oh, Richard, you know how much I've been looking forward to it." Riann clearly awakened to the fact that her supposed fiancé was being neglected. She turned a pouty, kittenish face to him and smoothed her hand over the few wisps of hair clinging to his balding dome.

His face softened. "But, sweetheart, don't you think it's a bit rude to leave the rest of your guests while—"

"But I'm not leaving them." Riann's voice had lost a little of its purr. "We'll be in the next room, and besides, you'll be here. And you are the host, after all." She let her hand rest over his heart.

"But they're your friends."

Riann stiffened and yanked her hand away. "Well, if you really can't see your way to helping me out, I guess I'll have to—"

Dick caved. "Of course, I'll help you. I—"

Riann squealed and leaned over to kiss his cheek. Instead, Dick twisted at exactly the right moment to shift the kiss from cheek to lips. Before she could pull back, he slid his hand around to her backside and, cupping it, pulled her against his body. Riann made a muffled sound. When Dick finally released her, she batted at his shoulder and mumbled, "You are so bad."

Dick patted her butt. "Don't you forget it."

For the first time since meeting her, Arie actually felt sorry for Riann.

Wyatt didn't. He grinned at Dick's retreating back. "Still think it's worth it, darlin'?"

"Don't be an idiot," Riann snapped. "Of course it is."

"I don't see a ring on that pretty little finger yet. I'd hate to think you're wasting your time and, shall we say, talents on that Viagra-popping asshole with nothing to show for it. I bet he spends more time playing with his choo-choo than with you. Or is that the way you want to keep it?"

"It could be worse," Riann said. "I could be wasting my time on some dirt-poor asshole and *really* have nothing to show for it." Riann spun on her Manolo Blahnik pumps and stalked off.

Wyatt hooted with laughter, but Arie saw a muscle twitching over his left eye.

He turned his focus to Arie as if seeing her for the first time or at least, seeing her breasts for the first time. As he stared at them, a slow smile slid across his face. "So you're Riann's new psychic friend."

Arie had spent years trying to get used to men who boob-talked. She'd never succeeded. She had, however, learned to restrain the nearly irresistible urge to punch them in the throat. Instead, she reached up and poked him in the middle of his forehead. Hard.

Not all urges needed to be restrained.

Wyatt's eyes sprang open. "Hey!"

"Looka eye, always looka eye," Arie said, pointing at her own.

Wyatt's grin widened, lighting his face with joy. Arie had a sudden insight into what he must've looked like as a young boy. Better yet, he'd finally discovered she had a face.

"Did you seriously just quote *The Karate Kid*?"

"You're lucky I didn't crane kick you in the danglies. Didn't your mother teach you better manners?"

"Considering she ran off when I was three," Wyatt replied, "she didn't have a chance. But I'm always open for lessons."

"Oh. I'm sorry."

"Don't be. I was acting like a jerk. I'm going to head over for another drink. Are you ready?" Wyatt wiggled his empty glass in the air.

"I'm good."

For a split second, Wyatt's eyes dipped again to her cleavage, then shot back up. "Yeah, I would say you are."

He walked away before she could deliver the aforementioned crane kick.

Arie watched him head directly for Kelli and begin flirting her up. Kelli didn't seem to mind, but her eyes kept tracking Chad.

This is crazy. Dick obviously adored Riann, who was openly flirting with Wyatt, who was trying to pick up Kelli, who was stalking Chad, who only wanted to get drunk. It was like a thwarted-love conga line.

She was exhausted.

Unfortunately, Riann left her to "absorb energies" for another hour, and given her nerves, Arie may have had a tad too much to drink. At least her wallflower tendencies had fallen by the wayside.

Chandra found her in the middle of a group of people listening with rapt attention to Arie's description of her biotech job and the difficulties that arose when bluebottle flies discovered dead flesh. One woman, hand clamped over her mouth, had turned an ominous shade of green.

Chandra dragged Arie into the hall and then through another door into Dick's man cave. The wedding party had been gathered and sat around what looked like a poker table with an antique lace tablecloth thrown over it. Lit candles had been scattered at tables around the room. Arie's red crystal ball, with its hidden snippet of Marissa's blood under the frame, waited for its mistress in front of the only open chair.

CHAPTER TWENTY-EIGHT

Arie took a deep breath and wished she hadn't drunk that last glass of wine . . . or the two before it.

She sat down and placed her hands on either side of the crystal ball. When she closed her eyes, the room rose and fell with a soft undulation that had nothing to do with a death vision, so she popped them open again. Another deep breath.

Chandra turned off the lights. Although the candles flickered, a shroud of darkness descended on the room. An eerie silence broken only by nervous shifting of the participants descended over the group.

Kelli giggled.

"Silence," Arie said.

Her voice rang in the gloom. *Damn.* She'd even startled herself. The nervous shifting stopped, and she sensed them turning their undivided attention to her. Arie pulled the crystal ball closer. The flickering candlelight danced like imps in the depths of the blood-red crystal. Arie drew another shaky breath. Looking up, she ran her gaze around the assembled guests.

"Are you certain you want to do this? When you speak to the dead, you are opening doors that are better left unopened."

Somebody gasped. Arie waited, running her gaze from person to person.

"Yes." It was Chad.

The others nodded somberly. Outside, the party could still be heard. People laughed, their voices rising and falling—discordant, but not unpleasant. Inside, all was still.

"All right," Arie said. "Close your eyes, and each of you concentrate on Marissa. Think about a memory you have of the two of you. Remember where you were, what you are doing or saying. Think about what you were wearing. Were you eating or drinking something? Are there certain smells you remember?"

Arie paused for several long moments. "Keep that memory close to your heart."

Arie took a deep breath and steadied herself. She leaned forward, and as soon as her gaze touched the crystal ball, the red fog rose and whirled around her.

Flash.

The rich, cloying smell of maple syrup fills her nostrils. Pancakes. I love pancakes. How did you know?

Arie felt Marissa's giggle floating like bubbles inside her. She put her hand to her throat and forced it down like vomit.

Flash.

A small, rather barren bedroom. A poster of a curly headed hunk wearing white sunglasses and a black leather jacket is tacked to the wall. Its bottom left corner curls up like an autumn leaf. Justin. Underneath, a cheap particleboard bookcase leans precariously against the wall; it bears the weight of three eighteen-inch-tall trophies sporting tiny gold cheerleaders suspended forever in midleap. The remaining shelf is crammed with paperback Stephen King novels and a tattered Raggedy Ann doll, whose little black button eye is missing. The diary—bright, shiny red leather—sits next to the doll. Rags . . . have to keep it safe. If they ever find out . . .

Flash.

On the lake, floating. Drifting. The sun is hot on my face and shoulders. It feels like my skin will sizzle when the cool water drips from the paddle as I swing it to the other side. His kayak bumps mine, and we laugh. On the dock now. I'm watching the sun go down. It turns the lake into pink frosting, and I want to eat it right up. He comes up, hugging me from behind, and I nestle into his strong arms. I twist around, and our kisses burn as hot as the sun. Oh, Wyatt . . .

Flash.

The journal. It's old now—the red leather cracked and faded. The lock is still silvery-bright and shiny, and so is the tiny key.

Flash.

Another key. Dull metal. Bigger. The smell of bleach fills my nose and mouth.

Flash.

A two-inch thick pile of papers, stacked neatly on the edge of the desk. Rags . . . she wants my book. She can't . . .

Flash.

His head rests on my lap. I run my fingers through the curls, so thick my fingers catch. Women would kill for this hair.

Brant's laughing face tilts to mine. He reaches up and draws my face to his.

The realization that she was about to lock lips with her own brother yanked Arie back to herself. She shoved herself away from the crystal ball, sending it spinning across the table. Wyatt lunged and caught it before it tumbled from the table.

Brant's face. Younger, leaner, and with an expression that hurt Arie's heart. Hurt, because she'd never seen him look that way before: at ease and filled with quiet contentment.

"Are you okay?" Chandra gripped Arie's shoulder.

Arie could only manage a nod, so she was basically lying with her head. Mitch rose and left the room, turning the lights on as he went. When he returned, he brought her glass of water.

"I'm going to need a minute," Arie said.

"It's okay. I've got some of it written down." Chandra held up a notebook.

"You mean I talk when I'm . . . ?" Arie shuddered with horror. *What had she been saying?*

"Not really," Chandra said. "Isolated words and some phrases. I took notes in case you needed some reminders. It sounded pretty intense."

Arie held her hand out for the notebook. After scanning it, she took a drink of water and composed herself. Chandra was right; it was just isolated words. *Pancakes. Justin. My rabbity can doll.* Arie smiled at that. *Kissing me. His face.*

"Who is Justin?" Chad's face was red and twisted with some strong emotion. *Anger? Fear?*

Arie smiled again. "Justin Timberlake. She had a poster tacked to her wall."

Riann gasped and put her hand over her mouth. "She did. That's so amazing."

"Are you kidding?" Kelli said. "Every girl in America had a poster of some boy band on their wall. It was the nineties."

"I didn't see any other posters," Arie said. "Just the one of Justin. He was wearing these white sunglasses and, um, a black jacket. A leather one. And it was her Raggedy Ann doll, not 'rabbity can.' She had a bookshelf underneath the poster. A cheap one, kind of. She had some cheerleading trophies and the Raggedy Ann doll. It was missing an eye."

"I gave her that doll," Riann said in a small voice. She started crying, great gulping sobs, and laid her head on her arms on the table.

"The doll," Kelli whispered. Her face was as white as her dress. "I accidentally . . . I mean, one day her eye just fell off. It wasn't my fault. But Marissa . . . she put her away on the shelf, so I wouldn't mess with her anymore."

"What else did you see?" Chad asked, his voice tight and still thick with anger.

"Um . . . she liked pancakes," Arie said. "I smelled maple syrup. I think somebody made pancakes for her."

She glanced around the room but was surprised when it was Mitch who caught her eye. He slid a glance toward Chad and gave his head the tiniest shake, telling her to move on.

Holy cow. How many guys had Marissa gone out with?

"She went kayaking on a lake. It was a really hot summer day."

This time, Arie was careful not to look directly at anybody.

"We never went kayaking," Chad said. "This is stupid."

Arie peeked at Wyatt. His face was expressionless, but when he saw her glance, he winked.

Flustered, she looked away. Chad's rising anger was palpable. In an effort to appease him, Arie said, "And she showed me her ring. It was stunning. An emerald-cut solitaire, right?"

At this, Chad took a deep shuddering breath. His eyes filled with tears. He started to say something but stumbled to a halt.

"She loved it," Arie said. It was the truth, even though that particular image hadn't come that particular evening. Besides, she didn't want Chad to storm off before she'd had a chance to bring up Brant. Riann had calmed down and was wiping her eyes with tissues Mitch had brought her from Dick's desk.

Now or never.

"There was another man," Arie said. The room froze. "Not anybody recent. Someone . . . I think he was somebody from her college days." She turned to Riann. "I saw him before, remember? I think you said his name is Brant. Who is he?"

Chad laughed, but it sounded strained. He leaned back in his chair and twisted the tension out of his neck. "He was an old college fling. It was over ages ago. She told me all about it. The guy couldn't take it when her book took off, and she started making money. I guess he was old-fashioned that way. But whatever. He wasn't anybody important."

But Arie had caught the secretive glance Riann and Kelli shared. Even Wyatt had grown too still. Out of them all, only Mitch looked natural.

"Well," Riann said. "I'd better get back to the party. Richard must be missing me." She pushed herself away from the table and circled the room, extinguishing the candles.

The rest of the group rose slowly. Arie and Chandra hung back, letting Marissa's friends work their way out the door. Wyatt was last. Before he crossed the threshold, he turned and stared at Arie. Their eyes met. He looked at her thoughtfully, then forced a smile and walked out the door.

CHAPTER TWENTY-NINE

Wyatt called Arie the next afternoon, but she didn't realize it until several hours later. Earlier that morning, Guts had called her and Grady in to work a biohazard scene at a local factory. Some assembly line guy had gotten the edge of his shirtsleeve caught in the machinery during a repair job and lost a finger. Unfortunately for Arie, she found it.

It wasn't until later that evening that Arie checked her voice mail and discovered Wyatt had called. Her heart thumped, but she told herself she was being silly. Before she could give herself too much time to think—and therefore chicken out—she dialed the number he'd left.

He answered right away. His voice, soft and low, didn't help her heart rate. She could almost feel his amused smile through the phone as she stumbled her way through the greeting. She ended with, "So, yeah. I got your message, and, uh, so I called you. Because . . . um, you left a message."

To his credit, it sounded as though he tried to muffle his chuckle.

"I was wondering if you'd like to join me for dinner," he said. "I know a great little place. They serve Italian, but if you'd rather have something else, we could do that."

Long pause.

"Arie? You still there?"

"Oh. Yes, I'm . . . yes, we could do that."

"Have you eaten yet?"

"Have I . . . ? You mean, tonight?"

"How about I swing by? It's nothing fancy. Just a nice, quiet meal. I can be there in thirty minutes."

"Sure," Arie said. "Yes. That'll be . . . a half hour?"

This time, the chuckle escaped. After they hung up, Arie stood in the center of the kitchen, holding her phone and waiting to see if she was actually going to have a heart attack. She was kind of okay either way, what with not minding death and all.

When her body finally resumed normal functioning, she realized she'd needlessly whittled away precious preparation time, and that smelling like disinfectant was probably not the best first date impression.

Not that this was a date. Because it wasn't. She knew that. At least, she didn't think it was.

But then, what was it? Or, better question, what was Wyatt really after?

Some other questions occurred to Arie as she scuttled around trying to get ready. The "how did he get my number" one was easily answered. Riann, of course. It would have been nice for her to have asked Arie before giving out her personal number, but it was doubtful that subtlety even occurred to Riann. If she'd questioned anything, it would have been Wyatt's taste—or maybe his sanity.

The other questions—what did she want to get out of this, and did Wyatt have anything to do with Marissa's death?—proved much harder to answer.

Wyatt had chosen well. Spinnaker's was exactly as he'd described: nice, but not fancy. Unfortunately, Arie was so nervous, she doubted she'd be able to enjoy it.

Although Wyatt was a smooth conversationalist, the waiter's appearance was a relief. Arie stuck with ordering a simple chicken Alfredo. There wasn't an Italian restaurant in the world that could screw that up, and she wouldn't have to worry about slopping red sauce all over her shirt.

Arie expected that, as soon as the waiter left, Wyatt would bring up the reading. She still hadn't figured out what his angle was. Even though he was attentive and borderline flirty, her gut told her he was after something else.

Instead, he fell back on the age-old "what do you do for a living" icebreaker.

Well, this should be fun.

"I'm a hazardous waste technician," Arie said.

"You're a . . . ?"

Arie repeated herself, enjoying the look on his face. Then she explained and watched his face morph from oh-that's-what-it-means enlightenment at her explanation to eww-that-sounds-so-gross disgust. In fact, his skin turned almost as green as the salad the waiter plunked down in front of them.

"Maybe we shouldn't talk about it before we eat."

"Oh, no, that's okay. I mean, I did ask." He pushed his salad away.

Arie covered her mouth to keep from giggling, but he caught her. Then, to her relief, he burst into laughter.

"Okay, you win," Wyatt said. "That is so gross. I've worked a lot of tough jobs in my life, but I couldn't imagine ever cleaning up that kind of stuff. How can you stand it?"

Arie shrugged lightly. "It's a job. And, well, somebody's got to do it. Besides, we wear head-to-toe biohazard suits and gloves and facemasks. We never actually touch anything."

"Does all that gear keep out the . . . you know . . . the smell?"

"Nope."

The waiter set their steaming plates in front of them. "I hope you have a good appetite." Then he looked confused as they both cracked up.

Midway through the meal, Wyatt finally asked. He chose the right moment. They'd gotten over the awkward phase of first dates, and Arie was feeling pleasantly sated by the delicious food.

"So," Wyatt said. "You're psychic, huh? What's that like?"

"I'm still getting used to it."

"What, it's like a new thing? How does that work?"

"It's a long story." Arie realized she'd lost her appetite and pushed her plate away.

"I bet. Listen, I gotta tell you. Before last night, I wouldn't have believed any of this stuff. But that whole séance thing was pretty freaky."

"I don't mind talking about the reading yesterday." After all, that was what this whole thing was about, wasn't it? Of course, *he* didn't know that.

Wyatt's hazel eyes crinkled at the corners when he smiled. A girl could get lost in those eyes. Arie reminded herself that, apparently, Marissa already had. Past tense. Had.

"I have to admit, it was pretty uncanny," Wyatt said. "It even shut Kelli up, which is next to impossible."

He hadn't seemed as though he'd been pushing away the young heiress the night before.

"She's young. And she's grieving. We should give her the benefit of the doubt." Arie had no clue why she was defending Kelli. Except, no matter how bratty the girl was, her sister *had* just died. And in a particularly gruesome way.

"I know. But if you knew her, you'd realize that's Kelli. She's always been a spoiled brat. In fact, she's even worse now that she knows she's getting all Marissa's money. And she doesn't even act sad."

"People grieve in different ways. Maybe she—"

"Kelli's been mooching off her sister her whole life. She even wanted to live with her. Marissa said no way. I think she even offered to send her to college, but Kelli said she wanted to 'enjoy life for a while.' Can you believe that? College. I would've given my left . . . anyway, now Kelli says she's trying to write a book. She thinks all she has to do is write books like Marissa, and she'll strike it rich." Wyatt snorted.

"Maybe she should read Marissa's book instead. It's full of ideas on finding a rich guy to whisk you off your feet. Even I considered trying a couple of them." Arie laughed to show she was kidding. Kind of.

Wyatt smiled and shook his head. "Don't. You're too nice to be a gold digger, and that's all it was." Despite his smile, he sounded bitter. "A how-to book on screwing old rich guys for their money."

210

The pause was long and strained.

Wyatt was the one to break it. "You know, that guy you asked about?"

Arie's heart pounded. "What guy?"

"That Brant dude. Chad won't admit it, but he was a bigger deal than Chad wants to believe. Marissa was engaged to him first. Brant, I mean. And the thing is, the dude didn't have any money. Not a dime. He was barely out of college."

"So you're saying Marissa was only with Brant because she loved him?"

Wyatt pinched his lips together, but he nodded reluctantly. "And he was back. I saw him coming out of her place one night a few of weeks ago. I tried to get Marissa to tell me what the hell was going on, but she . . ."

Another pause.

"You loved her, too, didn't you?" Arie finally asked.

Wyatt leaned back in his chair, a distant look in his eyes. "She was . . . lovely. It didn't matter where she came from. She was beautiful and . . . magical." His eyes glistened with unshed tears. "I bet you didn't know Mitch met her first. They only dated a month or so, right after she broke up with that college dude. Can you believe that? He broke up with Marissa right when the money started pouring in. That's crazy."

"Mitch did?"

"No, the college dude. Mitch was a rebound fling. And then she met Chad. He stopped in at Mitch's place one day when she was there."

"That must've been hard on Mitch," Arie said.

Wyatt nodded. "Sure, but she was never as into him as he was for her. It never would've lasted. But after she met Chad, it was all about him."

"Not exactly *all* about him, was it?"

For the first time since they'd started talking about Marissa, Wyatt's eyes connected with Arie's. He smiled ruefully.

"Yeah, well . . . she and Chad had some rough patches. Chad grew up with money, you know. Never meant the same to him as it did to Marissa or Riann."

At Arie's pointed look, he acknowledged, "Or to me, either. Chad met Marissa a couple months after the money from her first book started rolling in. Nobody expected it to take off the way it did, but apparently, there are a lot of females interested in bartering their youth and beauty for a four-carat diamond ring and a platinum credit card. The older the dude, the better.

"Anyway," he continued, "Marissa started doing television interviews and magazine features. Things went crazy for a while. And she loved it, but underneath . . . she was scared to death. I guess it's not until you have it all that you realize how easy it would be to lose it."

"Did Marissa—" Arie broke off when she noticed Wyatt's attention shift abruptly over her shoulder. She turned and found herself staring directly into a man's crotch.

Snapping her eyes up, she met Detective O'Shea's blue eyes. For dignity's sake, she tried to pretend she liked the eyes better.

Had he heard her talking about Marissa?

O'Shea swung his gaze to Wyatt, who had straightened in his chair at the other man's approach. The two locked eyes. Testosterone surged.

"Good evening, Detective." Wyatt was trying to pull off casual, but it didn't take.

"Mr. Striker." O'Shea gave a tight nod then turned to Arie. "Ms. Stiles, good to see you again."

"You, too." Arie's mind raced. *How did he know Wyatt?* She felt Wyatt staring at her and assumed he was asking himself the same question about her.

"I didn't mean to interrupt," O'Shea said. They all knew he was lying. "I thought I would stop by and say hello." With another nod and a smile, he sauntered off.

Arie and Wyatt stared at each other. She asked first. "How do you know O'Shea?"

Wyatt's lips pinched together slightly. For a second, Arie wasn't certain he was going to answer.

"He had some questions. For Chad, mainly. I came along for, you know, moral support. How do you know him?"

"From work," Arie said. No reason to go into details.

There was another long pause, then Wyatt cleared his throat. "Hey, listen. About that thing you saw with Marissa and me. The kayaking. There's no reason to . . . I mean, I'm not sure how much you saw but—"

"You kissed her."

Wyatt bit his lip, Bill Clinton-style. "Yeah, well . . . like I said, they were going through a rough time. And so you know, they were actually split up then. So it wasn't like we were doing anything wrong. Not really. But . . . uh . . . I don't see any reason for you to go into details about all that with Chad. Do you?"

Not with Chad, maybe. But that didn't mean O'Shea wouldn't be interested.

"Or Kelli, either," Wyatt added.

Arie tilted her head quizzically. "What's Kelli got to do with it?"

Other than inheriting all Marissa's money, that is.

"Nothing. But like you said, her sister did just die. There's no reason to tarnish Marissa's reputation, is there?"

"No," Arie said. "No reason at all."

CHAPTER THIRTY

Arie sat huddled in her chair, hunched over her breakfast of iced coffee and a chocolate croissant. She needed caffeine to clear the cobwebs and chocolate to soothe her nerves. Chandra was of the dreaded species: Morning Person. Worse, the restaurant they'd met in seemed full of them, lots of chattering and clanking of spoons and laughing.

Good lord. Didn't anybody sleep in anymore?

"Why are the cute ones always such scumbags?" Chandra said.

She'd been talking for at least five minutes while Arie yawned and struggled with reopening her eyelids after every blink. She'd ingested just enough coffee to be able to decipher her friend's words from the background noise of the shop, but the cheerful, chipper tone still made her flinch. She took another slug of coffee.

"Right?" Chandra said.

"Yes. Right."

"Were you even listening to me?"

"Kind of." No.

Chandra sighed. "Try harder. I have to leave soon."

"Okay, okay." Arie pulled a piece of paper from her purse and passed it over to Chandra. "I did this last night."

"Ooh, a suspect list. This is so Agatha Christie."

Arie sucked down the remaining third of her iced caramel macchiato with a quad shot of espresso. She needed another.

"Four names, huh?" Chandra said. "Are they in order of preference?"

"Not really. I put them down as they came to me."

"Okay, so Wyatt Striker came to you first, huh?" Chandra smiled.

"That's because I'd just seen him. And you can wipe the smile off your face. He's a flirt, but unless I win the lottery, he wouldn't pay me the least bit of attention. Except maybe . . . "

"To sleep with," Chandra finished. "He's obviously after Kelli now, and I doubt he gave her a second look before Marissa died. Why does being a male gold digger seem worse than a female one? That's jacked up, isn't it? To have a double standard for something that's already despicable."

"Because society supposedly has higher expectations for guys."

"That sucks on multiple levels."

"Yup," Arie said. "Anyway, if Wyatt did it, it would be a crime of passion. The only way he'd have a chance at Marissa's money is if she was alive. Whoever killed her was definitely in a rage, but I think if it was Wyatt, he would have done it when she went back to Chad after their fling."

"Wait a minute. You said he needed Marissa alive if he was going after the money, but don't you think he stands a better chance now that Marissa's out of the way?"

"You mean—"

"Kelli," Chandra said. "It's obvious he's chasing her, even if he can't really stand her. That kind of shows you what he'll do for money, doesn't it? With Marissa, he'd have had love and money. With her getting married, he's stuck being a man-whore again."

"He knew about Brant. Kelli knew, and she could certainly have told someone."

Chandra's eyes grew big. "Brant?"

Arie grimaced. She hadn't meant to talk about that—not even with Chandra. With a sigh, she filled her friend in on her visit to her brother's place in Madison.

While Chandra absorbed the new info, Arie got a much-needed refill. As soon as she sat down, Chandra picked up the list and continued.

"Chad, of course." She lifted her eyes to Arie's. "Especially if he found out about your brother, which he probably did. It's obvious Kelli wants him. I could easily see her throwing her sister under the bus by spilling the beans to Chad."

"Me, too, but do you think she would risk losing all that money? Plus it would be too obvious if Chad suddenly learned about Brant. Kelli was the only other one who knew they were meeting in her apartment."

"So did Riann."

"But Kelli wanted both the money and Chad," Arie said. "I think she wanted to *be* Marissa."

"Well, if she didn't tell Chad, maybe it really was Riann. She was angry enough over Marissa's so-called hypocrisy. Either way, Chad found out, confronted her, and then it got ugly."

Luckily, Guts called Arie and Grady in the next day for another job.

Death was picking up.

The building manager at the new job, a nice lady named Brenda, let Arie and Grady into the apartment through a side door.

"It happened right in the front foyer." Brenda's voice was tight and high-pitched. "Mrs. Schults from across the hall heard a terrible crash, but by the time the police got here . . . " She shook her head, apparently deciding to let the grisly details speak for themselves. "I can't believe such a thing could happen in my building."

The apartment itself was barely furnished and seemed strangely impersonal. They crossed through the kitchen and then through a small living room. The only item that looked expensive was the sixty-five-inch LED TV mounted on the wall.

Bachelor, probably.

When she walked past the armchair she realized she was right. A jacket hung over the back as though tossed there in passing. The blood-smeared foyer lay beyond, but it was the jacket . . .

Wyatt's jacket.

Arie recognized it from the night before. She turned to Brenda. "Who . . . ?" She swallowed and tried again. "Who lives here?"

"His name was Striker. Wayne, I think. He was a good tenant. Quiet. Always paid on time. I can't believe someone would kill him right here in his own home."

Grady pulled out the paperwork, and the building manager turned her attention to it. She stood next to him in the living room, nervously clicking a ballpoint pen, which set Arie's teeth on edge.

She moved to the edge of the foyer, examining the space as if evaluating it for cleaning. Blood pooled in three spots and had stained a small section of the carpeting beyond.

"How did he die?"

Arie's voice bounced off the tiles, louder than she'd intended. It startled Brenda, and she dropped the pen. Grady picked it up.

"One of the EMTs said it looked like he was knifed," Brenda said. "We would've heard a gun, I imagine. Or at least, Mrs. Schults would have. She's sixty if she's a day, but her hearing is still sharp as a tack. After all, she heard the crash."

Arie turned her back on the other two, facing the entryway but trying not to look at the blood. Not yet.

This time was different. She knew Wyatt. Not well, of course, but enough that she was entirely freaked out at the thought of seeing his memories through her own eyes. What if she saw herself? What if seeing herself set off some weird fifth-dimension sci-fi event like time traveling or something?

Arie took a deep steadying breath. She was losing it.

Behind her, Grady escorted the building manager back to the side door. As he left, he called over his shoulder, "I'm gettin' the equipment. Be right back."

Arie didn't have time to screw around with hysterics. He'd be back in just a few minutes. She took another deep breath, got down on her knees, and stared into the closest puddle.

She was immediately enveloped in the red haze. Rage shot through her body like an electrical current.

Flash.

Dad is after me. No good running, he'll . . . it'll be worse. It wasn't me! I didn't do it! Please, don't! But he's already swinging. The belt whistles through the air, then cracks across my head and shoulders. I fall down and curl up. It's better if he can only get my back.

Flash.

"Holy, holy, holy."

Flash.

The bookshelves rise up above me like a cage, but one I never want to leave. My fingers bump across the spines of the books while my eyes scan the white tab on each, looking for the right combination of letters and numbers. It's like a code that only secret agents—and librarians—understand. My finger stops. I found it. I pull the book down and open it, looking around to make sure no one is watching, and bury my nose between its pages.

Flash.

Marissa splays across my baby blue sheets like a diamond ring winking at me from a Tiffany's box. So lovely. She smiles and holds her hand out. As if she needs to ask . . .

Flash.

The doorbell. What the hell? Who's bugging me at this time at night? I open the door. What do you want? Like I care. Might as well get a beer. This is probably going to take a while. I head for the kitchen. Bam—something punches me in the back. It burns. I spin, but my heart sinks because I already know it's too late. I can't believe—an arcing gleam of silver streaks past my eyes, and another punch lands—this time to my throat. It's . . . it's a knife. I'm cut. This is crazy. My legs give out, and I fall. A blizzard of strikes. The knife rising and falling—my arms, legs, chest. I try to raise my arms, but they don't . . . I curl up. Maybe if he can only get at my back . . .

The side door slammed, pulling Arie out of the vision. She scrambled to her feet. Grady walked in carrying two crates with their cleaning equipment in his arms. He set them down on the floor near the entryway.

"At least we don't have to bother with setting up a clean zone." He tossed Arie a biohazard suit.

Arie kept her face averted as she pulled it on. To say she was shaken would've been an understatement. She doubted she would ever get used to being murdered, even if it was only in her mind.

Luckily, the job itself was pretty straightforward. Grady set to work cutting out the patch of carpet over the spot where Wyatt had died.

"Something wrong?" Grady stared at her.

Arie jumped. "No, nothing." She grabbed the spray bottle of disinfectant and started squirting.

After the initial shock, Arie felt numb. She concentrated on her job and was careful to not look directly into any of the blood. As expected, it had turned out to be a quick job. In fact, they had finished and were just packing away their supplies when Grady's cell phone rang. He'd already degloved, so he answered it.

Arie could tell from Grady's side of the conversation that it was Guts. Maybe they'd gotten another job already, which would be nice. Instead, Grady turned a quizzical look her way.

"Okay, boss. Sure." He ended the call. "Guts wants you back at the office."

"Me? What for?"

Grady shrugged but didn't meet her eye. "I don't know. He just said for you to head back. Don't worry about the rest of this." He waved his hand at the crates and the contaminated carpet they'd rolled and then duct taped.

"Are you sure?"

"Yeah, I got it. Guts said you were supposed to come right away."

"Grady? Am I in trouble?" Arie's heart thumped. This felt like third grade, when she'd been sent to Principal Richter's office for putting a pine cone on Mary Crossman's seat. And it had seemed like such a good joke.

He finally faced her. "Look, I really don't know. He said for you to stop what you're doing and come into the office. As far as I know, you ain't done nothin' wrong."

It helped, but only a little.

CHAPTER THIRTY-ONE

Arie's confusion lifted as soon as she entered the main office and saw O'Shea leaning on the desk. The fear didn't go away, though. In fact, it expanded.

"Uh, you can use my office as long as you need." Guts slid his bulk from behind the desk and exited as quickly as he could.

All the moisture in Arie's body relocated from her mouth to her kidneys. If she were to die now for the second time, it would either be from dehydration or embarrassment at wetting herself in front of Connor O'Shea.

The detective gestured to the hard-backed chair in front of the desk, the same chair Arie had interviewed in a month or so ago.

Time flies.

"I have a few questions for you." O'Shea didn't wait for Arie's nod before continuing. "Let's start with last night. What were you doing with Wyatt Striker?"

"We were . . . I guess you could call it a date."

"A date." It wasn't a question. "And how did that happen?"

"What you mean? He asked me out, and I accepted. How else do dates usually happen?"

"I see," O'Shea said. "Let's do it this way. How did you meet him?"

Arie swallowed hard. "I . . . uh . . . we met at my job."

"Your job. You're telling me you met Striker while you were cleaning Marissa Mason's apartment?"

Crap.

"Not exactly. I met him working for Riann Foster. I'm her . . . I guess you could call me her assistant. It's only a couple of hours a week. I—you know, things like scheduling her appointments, helping her arrange things. She's planning a wedding but . . . her own, I mean. Even though it doesn't look like Dick is ever going to—"

O'Shea's face scrunched up like an origami piece sculpted by a five-year-old with absolutely no eye-hand coordination. "What the hell are you talking about?"

"I met Wyatt at a party Riann gave."

"You were a guest?"

"Not exactly." Although it was thirty years too soon, Arie experienced her first hot flash. Sweat beaded along her hairline, and her armpits felt soggy. No wonder her mother was so crabby. "Riann wanted me there to . . . uh . . . " *Oh, double crap.* "To give a reading."

O'Shea crossed his arms and stared at her under lowered brows. Arie stared back.

Finally, he said, "A reading."

"You repeat things a lot. Is that, like, an interrogation technique?" Arie attempted a laugh.

O'Shea added tight lips to the lowered brows, and Arie's little let's-pretend-this-isn't-serious chuckle died a sad, lonely death.

Oh, well.

"I do psychic readings. That's how I met Wyatt. I was doing a group reading for Riann Foster's party."

To his credit, O'Shea didn't openly roll his eyes. He did, however, stare up at the ceiling and nod his head in short, little microbursts of exasperation.

"I don't care what you think." Arie sat up straight and gave him a regal chin tilt. "Anyhow, that's how I met him. You can ask Riann."

"So, after your date. What then?"

"I went home."

"Alone?"

"No, of course not."

O'Shea's look of surprise jolted Arie's awareness of what he was really asking.

"Oh! Not with him. I mean, I definitely didn't go home with Wyatt."

O'Shea's expression didn't change.

"I didn't go home with anyone. But I wasn't alone. That's what I meant. I live with Grumpa."

O'Shea's face relaxed a tiny bit. "Your grandfather can vouch for your presence? What time did you get home?"

"Uh, I don't think he can. Vouch for me, I mean."

The detective sighed.

"Look, he's eighty-three years old. He goes to bed early." *Sometimes.* "If he would have heard me, he probably would have gotten up and yelled at me."

O'Shea paced the tiny area behind Guts's desk. As he walked, he twisted his neck from side to side to pop the tension out.

"I'm going to need his name and contact information."

"Grumpa's? Why?"

"Maybe he heard you come in, after all."

"I doubt it. And anyway, you can't really think I had anything to—"

O'Shea flung up a *stop* hand. "Let's take a minute, and look at the situation. You're hired as the entertainment for a party given by Riann Foster, a murder victim's best friend. Wyatt Striker asks you out, and is likewise murdered the next day."

"Oh, come on—"

O'Shea slammed both hands on the desk and leaned over it. "Oh, wait. Let's not forget that you're related to a man who has a romantic history with the first murder victim and was apparently stalking her in the days before she was killed."

"Brant didn't kill Marissa."

"How do you know that? Did Marissa's ghost tell you that from beyond the grave?" He snorted, then rubbed his forehead.

Arie took a deep breath. "Look, I may not know exactly what was going on, but I do know my brother would never hurt anyone. I don't need to be psychic to know that you're on the wrong track. And you don't have to be so rude. Just because you don't believe—"

"Rude? You really don't get it, do you? Your brother has been taken in for questioning. And you"—O'Shea pointed a finger at her—"I could easily take you in for obstructing."

Arie gasped. *"Me?"*

"Obstructing, or even maybe as an accessory. You *literally* cleaned up the crime scene. And then I find you showing up at the funeral, going to parties with the deceased's family and friends, and dating the next guy who shows up dead."

Arie stared at him with horror, tears welling in her eyes.

"Shit." O'Shea rubbed his face with both hands, then propped them on his hips. "Look, I need you to understand this isn't some game. Your brother is already . . . never mind that. But I'd better not find that you've been running around muddying up my investigation. If you know anything, you need tell me right now."

"I know my brother didn't kill Marissa."

"Then if you want to help, you'd better make sure he gets a good lawyer. Otherwise, stay away from my case."

More tears broke loose as soon as Arie made it into her car. She swiped impatiently at them with a tissue she found wedged in the back of her seat. She didn't have time for a meltdown. She had to get to her parents.

Her dad's car was gone, but Arie found Evelyn sitting at the kitchen table. The sight of her—no makeup, her face ravaged from crying—scared Arie more than anything else had done. Her mom just sat there, staring out the patio door into the empty back yard.

"Mom, it's going to be okay." Arie sat next to her and gently took her hand.

Evelyn turned reddened eyes to her daughter. "Do you know?"

Arie nodded.

"How?"

"It doesn't matter," Arie said. "Where's Dad?"

"He's at the bank. The lawyer needs a deposit or something, and we have to figure out how to do that bail thing. Do you suppose you could Google it?"

Arie had never seen her mother so bewildered and at a loss about how to manage a situation. "It's going to be okay. We'll figure it out. Are you saying Brant already has a lawyer?"

Evelyn nodded.

"A good one?" With O'Shea's comments in mind, Arie couldn't help asking.

"It's Randy Bradley. From the Elder Board? You must remember him; he married Alexandra Greenman two years ago. She organizes the bake sale every spring."

"But is he a good lawyer?"

"I already said he was," Evelyn snapped. "He saw Brant first thing this morning. And then he called your father so we could get right to work on getting the bail money."

"What did Brant say?"

"We didn't get to talk to him. But Randy says . . . " Evelyn's voice trailed away.

"What?"

Evelyn crossed one arm around her stomach and used it to prop the other, which she pressed to her mouth. Tears slid down her cheeks.

"Mom, what did Mr. Bradley say?" Arie reach out and pulled her mom's hand from her face.

"He said they found something at Brant's, something they say he took from that girl the night she was . . . it's ridiculous! Who is this Melissa anyway? Brant never dated anyone like that. We would have known."

"Her name is Marissa. Was, I mean. And they were engaged. I met her once. But I don't believe—"

"What do you mean, you met her? This is crazy. Brant doesn't keep secrets from me. I'm his mother."

"It was a long time ago. It was a college thing. Did they say what it was that Brant took?"

"He didn't take *anything*," Evelyn said. "Brant doesn't steal things. And I don't care what you say. He didn't have anything to do with that girl or her murder."

"But do you know what it was? The thing they said he took. What was it?"

"A ring. A stupid . . . a pink cameo ring. What the hell would Brant want with something like that? It's ridiculous."

CHAPTER THIRTY-TWO

When Arie got back to Grumpa's, she was surprised to see a car in the driveway. She peeked in as she passed by. A suit jacket had been slung over the passenger seat in a way that was sure to cause wrinkles. A stack of folder files and paperwork was piled on the seat.

Grumpa and Detective O'Shea sat at the kitchen table, each with a mug of steaming coffee. O'Shea's notebook lurked like a snake next to his elbow. Arie also spied a familiar carton on top of the recycling bin. They'd used up her hazelnut creamer, the bastards. They both smiled pleasantly at her, and O'Shea gestured to the empty chair next to him.

"I'm fine." Arie leaned against the counter instead. She needed the support; her legs were buckling at the thought of what information O'Shea might have gotten out of Grumpa.

"They've arrested Brant." She tried to warn him. "They think he killed a girl."

"So Detective O'Shea was telling me," Grumpa said. "And some other guy got killed, too, I understand. The detective here seems to think you might know something about that."

Grumpa tried to *tsk-tsk-tsk*, but his dentures mutinied on the second *tsk* and almost slid out of his face.

"I never said that, Mr. Wilston," O'Shea said. "I'm just following up on Ms. Stiles's assertion that she came right home after she left the restaurant."

"Well, you implied it," Grumpa countered. "I guess you were trying to scare an elderly man with the thought of tossing his dear little granddaughter in the clink. Who would take care of me then, huh? I'd be left all alone to fend for myself. Al-l-l-l alone. I can hardly imagine such a thing. Can you, Arie?"

He smiled at her.

Arie inhaled sharply. Who was he kidding? He'd never wanted her to live with him in the first place. Was he really threatening her? *Why, you nasty old—* She took another deep breath and forced her glare into a sweet smile. "Now, don't you fret, Grumpa. No matter what happens to me, you can be sure Mother will take care of you. In fact, if I'm not available, I'm certain she and Dad will move you right in with them. That way, Mother could take care of you twenty-four seven. She'd probably put you in the guest room right next to theirs. That way you'd never be too far away. You know how attentive she can be. You'd never have to worry about being alone again."

Grumpa huffed and worked his dentures back and forth. "Well . . . I guess it's a good thing we don't have to put her to all that trouble, isn't it?" He turned to O'Shea. "Because I was here when Arie came in last night. She woke me up. Does it all the time. She's very inconsiderate."

O'Shea sighed but didn't reach for his notebook. "I see. And what time was that?"

Before answering, Grumpa took a long swallow of coffee, then started coughing. Arie rushed to his side and patted him on the back. O'Shea looked on, singularly unimpressed.

That is, until Grumpa's teeth shot out, skittered across the table, and landed in O'Shea's lap.

As the detective yelped and lurched out of his chair, Arie leaned down to Grumpa's ear. "Eleven," she whispered. She was afraid he was hacking too loudly to hear, but his coughing fit had subsided as suddenly as it had started, and she couldn't risk another try.

O'Shea glared at the two of them. Without taking his eyes from the pair, he stooped and—not without revulsion—picked up the dentures and slapped them on the table in front of the old man.

"Oh, thank you," Grumpa said, fully recovered now. He dunked them in his coffee and popped them back in his mouth. "Now, then. What was the question?"

O'Shea's scowl made him look like a dark angel. He washed his hands at the sink but didn't bother resuming his seat. Didn't repeat the question, either.

Instead, he pointed at Arie. "You. Walk me to my car." Still glowering, he turned to Grumpa. "Thank you for your time, sir."

At least, that's what Arie thought he said. The gritted teeth seemed to make enunciating difficult.

Grumpa smiled sweetly and waved bye-bye.

O'Shea didn't speak until they reached the car. Instead of getting in, he leaned against it and crossed his arms. His eyes bored into hers. Although the striking blue reminded Arie of the vivid colors she'd seen on the Other Side, they didn't offer a speck of the peace or tranquility she'd found there.

"I should arrest both of you and throw your asses in jail for that stunt."

Definitely no peace or tranquility.

"Look, you have to believe me. Brant wouldn't kill anybody. And neither would I."

"I hate to state the obvious, but I'm a homicide detective," O'Shea said. "I can't trust what people tell me, even if I wanted to. And after that little performance in there, I'm sure you can understand why. Besides, I believe what the evidence tells me to believe."

"Okay, fine," Arie said. "But sometimes, the evidence lies. Brant's lawyer told us you found one of Melissa's rings at his place. A pink cameo, right? Somebody planted it."

O'Shea shook his head. "Look, Arie. Sometimes even the people we love do things that we could just never imagine them doing. No matter how close you are to someone, you never really know."

"I know you won't believe this, but I'm not blinded by sibling bonds. I remember seeing that ring in Marissa's apartment when we were cleaning it. If you guys found it at Brant's, somebody else put it there. *After* she was killed."

A shadow flickered in O'Shea's eyes, but then it was gone.

"First of all, I've got two separate witnesses. Riann states Marissa wore the ring the afternoon before she was murdered, and Kelli confirmed it was missing from Marissa's jewelry box. That's two witnesses who, unlike yourself, I have no reason to distrust.

"Secondly, you can't expect me to derail the entire investigation on the word of our primary suspect's sister who just happened to be *literally* cleaning up the crime scene after him and *coincidentally* dated another murder victim the night before he was killed." He leaned in until their noses almost touched. "Lady, you are in this up to your"—for the briefest moment, his eyes dropped to her chest—"eyeballs."

They pulled back and eyed each other warily.

Arie almost couldn't believe what he'd told her. *Riann and Kelli?* What a couple of liars.

"Kelli was messing with Marissa's jewelry when she and June came over the second day we were cleaning. June saw her, too. You can ask her. She may not have seen Kelli with that particular ring, but the little brat couldn't wait to play dress-up in her big sister's jewelry box. And Riann had a huge argument with Marissa the afternoon she was murdered. June heard that, too."

"If you're talking about the wedding planner, we already have her statement. She didn't say anything about either subject."

"She was afraid to. She didn't want to risk losing the contract for Riann's wedding."

O'Shea groaned and scrubbed his face with his hands.

"If you'll just ask June—"

"I'll look into it. But in the meantime. . ." O'Shea pointed at Arie. "You stay out of this. I mean it. If I catch you near any part of this, I'll toss your cute little ass in a jail cell and leave you there to rot."

Cute little ass?

He got in the car and slammed the door. The tires chirped against the cement driveway as he reversed out to the street. Rubber burned as he sped off.

Of course, Arie was going to stay out of it. She had no intention of doing anything else. But first, she decided, she'd have a little chat with Riann about falsifying evidence and setting her brother up. And she knew exactly how to do it.

CHAPTER THIRTY-THREE

"I feel so bad." Then Arie said the words into the phone that she knew would guarantee Riann's full attention. "I feel like I've cheated you."

"Cheated me? How?" Riann's voice had a sharp edge.

"Part of what you've been paying me for is your readings, but it occurred to me that they've been mostly about Marissa. I mean, that's understandable. She's what brought me to you, but it's possible that the force of her character has been slanting the readings a bit. I wouldn't want you to—"

"No, you're right," Riann said. "You're absolutely right. I never thought of it, but . . . you know, it's just like Marissa to do that, too. She always hogged the limelight."

"Uh huh. Anyway, I thought maybe we should—"

"This afternoon?" Riann broke in. "I've got a workout with Evan at six, but we should have plenty of time before then."

"Be right there."

Riann was in a fabulous mood when Arie arrived. Her effervescence dimmed slightly when Arie pulled out a needle and told her they were going to prick her finger.

"What are you talking about? Where's your little crystal ball? Why can't we use that?"

"Because I'm afraid Marissa will keep blocking the, um, channel. I mean, she's used to coming through to us that way, so we have to try something different."

"You need my *blood*?"

"We have to try something totally different. And blood is, um, the drop of life. I'll need a bowl of water. "

"Right."

She was back in moments.

It took a little longer to get the drop of blood because Riann kept squealing and pulling her thumb out of reach at the last moment. Arie eventually jabbed out wildly, stabbing Riann's middle finger on the hand that rested on the table.

A single droplet of blood stained the white tissue.

But it was enough.

Arie felt the pull almost immediately. This time, though, there was no fog, red or otherwise, no chanting or voice from beyond. Arie wasn't seeing through Riann's eyes; her body wasn't feeling what Riann felt, or thinking her thoughts. In fact, Arie felt completely disconnected from all five of her senses. *The normal ones, anyway.*

It felt . . . blank. An entirely new and scary place. In much the same way that Arie hadn't been able to find words vibrant enough to describe the Other Side, now she couldn't seem to find words disturbing enough to describe the place Riann's drop of blood had taken her to. A murky, dark place. It felt like being locked in a closet and hearing the scratch of rats in the walls behind her back. Arie sensed things skittering around in the dark recesses of Riann's soul.

Secrets.

And then Arie was filled with a surge of raw emotions. She knew they were Riann's, but she didn't know how she knew, and they weren't what she might have expected.

Fear was the overriding one, and not the chronic anxiety felt by most discontented, insecure people. This fear was spiky with panic, the same primitive shriek of nerves that Arie had felt months ago when her brain had belatedly registered the sound of her rushing attacker on the night she'd been killed. Waves of terror caused her heart to accelerate. The tinny residue of adrenaline coated her mouth.

But something lurked under the fear. Arie could sense it. She tried to push past the terror, but that only caused panic to well up inside her own body. She tried to relax the way Chandra had taught her.

It helped a little. Instead of fighting Riann's fear, Arie pictured herself moving into it. Through it. She worked at staying calm.

Sadness and guilt lay beyond the fear.

Riann's sorrow felt heavy. A leaden thickness settled in Arie's chest. Tears welled, and her nose started to run. Like fear, the sadness triggered Arie's memories of times in the past when she'd suffered a great loss. The depression she'd fought when her soul had been forcibly stuffed back into her inert body flooded her heart again. No, not the depression she'd fought—the despair she'd *endured* because sometimes the only way to get past depression was to outlast the bastard.

Arie took a deep breath. She wasn't done yet. She couldn't risk letting herself drown in sadness. She had to move on and find out what that guilt was all about.

"What's going on? Do you see anything?" Riann's voice cracked through Arie's concentration like a fist through glass.

Arie gasped. "What?"

"I asked, what's going on? You've been sitting there for like twenty minutes. Usually, you say something."

Arie checked her watch. It had only been six minutes. Her insides felt as scraped and hollowed out as a Halloween pumpkin. She needed a few minutes.

"Can I have a glass of water?"

Sighing as though she'd been asked to be the surrogate mother for Arie's baby, Riann stomped into the kitchen. Arie heard water running. Apparently, she no longer qualified for the fancy gyno-water. Over the the sound of the tap, she heard Dick saying something to Riann. Unfortunately, she was too far away to hear what either of them said.

Arie gave herself a mental shake. Riann would return at any moment.

Arie hadn't expected to be able to psychically connect with Riann, not while she was alive. Maybe, Arie wondered, she could read Riann's blood because she *was* guilty. Maybe Marissa was still directing—

Riann appeared in the doorway. She crossed the room and held the glass of water out to Arie. No "is the glass half-full or half-empty?" dilemma here. She'd only sloshed about a quarter of a cup of water into it. Arie took a sip. It was warm.

"Come on, already." Riann sat down on the couch next Arie. "What did you see?"

"It was a little unnerving," Arie said truthfully.

Riann clasped her hands together with glee. "I bet it was. Did you see my future?"

"Not exactly." Arie gathered herself then plunged in. "You're hiding something, Riann. Something about Marissa's murder. You're lying about something."

The joy drained out of Riann as quickly as if someone had hit a delete button. A street-sly wariness crept in.

"Like hell I am."

"You are. Marissa was angry with you. You two argued. In fact, you fought with her the very afternoon of the day she died. And now, you're muddying the waters."

Riann looked confused as well as pissed. "Muddy waters? What are you talking about?"

"It means you're actively interfering with the investigation. Look, Riann, I'm not trying to upset you." *So much for being truthful.* Arie reached over and laid her hand on Riann's. "I'm just telling you what I saw. I don't want you to get in trouble."

But Riann wasn't falling for that.

"Whoever or whatever says I'm lying is a liar herself. Marissa and I were closer than sisters. In fact, I was closer to her than her *own* sister. How am I supposed to be interfering with her case? That's ridiculous."

Arie tilted her head and stared into the middle-distance as though tuning in to something from the "other plane" as Chandra called it.

"A ring is missing."

Riann went still.

"A pink ring." Arie turned her gaze back to Riann. "And there's something about Kelli. The message I'm getting tells me she's involved, too. You're both lying about something, and it has to do with a ring."

"That's ridiculous." Riann sounded far less sure of herself. "I don't know anything about . . . besides, I thought this reading was supposed to be about me. Why are you still going on and on about Marissa?"

"This *is* about you. It's about your unresolved feelings. If you were angry at Marissa when she died, it could affect your whole"—Arie scrambled to think of something that would sound suitably esoteric—"your whole aura. It could, um, mess with your psychic energy."

"My psychic energy?"

"And that would be bad. Very bad. It could change your whole destiny. It could, um, block you from all the fabulous opportunities that the universe has prepared for you."

Riann's eyes narrowed. "Are you saying that if Marissa and I had a little argument before she died, she could stop good things from happening for me now. Is that it?"

"Exactly," Arie said. "Of course, it would depend on what the argument was actually about. If you were arguing about something in particular, and then she died, all of that negative energy would still be unresolved."

Riann jumped up and started pacing. "You know what? It would be so like her. She always had to have the last word."

"What was the argument about?"

After several long moments, Riann finally turned to Arie. "You really think she can do that? Screw my life up from beyond the grave?"

"Everything here in the material world is a form of energy. Human beings are particles of energy. And energy doesn't disappear. You can Google that if you want to. Most of the time, after we no longer need our physical shell, our energy goes on to another place. But if something happens that keeps the energy trapped in this world, it can get stuck here."

"Like ghosts?"

"Sometimes. Sometimes it's memories that we can't seem to let go of. The point is, whatever you and Marissa were arguing about that day is blocking the universe from blessing you."

Riann bit her bottom lip so hard Arie was surprised it didn't pop. In a low voice, she said, "She was so stupid. She acted like such hot shit because she wrote a book. Big deal. It wasn't even her idea. We always knew what we were going to have to do to make it in this world. It's all we ever talked about when we were growing up."

"Finding a rich guy?"

"Oh, don't look at me like that," Riann snapped. "You have no idea what it was like, growing up the way we did. What's wrong with finding a rich man? They have a lot of good qualities. They're smart. Ambitious. I mean, if you have a choice between some poor slob and a rich guy, why not choose the rich guy? It's dumb to pretend like you wouldn't. So, yeah. The only difference was me and Marissa admitted it. That makes us more honest than you."

"Then what did you argue about?"

Riann's face reddened. "Because she was such a little hypocrite." She shook her head. "I mean, she went on all of those TV shows and acted like she still believed in all of our *Rich Bitch* stuff, but underneath? After all that, she goes and decides to marry for love. Okay, fine. She made a shitload of money off the first stupid book, so great. Why not marry Chad? What do I care? I mean, good for her, right?"

Arie nodded, but Riann was too engrossed in her tirade to pay any attention.

"But it was like she forgot what the world is like for the rest of us, you know? She started making these nasty little remarks, and I was supposed to pretend I didn't know what she was really saying. She did it in front of Richard, and she knew how risky that was. She could've blown the whole thing for me. She treated Wyatt like crap, too, because he was basically trying to get by the same way she always said she would. I mean, she wrote a whole book about finding a rich husband, and all of a sudden, she's acting like she's so much better than me.

"And then. . ." Riann's voice dropped nearly to a whisper. "After all that bullshit about marrying for love, you know what she did?"

Riann stared at Arie.

Almost afraid to breathe, Arie shook her head.

"She starts running around on him. On *Chad*. Chad is . . . he's amazing. I mean, he's handsome, and he's nice. He's not what I would call rich-rich, but he comes from money. You know what I mean? Plus, he loved her. It was, like, so obvious. Everybody could see it."

"That's what you argued about?" Arie asked. "Marissa was cheating on—"

"It must be nice," Riann continued, "to have all that money and everything you always wanted without having to . . . she got *everything* she ever wanted. She was even writing another book about why women want rich guys. Only this time, she was getting all psychological and shit. I mean, come on! Who doesn't want to be rich? What does that have to do with your childhood? Why did she have to go digging all that stuff up?"

"Stuff about her childhood?"

The struggle to tell or not tell warred for a long moment on Riann's face. "And mine, too, damn it. She . . . she kept something of mine from when we were kids. Something that was private. And she wanted to use that for examples. So, yeah, that's what we were arguing about. She just . . . she wouldn't listen."

"Riann, did you—" A movement in the doorway caught Arie's eye.

Dick stood there.

For a heartbeat, Riann looked dazed as she struggled with the abrupt transition from rant to reality. She snapped her mouth shut and put on her "happy" face.

"Hello, sweetheart. Are you almost ready?" Dick came farther into the living room.

"I, um . . . I think so." Turning to Arie, Riann said brightly, "We're finished here, right?"

"Well—"

Riann crossed the room and kissed Dick on the cheek. She linked her arm through his and rubbed her breast against his shoulder.

Dick's turn for a dazed expression. His seemed happier, though.

"Riann?" Arie said.

Dick reached up to and covered Riann's hand with his own, which strategically placed his wrinkled old knuckles directly on her nipple. Arie looked away, but not before she saw him put those knuckles to use. Riann squealed.

"Um, Riann?" Arie tried.

Giggling, although to Arie's ears, it seemed strained, Riann shifted away from Dick. "I'm sorry, Arie. But we'll have to pick this up later."

"But maybe we should—"

"She said later," Dick broke in, apparently irritated at Arie's *nipplous interuptus*. He turned and shuffled out of the living room.

"Riann . . . ?" Arie tried again, but the woman was already heading out the door.

"Don't worry," Riann said over her shoulder. "Everything's going to be just fine."

CHAPTER THIRTY-FOUR

Although Arie had discovered what Riann and Marissa were arguing about, she still hadn't gotten Riann to admit her part in setting Brant up. Even if she told Connor—Detective O'Shea, that is—it still wasn't enough. If Dick hadn't walked in, she might have had a chance to find out precisely how Brant had been set up.

She had to figure out how to talk to Riann without Dick walking in and grabbing body parts.

Arie tried to time her arrival at the gym for right after Riann's workout session with her trainer, but traffic had backed up during rush hour, and she was later than she would have liked. Afraid she'd missed her chance, she waited until the desk attendant was distracted and darted for the women's locker room.

She was in luck.

Not only was Riann still there, but given that it was the dinner hour, the room had emptied of other people. The smell of chlorine slammed into Arie's nose, making her heart race.

Chlorine? Something about the smell . . .

Riann must have just showered. She was wrapped in a big fluffy pink towel, and another was turbaned on her head. When Arie walked in, the other woman had her back to the door, tugging futilely on a padlock of locker 247. On the bench across the way sat an orange Prada gym bag that Arie had seen in Riann's office. A different locker just above the bag stood open. A series of little water puddles trailed across the tiled floor from the bench to where Riann stood.

"Riann?"

The half-naked woman squealed and spun away from the locker so fast her turban unraveled.

"Holy shit! You scared the crap out of me."

"Sorry. I didn't mean to."

Clutching her towel, Riann returned to her gym bag, tugged the zipper open, and pulled out a pair of lacy black underwear.

The chlorine was giving Arie a headache. She glanced over at locker 247—the one that Riann been messing with. If that wasn't her locker, why—?

"I said, what the hell are you doing here?" Abandoning modesty, Riann dropped her towel on the bench and began pulling her clothes on. Her still-damp body caused her leggings to twist around her calf. She yanked so hard she almost pulled her own feet out from under her.

Riann flopped down on the bench. "Son of a bitch. I broke a nail."

"I'm sorry for bothering you here, but I'm really worried."

"Look, I already told you about the argument. I told her she couldn't use my . . . Anyway, she didn't like it, but it's not like our friendship hadn't survived worse.

Whatever. Tell the universe I said I'm sorry, okay? And now it can leave me alone."

"I wish it were that easy. But I don't think it's the argument alone that's blocking your opportunities. There's the part about interfering with the investigation. I think that's the part Marissa is maddest about."

"I still don't know what you're talking about," Riann muttered. Arie couldn't see her face because she was pulling her shirt over her head.

"Yes, you do. You and Kelli have been lying to Detective O'Shea about that pink ring. That means the real killer—"

"Oh, for crying out loud. That stupid ring again? All I said was that I'd seen it on Marissa that day."

"I thought you told him it was missing?"

"No, Kelli said that. Look. What's the big deal? Marissa was wearing it that day. She put it on after that creeper started up with her again. I guess he'd given it to her back when they were together. Cheap asshole. Can you blame me for telling the cops her ex was stalking her?"

"But Marissa didn't think Brant was stalking her, or you wouldn't have argued with her about cheating on Chad. And why did you lie about the ring? You're talking about ruining a man's life!"

Riann's eyes narrowed. "Why does this matter so much to you?"

Arie tasted the sharp tang of chlorine that permeated the room. It made her want to gag. And then she got it. Chlorine—not bleach. It was chlorine she had smelled in the vision.

Arie stared again at locker 247. It was a padlock, not a combination lock. *The key.* In a daze, she turned back to Riann. "That's Marissa's, isn't it?"

"What you talking about?" Riann's voice came out in a raspy whisper.

"That's Marissa's locker. Why were you trying to get in? What's inside?"

Riann stood, fists clenched. "I suppose you saw that, too. You know what? You see too much. Get out of here."

"Riann—"

"Get. *Out*."

Keeping her eyes on Riann, Arie slowly backed toward the locker room door.

Arie's hands shook so hard she could barely start the car. She was afraid to drive, but she knew she had no time to spare. Now that Riann knew that Arie knew about the locker, she wouldn't content herself with leaving it alone. Arie had to get the key and get back to the gym before Riann could figure out some way of opening that locker.

What was in it? Arie thought she knew. She scrabbled in her purse for her cell phone. At the next red light, she dialed O'Shea's number. It went to voice mail, and she hung up. She should have left him a message, she knew, but her thoughts raced too fast for her to figure out what to say in a message. She'd try again when she got to Grumpa's.

As soon as she pulled into the driveway, she slammed the car into park and leaped out. Grumpa was in the kitchen, trying to open a can of tomato soup and cussing at the can opener.

"I'm starving here," Grumpa yelled as she bolted past him.

"I can't right now, Grumpa!"

The key was tucked away in her jewelry box, right where she'd left it. Arie stuffed it in her pocket and hurried back the way she came. Grumpa was still struggling with the can and opener, but Arie kept going.

"Sorry!"

She thought she heard him holler something in return, but it didn't register. As soon as her butt hit the seat, she called O'Shea again. This time, he answered.

"What can I do for you, Arie?"

O'Shea's voice sounded as smooth and rich as hot cocoa with whipped cream. Arie wanted to snuggle up with it, but she knew that what she had to tell the detective would probably end that potential once and for all.

"I don't know how to say this," she said.

"Oh, boy. That never bodes well. Just say it."

"Tell me, was Marissa writing another book?"

"Why?"

"She was, wasn't she? I think that might have been why she was murdered. To keep her from publishing it. And I think I know where Marissa hid it."

"First, tell me where it is," O'Shea said. "We'll leave the part about how the hell you know about any of this for later."

"Marissa has a locker at her gym. The problem is Riann knows about it, too. It's padlocked, but I think she's trying to figure out how to get in."

"Which gym?"

"Elite Fitness, over on South Street. I'll meet you there."

"There's no need for that," O'Shea said. "You've been too involved—"

"I have the key."

Through the strained silence, Arie thought she could hear O'Shea grinding his teeth again. He was going to have serious dental issues if he didn't curb that habit.

"Look, when I was cleaning, I dropped the knife behind her—"

"Not now," O'Shea interrupted. "Meet me there."

CHAPTER THIRTY-FIVE

Arie made it across town in record time, but O'Shea was still there before her. As she hurried up the sidewalk to meet him, she couldn't help tallying up the multiple body language cues he gave off. Hands fisted on his hips, eyebrows furrowed, and eyes glaring with a blue flame— it didn't take a psychic to see how angry he was.

"I can explain," Arie said.

Instead of answering, the detective spun on his heel and strode into the fitness center. When Arie turned toward the women's locker room, O'Shea grabbed her arm.

"Not yet," he said.

"But she could be—"

"We need a search warrant. One's on the way. In the meantime, I need to talk to the manager." He led the way to the front desk.

The svelte blonde at the counter caught sight of O'Shea from twenty feet away and powered up a glittering display of white teeth and twinkling eyes before he got there. The tight red yoga pants and clinging white tank top were a walking billboard for the benefits of regular exercise.

Arie hated her on sight.

"Welcome to Elite Fitness. I'm Becky. What can I do for you today?"

She spoke directly to O'Shea in a wispy Marilyn Monroe-lisp and managed to turn the pronoun into a sex offer. She didn't even flick a glance at Arie standing next to him.

"I'm looking for the manager," O'Shea replied. "Would that be you?"

Becky had what appeared to be a neck spasm and tossed her hair. "'Fraid not. But if you're interested in working out with us, I'm sure I can meet your needs." She leaned on the counter and used her elbows to create a cleavage press.

Arie snorted.

O'Shea shot her an amused look then turned back to blonde. "The manager?"

The blonde pouted. "Okay, but don't go away. I'll be right back." Her taut butt cheeks bobbed like apples as she strode into a back hall, presumably toward the center's offices.

"We'll be right here," Arie called to her back. "Both of us." It was possible her voice sounded a little irritated.

O'Shea's grin confirmed it. "Didn't anybody ever tell you that you'll catch more flies with honey?"

"It looks like you're more interested in catching honey than flies."

O'Shea laughed out loud. "Don't you believe it. Besides"—his eyes glided over Arie's curves—"she's not my type."

He turned away before Arie's fiery blush reduced her to a pile of ash.

The manager—a tall Ichabod Crane type who had obviously been hired for business savvy rather than any fitness knowledge—arrived at the same time as a uniformed officer with the warrant. After a brief introduction and even briefer explanation, O'Shea had Kevin Speck, the flustered manager, lead the way to the women's locker room. To Arie's annoyance, Becky tagged along.

As soon as they walked through the door and Arie caught sight of locker 247, her heart sank.

The hasp had been sawed through on the padlock, and it dangled uselessly from the lock plate.

"It must have been Riann," Arie blurted.

"Oh, my." The manager paled almost as white as the tiled floors. "I didn't approve that."

O'Shea pulled a pair of disposable gloves out of his jacket pocket and after donning them, pulled the lock off and placed it in an evidence bag. He swung the door open, revealing what everybody already expected to see: nothing.

O'Shea turned a cop-face to Arie.

"It must have been Riann." Even to her own ears, Arie's voice sounded quivery and guilty.

O'Shea turned to the manager. "If you didn't open this, who did?"

Speck shrugged, but a line of sweat had beaded across his forehead.

"You're in charge here, right?" O' Shea snapped.

"Well, yes, but I can't be everywhere."

"This is a homicide case," O'Shea said. "Somebody cut off this lock without, as you just pointed out, your approval. Let's start with this. Who has access to a bolt cutter?"

"Anybody could bring a bolt cutter in here. There's nothing to suggest it was a staff member."

O'Shea looked around Speck to Becky, standing behind her boss. He gave her a slow, sexy smile and waited.

"Clancy," she said.

Speck spun to face her. "Becky! This doesn't concern you."

The blonde dimpled at O'Shea. "It's a police matter. I'm supposed to give my full cooperation. Right, Detective?"

"Get back to the desk, Becky," Speck said.

The blonde rolled her eyes. As she turned to leave, she flashed the thumb-to-ear, pinky-to-mouth sign and mouthed "call me" to O'Shea.

He winked, then turned back to the manager.

"Find Clancy. Bring him to me."

Speck clearly wasn't pleased about having his tiny office commandeered, but he must have known better than to object. Clancy, the center's "maintenance engineer," looked like someone whose workout regimen consisted entirely of lifting potato chips to his mouth. If he'd taken the job at the fitness center hoping to tone up through osmosis, it hadn't worked. He started off the interview strong, but he quickly lost stamina and caved as soon as O'Shea threatened to take him to the station for questioning.

"How was I supposed to know? She said it was her locker."

"You know you're supposed to get clearance from me before something like that," Speck said peevishly. "There are procedures—"

"How much?" O'Shea asked.

Clancy's Adam's apple bobbed, and his eyes darted around the room. "I don't know what—"

"How much?"

The janitor swallowed. "Look, she said it was her—"

O'Shea snapped his notebook shut, rose, and pulled out a shiny pair of handcuffs. "Stand up."

"Fifty," Clancy squeaked. "Fifty bucks. But I swear. She said it was her locker."

O'Shea slid the notebook back out. "What's her name?"

"I don't know," Clancy said.

O'Shea sighed and shook his head.

"I really don't! But I can describe her. She's got that reddish hair but not too red, and she's real pretty. Kind of snotty, though. And, uh, kind of tall, but not too tall."

"That sounds like Riann," Arie said.

"Oh, come on," Speck broke in. "That could be any number of our members."

"If that's true," O'Shea said, "we're going to be here awhile. I'll need to interview each and every one of the women who came in today. I assume you keep some kind of record?"

Speck's mouth dropped open. "Every one of . . . ?"

O'Shea stared blankly at the manager.

"You know, now that I think about it, I think it must have been Riann Foster," Speck said.

"You don't say."

CHAPTER THIRTY-SIX

O'Shea had a pensive look on his face as he and Arie left the fitness center. Hoping to take advantage of his distraction, Arie eased her way over to her car.

"Where do you think you're going?" O'Shea barked.

"I, uh . . ."

"Come with me."

The detective led Arie over to the sedan and held the passenger door open for her.

"Oh, crap," Arie said. "Look, I didn't do anything." She backed away from the car.

O'Shea reached out and grabbed her wrist. "Relax. If I was going to arrest you, I'd have you in cuffs already. Get in. We need to talk."

Suddenly, being arrested seemed like the better option, and it wasn't because of the glint in O'Shea's eyes when he'd mentioned handcuffs, either. Well, not entirely.

But Arie wasn't looking forward to a chat with O'Shea and the questions that would come with it. She knew what it would sound like as soon as she started talking about her NDE and visions in blood. She'd be lucky if he didn't cart her off to the psych ward instead of jail.

Instead of joining her right away, O'Shea stood in front of the car, speaking into his cell phone. He turned once to look at Arie, but he didn't return the little finger wave she gave him.

After a few minutes, he slid in behind the steering wheel, and they twisted to face each other. The car was stifling in the summer heat. O'Shea started it, letting the air-conditioning run.

"Look," Arie said. "We don't have time for this. Riann will be getting rid of the manuscript. She probably already has. And there was something else she might have been after."

"And what would that be, pray tell?"

"Um, her diary. Riann's, I mean. From when she was a kid. For some reason she gave it to Marissa to keep when they were younger and now Marissa was apparently refusing to give it back. That's why she and Riann were arguing the day Marissa was murdered. Riann told me. I can testify to that."

O'Shea pressed the heel of his hand against his forehead and made a sound somewhere between sobbing and laughter. "A diary? I seem to remember—"

"I know, I know; you can yell at me later. But right now we have to hurry. Riann could be destroying everything right now."

"That's very possible," O'Shea said. "If so, there's nothing I can do about it until we get a warrant. She's had a pretty decent head start already, and I can't just barge in to a private residence. I've got an officer expediting a search warrant, and I'm heading over there as soon as we're done here. So the faster you tell me what I need to know, the better."

Arie sighed. "Like what?"

"Let's start with: tell me everything you know."

"What does that even mean?" Arie said. "Besides, you won't believe it, anyway."

"Okay, I'll start. Seven months ago, on December seventh, you were attacked outside Rack's Bar over on North Venice Beach where you bartended part-time. Some Good Samaritan heard you screaming and called 9-1-1. By the time the EMTs got to you, you were unconscious and had lost a ton of blood. Shortly after arriving at Memorial Hospital, you were pronounced dead by Dr. Samuel Jasperson at 3:28 a.m. At approximately 3:47 a.m., you moaned, which frightened a nearby CNA so badly he wet himself and ran screaming from the cubicle. The treatment notes state that you claimed to have gone to heaven, and were so despondent at returning to life that they placed you on suicide watch. Soon after—"

"Shut up! Please—"

"Arie—"

"Stop it." She covered her face with her hands and tried to remember how to breathe.

"I wish I could. I really do, but as you just pointed out, we've got a time issue here."

"But how did you find out? Hospital records are supposed to be confidential."

"I didn't learn that from the hospital. But keep in mind, for almost twenty minutes, you were a homicide case. With something that freaky, word gets around."

Arie huffed. "You think that's freaky? Wait."

"I can't. That time thing."

"Oh, right."

Arie took a deep breath. He already knew she did psychic readings. How much weirder would visions in dead people's blood be?

On second thought . . .

Arie told him anyway. The whole thing, not just the visions in blood. She made it quick, but she told him about the different colored fogs for different types of deaths, and the sounds and smells. Finally, she even told O'Shea about experiencing each dead person's memories as if she were reliving them—murder and all.

She had to give the detective credit. He didn't interrupt. In fact, he didn't speak for at least five minutes after Arie finished.

Finally he said, "And you didn't have this whatever-you-call-it before the NDE?"

"It's called scrying. And no, I never had anything like this."

"Okay, so these visions, or whatever, have led you to start digging around in my case?"

"I knew you wouldn't believe me—"

"I'll decide what I believe. I'm trying to understand what you've been up to and, more importantly, what other people might think you've been doing."

"You don't believe Brant killed her, do you?" Arie couldn't help smiling. "You wouldn't be so worried about other people knowing what I've been doing if you did."

"I didn't say that. The evidence still points in that direction, but I'm not going to get tripped up by some slick defense lawyer who'll say I didn't rule out every line of investigation. Like, for instance, whatever it was Riann took out of Marissa Mason's locker." He scrubbed his face with his hands.

If he keeps that up his skin will be raw. Probably not the best time to suggest face moisturizer.

"What was I supposed to do?" Arie asked. "Tell you I saw an old diary in a vision I channeled through Marissa's blood? How would that have gone over?"

"Okay, I'll give you that one."

"That's one of the things Marissa keeps showing me. At first, I thought it was hers. In the vision, I saw it on a bookshelf in her room when she was a kid. And by the way, both Riann and Kelli corroborated the things I saw in Marissa's old bedroom. But the point is, I screwed up by thinking it was hers. I'd hear her say things like 'keep it safe' and something about rags. She had a Raggedy Ann doll on the shelf next to diary, so I thought she meant that. But now I don't think so. Riann's real name is just plain Annie, but I think her nickname back then was Rags. It was *Riann's* diary Marissa was telling me about. Marissa was supposed to keep it safe for her. Not that *that* turned out so well."

"You expect me to believe someone killed Marissa because of a twelve-year-old's angst-ridden journal?"

"Maybe not just that," Arie said. "She was also furious with Marissa for being what she called a hypocrite. Marissa had started making snide comments about Riann and Dick. She'd been making fun of Wyatt, too. He was another one who wasn't adverse about marrying up. He'd even started sniffing around Kelli, although he made fun of her behind her back."

"I could see him doing that. He was an obvious man-slut." O'Shea gave Arie a steady look that seemed fraught with meaning. She blushed.

"Yeah, well . . . the thing is, Marissa was writing a kind of memoir, using her childhood, and therefore Riann's, to explore how women might grow up to be gold diggers. The problem is, when she tells her story, she's also telling Riann's. And Riann isn't too happy about that. Maybe she doesn't want Dick to know about her past. He seems to think she was some kind of angel, but my friend knew her in college and she was quite the opposite. If Marissa was holding on to a diary for Riann, supposedly to keep it safe, then Riann would be justifiably pissed about her going public with it. I think Riann's trying to find her diary and the manuscript. Or, rather, she probably already has."

O'Shea had already returned his face to its normal cop mode. He pulled out his cell, speed-dialed, and when the other party picked up, he said, "Add a diary or journal to the warrant. How soon will you be there?"

After a few more back-and-forths, O'Shea hung up. He turned to Arie, and she braced herself for another round.

"Time for you to go." He nodded dismissively toward the door behind her. "Keep your cell phone handy. Some things may come up that I need to ask you about."

At Arie's blank look, O'Shea nodded again. "Out you go now. I'll call if I need anything."

He barely waited long enough for Arie to get clear of the car before speeding off.

"You're welcome!" Arie yelled at the shrinking taillights.

At least he hadn't arrested her. Yet.

CHAPTER THIRTY-SEVEN

Arie fully intended to go home after talking to O'Shea. She had no doubt that he would make good on his threat to toss her (cute) butt in jail if she got in the way any more than she already had. She was pulling into Grumpa's driveway and trying to figure out what to make her roommate to eat since she hadn't been grocery shopping in days, when her cell phone buzzed.

It was her mother, and she wasn't making a lot of sense.

"Wait, slow down." Arie tried to slow the force of Evelyn's panicked flood of words. "He what?"

"He's going over there," Evelyn said. "Right now. And your father's at the church in a meeting. I can't interrupt him. It's the Elder Board. If this gets out . . . you have to go get him."

"Dad?"

"No! Pay attention, damn it. *Brant*. You have to get Brant before he gets in trouble."

Arie was stunned into silence at the cuss word, mild though it was. She'd never heard her mother swear before.

Evelyn huffed into the phone. "Are you listening? You need to get over there."

"Over where? I don't—"

"He's going over to talk to that dead girl's sister! He kept saying something about a ring, and that she lied or stole it or something. I don't know what he's thinking. I told him to stay away from the whole thing. He's going to make everything worse. What if they take him back to jail? He sounded . . . he's been drinking, Arie."

"Brant? Mr. Perfect is drunk?"

"Arie, I don't have time for your nonsense. You go get your brother right now, and you bring him home."

"Okay, okay. Where is he?"

"I already told you. At that girl's house."

"Ma, I have no idea where Kelli lives! How am I supposed to find Brant if I don't know her address?"

"You said you knew all about that girl. The one he was engaged to. Why can't—"

"I have an idea, Ma," Arie said. "I think I know somebody who can tell me where she lives. I have to go now."

Arie hung up and swung the car back toward Lac La Belle Road. If O'Shea had taken Riann in for questioning, she might be able to convince Dick that she had work she had to finish up for his fiancée. If the police were already there with the search warrant, Arie knew she wouldn't stand a chance of getting in. In that case, she didn't know what she'd do. Would O'Shea help her, or would it serve to pound another nail in her brother's legal coffin?

Ten minutes later, Arie parked in front of Riann's—well, really, her sugar daddy's—beautiful home. Arie's heart thudded against her tonsils when she pressed the buzzer on the Boyette-Foster's door.

For several long moments, nothing happened. She pressed again, then jabbed at it several times in frustration.

If she turned Brant into O'Shea, her mother would kill her, but if he'd been drinking and ended up at Kelli's, acting stupid, Arie didn't know what—

The door swept open and almost scared Arie back to death.

Dick stood in the doorway, looking shriveled and frightened. Given that Arie had just screamed in his face, that wasn't unreasonable, but it seemed more than that. In fact, he acted as if he hadn't noticed Arie's rather unconventional greeting.

"Oh, gosh, Dick, I'm so sorry. I didn't mean to—"

"They took my baby away." His voice sounded thin and reedy.

"Riann?"

"For questioning, he said. That Irish detective. I called Hinsdale, my lawyer. He's meeting them."

Arie edged her way past the elderly man. At the moment, he seemed like a lost little boy.

"They should have been back by now," Dick said. "I told Hinsdale to get her home to me as soon as possible. She must be having an awful time."

He made it sound like Riann was attending some boring but obligatory social event.

"I'm sorry to hear that," Arie said. "I'm sure she'll be fine. When did they take her . . . I mean, how long since they left?"

"I don't know." Dick turned abruptly and shuffled toward the kitchen. "But she should be back by now."

"Dick? I'm sorry to bother you with this now, but Riann wanted me to pick up something from her office."

Dick spun around. "You heard from her? She called you?"

"Oh, no. This is from before. From this afternoon." Arie sidled toward the hall leading to Riann's office. "If you don't mind?"

A phone rang.

"That must be her." Dick turned and headed for his own office. Over his shoulder, he said, "Wait. I'll be right back."

Arie pretended she didn't hear him and slipped into the room Riann had designated as her workspace. The first thing she spied was the orange Prada bag left in the corner. The second thing? Riann's address book beckoned from the desk.

Look for the diary and manuscript, or find Kelli's address?

Arie stood frozen in indecision until she noticed a stack of papers about a quarter-inch thick on the edge of Riann's desk. A squat black machine sat under the desk, waiting.

A paper shredder.

Arie darted to the desk and grabbed the top sheet. It looked like a page from the middle of a chapter, and it had "From Rags to Bitches" in the header. Before she could think what to do, she heard Dick hang up the phone in the next room. She folded the page and shoved it in her bra seconds before he walked in.

"What are you doing in here? I thought I told you to wait." Dick's eyes scanned the room.

"Did you? I thought you said for me to go ahead because you might be late." Arie picked up Riann's address book. "I just need Kelli's—"

"I told you. You have to wait for Riann to get back. She doesn't even like me in here." Dick's voice was firm and left no room for argument. Then he brightened.

"I tell you what. Let's have a drink. You can keep me company until Riann gets home."

He waited until she slid the book back on the desk, then stood back and let her pass through the door and down the hall in front of him. Arie had no choice but to comply.

"I'm sorry, but I really can't stop for a drink," Arie said. "I'm going to be driving. I need a couple seconds to get Kelli's address, and then I'll be out of your hair."

Dick blushed and ran a trembling hand over the remaining wisps of hair unsuccessfully camouflaging his bald pate.

Damn it. Arie wanted to swallow her tongue. "I mean, I don't want to intrude on your—"

"You're not intruding. Not at all. In fact, I'm sure Riann would want you to wait with me."

They had reached the kitchen. Like the rest of the lake house, the decor was modern, although in here, the stainless steel dominated over the white. She took a seat at the glass table. Although the chair was all metal rods and white leather, it was surprisingly comfortable.

Dick shuffled to a cabinet and took out a bottle filled with amber liquid. *Whiskey.* She schooled her face to not say "ick." Instead of the usual tumblers, he pulled out what looked like wine glasses and set them on the white marble counter.

As he poured, Arie saw she was right. It was whiskey. Balvenie Scotch, to be exact. Despite being a bartender for a short time, Arie had never heard of anything more expensive than Johnnie Walker Black. The whiskey she was being offered was in another solar system from her little moon. Maybe even an alternate reality.

Unfortunately, she didn't like Scotch, no matter the cost.

And she had to get to Brant. She wished Dick would let her get the address and go, but he was used to having his way. Arie didn't know whether that was because he was male, rich, or old. Or because he was a rich old man. At any rate, she wasn't going anywhere quite yet.

Dick set her glass down in front of her. She eyed the strangely shaped glass warily.

"It's a nosing glass," her host said with a smile. "It funnels the aroma of the Scotch."

"Oh." He was watching her, so Arie pretended to take a sip. "Mmm. Good."

"Well, it's not the fifty-year-old Balvenie, but it'll do in a pinch." Dick chuckled.

Arie did, too, just to keep him company. After chuckling, they seemed to run out of things to talk about. Finally, Arie thought of something to say.

"Was that Riann?" she asked.

He blinked in confusion.

"On the phone."

"I certainly wish it had been. It was a business call."

"I thought you were retired."

"If a man loves his work, he never completely retires. Besides, if I'm not making money, I'm losing money. There's a certain lifestyle I need to maintain."

Gold diggers could be spendy, Arie guessed. But she supposed Dick hadn't figured criminal defense teams into the original estimate.

"I love her, you know."

As if to mock all the money, energy, and time spent trying to arrest the effects of aging on the human body, Dick looked old and worn again. He fidgeted with his glass a moment, then took a large slug.

"She's excited about the wedding." Arie skirted the issue of whether Riann cared for Dick or not.

He raised rheumy hazel eyes to hers and smiled ruefully.

"I waited a lifetime for her. All the other women, and believe me, there were plenty, none of them are worth one of her. She thinks I don't know where she's come from, but I had a PI dig all that up before I got in too deep. But if she wants to keep that quiet, fine. She's come through so much. Why not let her have a little secret? She's looking for security, a safe place where she won't be hurt anymore. And I'm going to give her that place. Just as soon as . . . "

As soon as she gets back from the cop shop.

Dick took another long swallow and motioned for Arie to drink up. She raised the glass but didn't let the whiskey do more than wet her lips.

Dick turned away and stared out the window into the darkening night. "This couldn't have come at a worse time. She's been a bundle of nerves ever since Marissa died. That's understandable, I guess, but she needs to move on."

"They were very close. And Marissa was murdered, after all."

Dick set his Scotch down with a sharp click of glass on glass. "She was a virus."

"Marissa?" Arie was shocked at his sudden virulence, but he'd finished off his drink. She hoped he wasn't on any medications that would interact with the alcohol.

"Ready for another?" Dick asked.

"Uh, no. I'm still working on this one."

He frowned. "Well, drink up. It's seventeen-year-old gold. I'm not going to pour it down the sink."

Arie took a small sip. When his frown deepened, she took a bigger drink. She couldn't afford to piss him off before getting him to let her back into Riann's office. If she'd only hung on to that stupid address book instead of setting it down when he'd snapped at her.

"I'm going to have to get going pretty soon, Dick. I'm supposed to be picking someone up. If I could get that—"

"Don't be silly. You can stay a little longer. Riann should be home any minute, and then she can give you the go-ahead."

Dick smiled at her with a false amiability. Arie knew she was being manipulated, but she wasn't completely sure what his motive was. Was it as simple as a nervous old man who didn't want to be left alone during a frightening time, or something worse? Had he seen her stuffing the manuscript page into her bra? Maybe he was keeping her there until Riann got home to take care of it, or to stop her from going to the police with it. And where were the cops, anyway? Weren't they going to execute the search warrant?

Maybe they were all busy organizing a manhunt, with Brant as the prey? Whatever the reason, Arie knew she had to go, with or without the address. She'd have to think of some other way to find Brant.

"Oh! I almost forgot." Dick broke into her thoughts. "Riann left something for you when she got back from the gym."

"She did?"

"If I wasn't so upset, I would have thought of it earlier. Be right back."

Arie couldn't imagine what Riann would have left for her, and as the fear that Dick was going to come back clutching a butcher knife crossed her mind, he returned. He had something pink and fuzzy in his hand, so Arie relaxed.

Until the old geezer slapped one half of a handcuff on her wrist and the other to the metal armrest of her chair.

CHAPTER THIRTY-EIGHT

Arie leaped to her feet but only managed to trip and fall. The chair landed on her hip. She yelped and shoved it off, but it rolled, twisting her wrist.

"Ow!"

Dick stood above Arie, watching her struggle.

She knew, of course. She knew right then who the killer was, but if there was any way of convincing him that she didn't, she had to try.

"What the hell do you think you're doing? I don't know what Riann told you, but I'm not into this kind of thing."

So lame.

Dick seemed to agree. He snorted and then took his glass over for another shot of his seventeen-year-old gold.

Arie scrambled to her feet, dragging the chair with her. She yanked on the handcuff, trying to wiggle her hand out. *If it was only some kind of sex toy* . . . her stomach heaved at that particular thought. But if it was, then it was probably some cheap manufactured-overseas product. There had to be some fail-safe, right?

Wrong. At least, not one that Arie could find. Dick continued watching her, an amused expression on his face.

"Dick, you need to let me go right now." The nanny was back.

But Dick was made of sterner stuff. He smiled wider and took another swallow. With his glass, he gestured toward Arie's, which had overturned when she'd bolted up.

"Look what you did there," he scolded. "That's wasteful. And it's too bad because this would have gone a lot easier on you if you would have finished that off."

"Let me guess. You put something in my drink, didn't you? How original."

"No need to be sarcastic. You put yourself in this situation. Nobody asked you to come stick your nose into our business, did they? There wouldn't have even been a problem if it hadn't been for you and that weirdo juju stuff you pretend to do. I don't know how you came up with that crap, but I'm not as gullible as those dimwits."

"It's not crap." Arie placed herself behind the chair so she could hold on to the back of it. Her wrist throbbed.

"And I really did just come over to get Kelli's address. I never once thought you were the killer. So who's the dimwit now?"

Dick's eyes narrowed, and his lips twisted into a sly smile. "Well, I couldn't be sure. Better safe than sorry. People tend to underestimate old farts like me. Marissa sure did. So did Wyatt, for that matter. And Kelli? There's another little leech. Do you know all Marissa's money goes to her? That's Riann's money. That disgusting book was as much her idea as Marissa's. Not that she needs it, mind you. I'll take care of anything she'll ever want or need, but if she had her own money, people wouldn't be so nasty. Like that Wyatt jerk. I knew what he was saying behind my back. Who did he think he was? I made my first million before I was twenty-five, and it certainly wasn't my last. All that loser could do was try to find some rich titty to latch onto. He couldn't take care of himself. And he thought he was better than me? He thought he could take my woman?" Dick snorted.

"At least he didn't kill someone." Arie slapped a hand over her mouth. She hadn't meant to say that out loud. Worse, whether it was because of shock or whatever Dick had spiked her drink with, she felt a little woozy.

"Starting to feel it, aren't you? You know, before Riann, I sometimes had to be a little inventive with the ladies. They couldn't see past a few wrinkles the way she can."

"Maybe you should have shown them your bank account. That seems to have worked with Riann."

The sense of evil that thickened the air between them deepened. If Arie had been frightened before, the glint that slithered into Dick's eyes terrified her. She wanted to run, but her legs felt thick and sluggish. And there was the chair to think of. She tugged at the handcuff, but it held. Her wrist was starting to swell.

As if reading her mind, Dick slid open a drawer and pulled out a knife that looked big enough to slaughter a cow.

"Be careful, Dick. Some people might say you're compensating for something."

"Well, they'll only say it once."

He hefted the knife—cleaver, really—as if testing its balance. Arie supposed after two murders, he had gotten a feel for what worked and what didn't. Two murders that she knew of, that is. He was old. He could have been at this for years.

"This is stupid," Arie said. "What are you going to do? Kill me in the middle of your kitchen? We both know what kind of a mess that'll be. And what are you going to do with my body? Toss it in the lake? People know I'm here. It's the first place they'll look."

A shadow of doubt crept over his face, but only for a moment.

"I guess I'll have to cut you up into little bitty pieces and feed the chunks down the garbage disposal." He reached over and flipped a switch next to the sink. A raucous grinding sound split the air. He flicked it off. "We just had it repaired. It's working fine now."

"How nice for you."

Dick seemed to be working out the kinks in his little plan. It was time to go.

Arie picked the chair up, holding it lion-tamer style, and started backing out of the kitchen.

Dick matched her step by step, a tango of death. Her nerves shot sparks of adrenaline, trying to get her to run, but the chair . . .

As if reading her mind, Dick said, "How far do you think you're going to get carrying that chair? It's already getting heavy, isn't it? You might as well stop. I'll tell you what. I'll make it easy on you. We could use a blindfold. We've got plenty of them. You'll never see it coming. I'll make it easy and pain-free."

Despite Arie's firsthand knowledge of dying, she didn't take the offer. Besides, she was tired of being stabbed to death.

Arie's backward journey deposited her in the living room. Instinctively heading for the wide light space of the patio doors behind her, she backpedalled at full speed. At least until she rammed the small of her back into the waist-high platform of Dick's stupid model train.

Buildings and houses rocked and crashed to the floor, and a Soo Line locomotive tipped over onto its side.

"Hey! Watch out, you clumsy heifer."

Heifer?

Arie swung the chair like a scythe, mowing down a logging mill, a wide expanse of forestland, and half of a quaint, midcentury small town where a teensy circus had set up tents.

Dick shrieked with rage, a sound that simultaneously brought fear and glee to Arie's heart.

She ducked under the platform and pulled out train tracks and electrical wires with her free hand. Dragging the chair behind and crunching over clowns, barns, and other casualties, she scurried down the aisle, wreaking havoc on Dick's tiny world.

He was surprisingly agile for an octogenarian. He slid under the plywood and charged after Arie. He'd gone silent now, which was even scarier.

When she made it to the aisle nearest the patio door, Arie took one last swing at a mountain range, then she darted out of the display. As she fumbled with the lock, she saw a length of a two-by-four wedged in the track between the slider in the door jam.

No time to—

A sharp, stinging blow struck her shoulder. Something punches me in the back. It burns. Arie spun away, bringing the chair up to block Dick's next swing of the knife.

His face was twisted into a hideous snarl. He panted, but the hunt had made his eyes sparkle, and he showed no sign of tiring.

What kind of vitamins is the old bastard taking, anyway?

Arie reverted to backing away, holding the chair up to parry his blows. Her wrist throbbed with the growing pain, and her wounded shoulder made the chair wobble uncertainly. She felt blood running down her arm. She was getting tired. Fuzzy numbness pushed in at the edges of her focus and not from blood loss, although that would be a problem soon enough.

Arie kept backing away, trying to force her brain to come up with a plan, something more than defensive moves. She stumbled, and the chair slipped.

Dick slashed at the fingers holding the chair, but Arie managed to twist back up. The knife made a ringing sound against the metal chair leg. The vibrations hurt her wrist.

"Getting tired, aren't you?" Dick's smile looked feral. "That chair must feel like it weighs a hundred pounds. Can you feel your muscles quivering? They're getting tired."

Arie kept backing up. She was almost to the hallway, but then what? She knew the front door was locked, and there was no way she could keep Dick at bay while she unlocked it.

"And that shoulder . . . it must be burning by now."

As if leaping to its master's bidding, Arie's shoulder blade flared with pain. Tears filled her eyes.

"Oh, poor dear. It's real now, isn't it? You're going to die. Right here, right now. And it's going to hurt so terribly. I told you before I could make it fast and painless, but not after that little demonstration in there."

He glanced back at the destruction of his big-boy toy, and the fake solicitous expression that he'd donned to mock Arie slid off his face.

Taking advantage of his distraction, Arie scurried into the foyer. But Dick lunged at her face. She again parried with the chair. This time, one of the legs caught him across the cheekbone with a solid thunk. He slipped on the tile.

He hit the floor with a resounding crash and a soul-satisfying—to Arie, anyway—howl.

Arie backed up until she felt the door at her back.

"Don't leave," Dick yelled. "Can't you see I'm hurt? I need an ambulance."

"You're kidding, right? You don't seriously expect me to get you help."

"I think I broke my hip."

Arie snorted. "You mean you've fallen, and you can't get up?"

Relief flowed through her veins like morphine. She lowered the chair but didn't completely let go. He was a sneaky bastard, and she wouldn't put it past him to launch off the floor like a horror show serial killer. Arie couldn't even watch slasher movies, and here she was living one. Again.

"Not so easy and pain-free now, is it, Dick? Do you see what happens when you run with knives?"

Dick snarled and lunged toward Arie. Happily, this wasn't the movies, and the attempt only served to give him more pain. Much shrieking commenced.

A pounding at the door directly behind her caused Arie to join the chorus for a couple moments, but then she realized the cavalry had finally arrived.

She flung open the door.

CHAPTER THIRTY-NINE

"Are they at least charging Riann as an accessory?" Chandra asked.

Her mouth was coated with BBQ sauce from the chicken wings she was gnawing, but Arie'd known her long enough to decode her mumblings. Besides, who was she to judge? She was struggling to keep sauce from dripping down her chest and was pretty sure she had bleu cheese dip smeared all over her cheeks. There weren't enough napkins in the world to keep up with the mess, but wings were fifty cents on Tuesdays, and there was no way to resist that kind of deal, especially not when they tasted this good.

"Nope," Arie said when she was finally able to answer Chandra's question. "Dick said he did it and then refused to give details. He's got a lawyer now, of course. So does Riann. My theory is she stole the ring from Kelli and then sent it to Brant. She knew how bad everything looked for him already, so she probably figured his having it in his possession would tip the scales. She was almost right."

Arie reached for her bottle of Leinenkugel and almost slid off her seat. She hated high bar stools. They were made for tall women with lots of leg to flaunt. Being perched so high made Arie feel like a kid left to dangle her feet. Plus, her boobs already made her top-heavy, which threw her balance off.

"But if she knew Dick killed her best friend," Chandra said, "why would she feel she had to set Brant up?"

"She was afraid."

Arie thought about the vision that had risen from Riann's blood—the panic and the guilt. *Had* Riann known? She must have, on some level, anyway. Why else would she feel she had to protect Dick?

A woman in a denim skirt fell against Arie, almost toppling her off the barstool. The chicken wing basket skidded down the bar, but Chandra managed to grab it before it sailed completely off. After apologizing profusely, the woman's date guided her back to their table. They both laughed.

Chandra returned to the subject. "Okay, I get being afraid. But wouldn't that just make you want to turn him in more? I mean, how could you live with a murderer?"

"People are weird. O'Shea says by now, she's almost convinced herself that Brant really did it. If you lie to yourself long enough, you start believing the crap yourself. I don't think she could admit, even to herself, that Dick killed Marissa and Wyatt. She still can't. Did you know she's still living at the lake house?"

"So she's stuck with facing the truth or leaving her meal ticket? Still doesn't seem like a hard decision to make."

"It wouldn't be for you," Arie said. "But ever since she was a kid, Riann convinced herself the only way she could survive was to trade herself for a lifestyle. Dick was everything she'd been aiming for her whole life. That's why it hurt so bad when Marissa started making fun of her and then, worse, started writing a book that would expose her past and make a mockery of what used to be their shared dream."

The band started playing a cover of Trace Adkins's "Marry For Money." The girls looked at each other and laughed. It felt good. Laughter had been scarce lately.

"Speaking of O'Shea . . . " Chandra had a wicked smile on her face and also barbecue sauce, which Arie pointed out. It didn't deter her friend.

"There isn't anything to speak of," Arie said. "He took my statement, but that's it."

"Maybe for now, but there was something there. He must be a breast man. Not that there's any other kind, really, but—"

"He was doing his job."

Instead of taking offense, Chandra smiled knowingly. This time, she let the subject drop and called the bartender over for another round. She made a face when it arrived: one club soda and another Leinie for Arie. She'd lost the coin toss for designated driver.

"Is your mom talking to you yet?"

"If I speak directly to her, she will answer, but not if it's about Brant."

"It's not your fault he got arrested again. He's the one who got drunk and made such a ruckus at Kelli's. I'da called the cops on him, too."

"I know, but it was in the paper and all. I talked to Brant, though. He's doing better. He had a lot of questions."

"I bet. Did you tell him about the visions?"

Arie sighed, then took a swallow of beer. "No. There's no way he'd be able to wrap his mind around that. I haven't told anyone in my family."

I told O'Shea, and look how that turned out.

"You're probably right, but—" Chandra broke off and grabbed Arie's arm. "I see him!"

Arie spun toward the dance floor.

And there he was.

Arie gasped. Her sleuthing had finally paid off. He had a leggy blonde on one side and a sultry brunette on the other. They were each vying for his attention, which he seemed content to divide between them equally.

"Good Lord, he's in a *menage a trois*," Chandra said, awestruck.

"He is not. He's dancing with two . . . uh . . . ladies."

"He just grabbed the blonde's butt, and the other chick is trying to stick her tongue down his throat."

"This can't be happening." Arie felt light-headed.

The trio spun on the floor, expertly weaving through the other, more conventional dance partners. The man, at least, seemed fairly well known. As they wove in and out of the crowd, several of the other dancers—the men, mostly—made laughing remarks as he passed. Although Arie was too far away to catch the words, it was obvious from the laughter and the tone that the comments were equal parts sexual innuendo and that strange form of male respect that displayed itself in coarse innuendo.

The turquoise boots never missed a step.

"Your grandpa's a stud," Chandra said.

Arie gagged and turned away.

"Chandra, if you value our friendship, you will never say that again."

"Okay, what if he decides to bring one of them home tonight? Or both? They're looking really frisky together."

Arie put a hand to her throat and swallowed. She had a choice: switch to 7 Up and try to calm her heaving stomach, or drown all thought in alcohol.

What the hell? Chandra was driving. She caught the bartender's eye.

"Give me a shot of Jagermeister, and don't walk away."

The shot didn't help. Neither did the next two Leines that followed. To make matters worse, Arie's eyes kept being drawn back to the spectacle of her grandfather and his two babes. Eventually, she was able to look past him enough to notice the babes in question were only about twenty years younger than their escort, making them all eligible for Medicaid, should the need arise.

It also became obvious that any one of the three would have been able to dance Arie under the table—if she knew how to dance, that is.

"They're pretty amazing, aren't they?" Arie said over her shoulder to Chandra.

"I would say so," a low voice rumbled in her ear.

She knew that voice.

The band swung into Josh Turner's "Your Man." A hand reached down, took hers, and tugged her toward the dance floor. As he pulled her close, she finally looked up. O'Shea's brilliant blue eyes were laughing into her own.

"How did you—?" Flustered, Arie broke off. Maybe he hadn't known she would be here. After all, Bootz was forty-five minutes away from Oconomowoc. She herself had only come here to track down her wayward grandfather. There was no reason to think—

"A little bird told me," he whispered in her ear.

Thank you for reading *A Scrying Shame*.
I hope you enjoyed it!

Please sign up for my New Release mailing list or contact me via my website at <u>donnawhiteglaser.com</u>

If you enjoyed reading *A Scrying Shame,* I would appreciate it if you would help others enjoy this book, too.

REVIEW IT: I invite you to leave a review of this story. Reader reviews, both positive and negative, are vitally important to authors and to fellow bookworms.

RECOMMEND IT: Please help other readers find this book by recommending it to friends, readers' groups, and discussion boards.

LEND IT: This book is lending enabled, so please share it with a friend.

ALSO BY DONNA WHITE GLASER

THE LETTY WHITTAKER 12 STEP MYSTERIES:

The Enemy We Know
The One We Love
The Secrets We Keep
The Blood We Spill
COMING SOON: *The Lies We Tell*

THE BLOOD VISIONS PARANORMAL MYSTERIES:

A Scrying Shame
COMING SOON: *Scry Me a River*

The Enemy We Know: A Letty
Whittaker 12-Step Mystery
Book One

CHAPTER ONE

I heard him coming. The hall funneled the sound of his rage, racing just ahead of the man. Our clinic's manager screamed, "Letty! Watch out!" but he already filled the doorway. Despite training, I leaped to my feet. Waves of booze and the clamor of civilized people fumbling in the throes of chaos seeped around his mass. In the distance, the thud of running feet, objects careening into each other, and panicked versions of "what's going on?" littered the air.

After the first instinctive reaction, my training reasserted itself, and I recognized the intruder as a client I'd just begun seeing. Now he stood swaying on the threshold, jean jacket straining at the shoulders, barely covering a ratty T-shirt which offered sexual favors to my sister. His bleary, pig-mean eyes stared straight through me. So different from the shy, hurting man I'd met with a week ago.

We'd met together twice for counseling. Despite an initial complaint of marital conflict, Randy had kept the focus squarely on a seemingly trivial dispute with his boss. At the time, I'd thought he was avoiding the real issue, but we were still getting to know each other. Any attempt on my part to bring the subject back to his troubled marriage was charmingly, but firmly, deflected. Maybe he was ready to talk.

He slammed the office door so hard I flinched and bit my tongue. *Maybe not.*

"Where is she?" The dead monotone scared me more than if he'd yelled.

"Who?"

"You *bitch*." His teeth chewed at the word, turning his face into a lupine grimace. "You think this is a joke?" He pulled a hunting knife out from under his jacket, moving deeper into the room, still blocking the door.

"No, Randy," I said, eyes locked on the weapon. My voice sounded high and thin, squeaking past my closed throat, a far cry from the professional calm I wished for. "I don't think this is a joke. I can see how upset you are, but I don't know what you want."

"I want Carrie to stop this bullshit. Get that? Real simple. And I want *you* out of our lives. *Where is she?*"

It was hard to think. All the oxygen pumping from my thudding heart seemed directed to my extremities. My legs tingled in helplessness; flight was impossible.

My mind scrambled to mesh together the bits of information from our sessions with what he was saying now. "I thought your wife's name is Debbie?"

"What?"

"Debbie?"

"Don't play stupid with me. You knew the whole time, didn't you? You knew why I was here, and you played me for a fool. You think I don't know? The whole time you're yapping about trust, and you and that bitch are setting me up behind my back."

"Randy—"

"My name ain't Randy!" he exploded. "Quit pretending."

It finally sunk in that "Randy" had given me a fake name. So much for trust. I jettisoned any information gleaned from our previous sessions and pretended he was just an irrational stranger—which he was—leaving very little to go on. Just a name, really. The name of the woman I was supposedly conspiring with: Carrie.

It clicked.

Carrie, the client usually scheduled in this time slot, had canceled at the last minute. She and I had been working for the last four months on self-esteem issues, gathering her courage to deal with her relationship with her abusive boyfriend. She'd recently decided to get out and had begun making practical plans for her escape.

Guess who showed up?

His eyes darted around the room, hyperalert, as if he thought I had her stashed in the file cabinet. My office held an old metal desk, an ergonomically challenged chair, a tattered love seat, and a waist-high, two-drawer file cabinet *sans* escaping girlfriend.

Ethically, I couldn't even acknowledge that Carrie was a client. Stacked up against the stark reality of the buck knife, however, confidentiality seemed like a vague, misty concept. Problem was, I liked Carrie, and I refused to draw a map for her asshole boyfriend. And there was the added issue of not having a freakin' clue where she might be.

"Where is she?" he repeated.

Drunk, dangerous, and impatient. The unholy trinity.

What the hell was his name, anyway? She must have said his name a half-million times, at least. She'd even divulged having it tattooed in the shape of a crescent moon on her left breast. Why should her boob tattoo flash into memory and not his name?

"Look, I know you're upset. I want to help." I worked to keep my voice calm, dropping it low and soft in direct contrast to his anger.

"Don't you try that psych crap on me, you bitch! You've been trying to break me and Carrie up ever since she started seeing you."

Well, not exactly, but I doubted what's-his-name could distinguish the fine line between encouraging Carrie to make her own decisions and telling her to leave the jerk who kept throwing her against the wall whenever she disagreed with him.

"It's not crap to tell you that the police are coming. You know that, right? You can make this so much better for yourself if you just give me the knife." My eyes were glued to the weapon—it looked like something that could gut a deer with one flick of the wrist. My stomach rolled, the acids within sloshing loosely from side to side.

"Give *you* the knife? Why? So you can stab me in the back with it? You bitches are all alike. First chance you get, you kick a guy in the teeth." The blade whispered evilly as he sliced it through the air. I hated that knife.

"I wouldn't hurt you," I said. Sweat rolled down my face, tickling.

"Bullshit! You're taking Carrie away!" His face flooded with incredulity, and the next few seconds blurred as he charged forward. Flipping the desk chair aside like it was made of Styrofoam, he pinned me against the back wall, the knife a silver glint below my chin. Its tip nicked my skin, not cold as I had anticipated, but burning a slender line across the thin layer of flesh guarding my throat.

"You just don't get it, do you? I love her. And you got no right coming between a man and his woman. That's a sacred thing, and you can't just—"

"I'm not taking Carrie away. She's—"

"Liar!" Rage twisted his face into a grotesque mask, barely human. "You think I don't know? You think I'm stupid because I don't have a stinkin' diploma stuck up on my wall?"

He smashed the knife into the glass frame above my head, shards splintering like frozen rain on my hair and the floor below. He'd just killed a cheap Monet print, but now didn't seem like the time to point out the error.

"You think you're so special, don't you? Got your college education, and your tight little ass that you like to shake in front of all the men. Bet you make them crazy, huh? Make them come back for more, just 'cause they got the hots for you. Do you wear that long, black hair up just so's we wonder what you look like at night, when it's down?

"And then you act all concerned about me, like you care. Just like *her*. I'm not stupid." His voice dropped again to that frightening, raspy whisper. "I know what she's planning. She's been checking into those shelters like she thinks that's gonna keep her safe. I bet you been workin' on her, trying to get her to go to one of them places."

The knife skimmed my throat again; I couldn't even shake my head to answer without slicing it off. Tears of frustration pooled in my eyes, ready to fall. Carrie and I had talked about the possibilities of domestic abuse shelters, but that was weeks ago. At the time, she wouldn't even take the brochure that I'd tried giving her, for fear that her boyfriend would find it. *Was her cancellation today part of an escape plan that she hadn't trusted me with?*

"Did you try her at work?" The question popped out of its own volition.

"Huh?"

"Well . . . she canceled her appointment. Maybe she just got called in to work."

Stopped him cold. Suddenly, as we stood there in a grotesque parody of an embrace, the wail of police sirens filtered through the office's strip-mall thin walls of the office. No soundproofing, another cheap aspect of our working arrangement, but I loved it now. His eyes locked on mine, briefly, and a disturbing emotion rippled between us. He stood there only a few moments more, but it felt like hours; his breath fanned my cheeks while his body held mine hostage. Rearing his head back, he spit full in my face, then bolted for the door. Turning right, away from the front lobby, he ran toward the back fire exit. I heard shouts, and a thunk as something heavy tipped over. Seconds later, several police officers flew past the office door in pursuit.

Now that the time for panic was officially over, it took possession of my body, unhinging my knees, crashing me down to the floor. I cowered there, heart pounding, adrenaline turning my mouth tinny, shaking so hard my joints ached.

The sound of more running feet jolted me to my knees, but it was just my supervisor Marshall sprinting down the hall. The back door slammed, and then Marshall was at my side.

He guided me into the chair. I watched disinterestedly as his mouth made noises over me. My brain tuned him out until a shout of astonishment from him pulled me back to focus. Marshall knelt beside my chair, holding my right hand. For a brief spasm of time, I imagined he was going to propose. That is until I saw the bright red blood pooled in the cup of my upturned palm, seeping over the side and into his beneath like a water fountain in a particularly grisly park. My first instinct was that I'd been stabbed, but then I spied the glass shard sticking straight up, cleaving the pad of skin between my thumb and forefinger. I couldn't stand the sight of the alien object stuck inside me. So I pulled it out. More blood.

Marshall's noises grew more agitated, but this time a wave of dizziness blocked him out. A uniformed policeman pushed into my tiny office, crowding us, using up more air. My ears started ringing, and the cop pushed my head between my knees. I closed my eyes, concentrating on not throwing up, while someone squeezed the cut on my hand real hard.

"Wayne," I said to my knees.

Someone's head orbited into my vision. "What?" the someone said.

"His name is Wayne."

ACKNOWLEDGEMENTS

I'd like to thank Kindle Press and the Amazon Scout program for choosing *A Scrying Shame* for publication. And for all of those readers who took time to nominate *Shame* or to support my other books, you have my eternal gratitude!

To my friends and fellow authors: Marla, Madison (TJ Peacock & Lisa Rayburn Mysteries), David Tindell (*Quest for Honor*), Marjorie Doering (Ray Schiller series), Katie Mettner (Snowberry series), Helen Block, Darren Kirby (*Coordinates for Murder*). With every book I write, I become more and more indebted to each of you. There is simply no way I would have continued down this path without your support and encouragement. Your critiques keep me on my toes and our business meetings keep me motivated. You are all a blessing in my life, and I thank God for you all.

To Fiona Quinn, author of the Lynx thriller series and the writers' resource blog ThrillWriting: Thank you for holding my hand and keeping my chin up during the Scout campaign. You were kind, generous with your time, and patient with my multitude of questions. I can't thank you enough!

Finally, to Joe, Levi, and Leah. You are my world.

Made in the USA
Middletown, DE
16 July 2021